CANYON QUEST

The Exciting Start of the Last Chance Detectives!

BY JIM WARE

TYNDALE

Tyndale House Publishers, Inc.
Wheaton, Illinois

JIM WARE, a graduate of Fuller Theological Seminary, is the author of *God of the Fairy Tale: Finding Truth in the Land of Make-Believe* and four novels for children. He lives in Colorado Springs with his wife Joni and their six children. He has also written several episodes of the popular *Adventures in Odyssey* radio drama for children, and is co-author (with Kurt Bruner) of *Finding God in the Lord of the Rings* and a companion volume, *Finding God in the Land of Narnia.* A Celtic music enthusiast, Jim plays the guitar and the hammered dulcimer and is likely to show up wherever there's an opportunity to play a few jigs and reels.

1

The Worst Thing About Ambrosia

"Seventy-nine, eighty, eighty-one, eighty-two . . . *eighty-three.*"

Mike Fowler stopped counting and looked at the money where it lay spread out across his cowboy-patterned bedspread. Beside it sprawled a wrinkled Greyhound bus schedule and a AAA road map of the Mid-Western states. Mentally he added it up again. $53.83 in change and single bills. His entire life's savings. *Not a lot*, he thought. *But enough.*

Once more he checked the contents of his backpack: two changes of clothes; a water bottle, an orange, three Snickers bars, and a packet of dried fruit snacks; and the leather-bound pocket Bible and compass—a big, beautiful, hand-sized compass in a shiny brass casement with a pure glass crystal—that his dad had given him on his sixth birthday.

11:42 P.M. The numbers on the digital alarm clock glowed a fuzzy red in the soft darkness. It was the eve of his 12th birthday, and while the rest of the household slept, Mike sat huddled on the bed with his flashlight, pinning down the final details of a plan that had been taking shape in his mind for years.

A plan to get out of Ambrosia.

Mike hated Ambrosia. He hated the hot, dry winds and the barren landscape that hemmed the town in on every side. He loathed the monotonous cactuses and yucca and the endless flatness of the Arizona desert—a flatness interrupted only by the few arid red buttes and mesas that rose starkly out of the shimmering waste like the cracked and eroded bones of long-forgotten primeval monsters. He cringed at the sight of the searing sun, the unyielding blue of the daytime sky, and the oppressive swarms of winking stars at night. He hated every last bit of it.

Once more Mike consulted the bus schedule for late-night departure times. There was a coach leaving for Columbus at 1:38 A.M. *Perfect.*

He sat back on the bed, ran his fingers through his sandy brown hair, and went over the plan in his mind. He pictured the dingy Greyhound station down on Ambrosia's drowsy main drag. Main Street, Ambrosia: once a busy stopping point along historic Route 66, now a dilapidated relic, bypassed completely by the new Interstate 40. He couldn't bear the sight of its peeling storefronts and cartoonish neon signs, blinking garishly in the purple desert twilight. He winced every time he passed the Teepee Motor Lodge, a tacky cluster of slapdash, zigzag, wood-and-stucco wigwams huddled together in a narrow space between two crumbling sandstone cliffs at the east end of town.

Yes, thought Mike. Ambrosia had everything—everything banal, boring, and repulsive. Like the Galaxy Drive-In, a crater-based outdoor movie theater, which was one of the ugliest things he'd ever laid eyes on. Its futuristic marquee—futuristic for the 1950s—was like something out of an episode of *The Jetsons*. He fingered his money and told himself that he couldn't wait to get away.

Ambrosia wasn't anything like home. Home, in his memory, was a green and fragrant paradise: a land of gentle rolling hills, thick-boughed, broad-leafed trees, and shady lanes lined with snug wood-frame houses, each with a white picket fence, brick walk, and trim green lawn. If he closed his eyes, Mike could still smell the damp brown earth and the fresh green grass of home. He could feel the damp itchiness that came from tumbling and wrestling with his dad on the lawn during long summer evenings, when tall, puffy clouds, full of night rain, hung thick and gilded and pink above the western horizon. He could remember sitting out on the front porch with his dad, memorizing psalms and verses out of the Bible, while the sprinklers hissed and filled the air with a gentle mist. People didn't have lawns in Ambrosia. They had rocks or gravel or "xeriscapes"— patches of spiny, spiky, scrawny plants that looked like they came from another planet and reminded you of the kind of place where a horned toad might feel at home. Mike hated xeriscapes.

What made all of this even more unbearable was the fact Jamie Fletcher didn't live in Ambrosia. Jamie had been Mike's best friend back at home. He'd never been able to find a friend like Jamie out here in the desert. He hadn't even tried. He didn't want to.

Mike still liked to talk to Jamie on the phone as often as he could wheedle his mom into letting him call. But that didn't happen very often. Mike's mom didn't have a lot of money for long-distance phone bills. Neither did Pop and Grandma Fowler.

So Mike hated Ambrosia. He hated everything about it.

Everything, that is, except the B-17.

The B-17 belonged to Pop. It was a real "Flying Fortress"—the same plane he had piloted over France during the Second World War. Now it sat on display out in front of the Last Chance Gas and Diner, the family business where Mom kept the books and waited on tables, and where Mike spent a lot of time hanging around with Pop and wiping windshields.

No question about it. The B-17 was the one thing about Ambrosia that Mike definitely did *not* hate. It was sleek and silvery and wonderful. Just looking at it stirred his imagination and filled him with dreams of being a pilot himself someday—like Pop and his dad.

During his years in Ambrosia, Mike had spent hours upon hours poring over the picture books of airplanes and aircraft he'd discovered in his bedroom—the same room his dad had occupied as a boy. He'd memorized every model in *Jane's Pocket Book of Major Combat Aircraft* and *Jane's Pocket Book of Helicopters*. He'd have given anything for a look inside the B-17. But he'd never had the chance. The B-17 was off-limits. Pop had put padlocks on the doors to keep kids, vagrants, and curiosity seekers out. So the B-17 didn't really do Mike a whole lot of good.

At any rate, he told himself, even the B-17 couldn't change the very *worst* thing about Ambrosia. Because the very worst thing about Ambrosia was the thing that had brought him to the hot, dusty little town in the first place. It was a thing that had shaken his whole world and changed his life forever—a thing Mike couldn't put out of his mind if he lived to be a hundred.

Never would he forget that late winter afternoon, not long after his sixth birthday, when his mom had come in with red eyes and made him sit down at the end of the living room couch. She had bad news, she said. She told him to be brave and to pray and trust in the Lord.

The wreckage of his dad's F-16 fighter had been recovered, she told him. Somewhere in the Middle East. Of John Fowler himself not the slightest trace had been found. That's why they had to go away to Arizona to live with Pop and Grandma Fowler. Away from Jamie Fletcher and the white picket fences and the summer lawns and the winter snows. Away to the land of cactus and baked rocks and corrugated metal roofs. It was the only way they'd be able to make it, she said . . . without Dad.

Without Dad. *That* was the thing Mike *really* hated about Ambrosia. *With* Dad, even Ambrosia might have been tolerable. As hard as it was to believe, Pop had often told him how much John Fowler loved growing up in this withered little town . . . what a fanatic he had been for desert exploration, and how he had left the marks of his adventures and exploits all over the place. Deep down inside, Mike almost felt that *he* could have loved Ambrosia too, if only his dad were there to help him . . . to hike with him over the bluffs, guide him through the rocky wastes, teach him the names of the desert flowers, and lead him into the mysteries of the Navajo country. But he wasn't. He was gone. And now there was nothing left of him but the compass and pocket Bible he'd given to Mike on that special birthday so long ago.

So Mike hated Ambrosia. Because without his dad, Ambrosia was nothing but a dull, dry, boring, desert waste.

Grimly, Mike smiled. Then he carefully tucked the money back into his wallet, stuffed the map and bus schedule down into his pack, and clicked off the flashlight. Climbing into bed, he pulled the covers up to his chin, bit his lip, and stared into the quiet darkness, listening to the swish of the curtains as they stirred in the breeze at his window.

Everything's ready, he assured himself—a little nervously, perhaps. Tomorrow was D-Day. His 12th birthday. The day he'd been looking forward to and praying about for so long. The day he'd put his well-laid plans into action. There was only one thing left to do.

Make the phone call to Jamie.

Mike closed his eyes and tried to sleep.

2

The Gift

Happy birthday, dear Mike,
Happy birthday to you!

"Now make a wish and blow out the candles!" said Gail Fowler, shaking a blond curl away from her face as she bent forward to set the cake on the table in front of her son.

"And make it good!" added Pop, setting the flash and aiming the camera.

Mike glanced up at the faces gathered around the table as the last notes of the song faded into a suspenseful silence. Each one was dear to him . . . Mom, Grandma, Pop. Now that it came down to it, he honestly didn't know how he could bring himself to leave them. But then each was also a nagging reminder of his exile, his captivity, and the terrible thing that had brought him to Ambrosia in the first place. Mike licked his lips and realized that his mouth had gone dry.

They'll understand, he thought. *I just can't stay here*

anymore. I'll call them when I get to Jamie's. Everything will be okay after that.

And yet, as hard as he tried to make himself believe it, he knew it wasn't true. They wouldn't understand. They wouldn't be pleased. They'd come after him and catch him and bring him back again.

Feeling as if time had stopped, he surveyed the faces once again. One by one he took in their distinctive features: Pop's crinkly, smiling eyes, ice blue and sparkling under bushy white eyebrows; Grandma's soft gray hair and intricately lined forehead, arched upwards in a network of expectant wrinkles; his mother's girlishly rounded cheek, smooth and glowing in the yellow candlelight.

Outside, the sky was dark and the stars were already shining. It was after hours at the Last Chance Diner, and they were celebrating his 12th birthday.

For a moment Mike sat staring down at the cake. It was iced in white and several shades of blue. In the very center, right in the middle of a long gray runway, sat a small plastic airplane. He swallowed hard; looking at it, he couldn't help remembering all the other plastic airplanes on all the other birthday cakes he'd ever had. He closed his eyes, inhaled deeply, puffed out his cheeks, and blew. The camera flashed bright and white while Mom and Grandma clapped and cheered.

"Twelve at one blow!" exclaimed Pop, clapping Mike on the shoulder as the white smoke swirled around their heads. "Quite a pair of lungs you've got there!" He leaned forward with a wink. "So what did you wish for?"

"Roy!" put in Grandma, scowling playfully. "You *know* he can't tell. Otherwise it won't come true!"

Mike looked up at his grandfather.

"Actually," he said, "I've got *two* wishes. And I'm not afraid to tell you the first one." He looked straight at his mom and tried to smile, but when he spoke again, it was with an involuntary crack in his voice. "Can I use the cell phone to call Jamie tonight?"

Gail laughed. "I suppose that can be arranged," she said. She reached into her purse, produced the phone, and laid it in his open palm.

Mike stared down at it. Then, pocketing the phone, he added more soberly, "I guess you *know* what my other wish is."

Gail smiled in answer. A sweet but sad expression came into her deep brown eyes. "I know," she said quietly. "And I know that *you* know I know."

"Well!" said Grandma brightly. "Why don't I go get the ice cream?"

"And why don't I help?" said Gail. With that, she slid out of the booth and followed Grandma out to the kitchen.

Underneath its blue-and-white icing the cake was chocolate with a raspberry filling—Mike's favorite. His mom served it up on paper plates with rocky road and Neapolitan ice cream. And then came the presents: a knitted sweater from Grandma Fowler; a new pair of jeans, a Discman, and an illustrated edition of *Tom*

Sawyer from his mom; and birthday cards with checks from his aunts in Indiana. Mike carefully stowed his loot, stuffed the used wrapping paper into a plastic trash bag, and told everyone how thankful he was for the wonderful gifts. Then he licked his lips again and gulped down a full glass of lemonade. He couldn't help thinking about the road that lay ahead of him. And about the one thing in the world that could have made this birthday a happier occasion.

Once Mom and Grandma had started clearing the table, Mike saw Pop lean back in his seat and give him a sidewise glance.

"Well," said Pop, dropping his chin and peering at his grandson over the rims of his spectacles. "Guess it's time for *my* present."

Mike gave him a quizzical look.

"Here," Pop continued, reaching over to the deci-mated birthday cake and plucking the model airplane from its gray-icing runway. "From me. Don't say I never gave you anything." He chuckled and plopped the tiny aircraft, clumps of frosting still clinging to its plastic landing gear, into Mike's open palm.

Mike stared at the little plane for a moment, wonder-ing whether this was another joke. Sometimes it was hard to tell when Pop had come to the punch line.

"Oh, that's not all of it," Pop added in a moment, watching him closely. "Of course not. Not yet. It's just sort of a pledge or down payment—what the Good Book calls an 'earnest.'"

He paused and reached into his hip pocket. "This goes with it," he said, pulling out a piece of blue lanyard. At its end dangled a shiny silver key. "Come on," he said, tossing the key to Mike and getting to his feet. "Let's go have a look."

Still at a loss, Mike stood up and followed Pop out the door of the diner, past the gas station, across the parking lot, and over to the rocky, stubbly lot where the old B-17 lay gleaming in the cold desert starlight, its nose tilted upward expectantly, as if awaiting a chance to rocket away into the night. Pop led him around to the crew door, which was still secured with a big padlock. Then he turned to Mike with a nod. "Go ahead," he said. "Try it."

"You mean . . . ?" said Mike.

"That's right. Go on."

Mike fitted the key into the hole and turned it with a click. Off came the padlock, and the door swung open. He leaned inside and peered into the dark, empty cabin. Hesitantly, he glanced back at Pop.

"Oh—here," said Pop, pulling a flashlight from his jacket and handing it to Mike. "We'll get the lights rigged up later. I'm right behind you."

Mike switched on the flashlight and stepped cautiously into the plane, swinging the yellow beam from side to side along the length of the cabin. He couldn't believe this was happening to him. He was actually inside the B-17!

He held his breath as he surveyed its interior. It was

a narrow, tubelike space crammed with all kinds of fittings and furnishings: a carom board, a couple of chairs, the original guns (without ammunition), the old radio operator's table, a few woolen blankets, a metal file cabinet, and a small bookshelf. A row of utility shelves had been built in between the steel ribs of the upper walls. Here and there hung various posters, maps, and charts. Mike could do nothing but stare.

"Lots of memories in here," said Pop from over his shoulder. The whole place rang with a dull, hollow metallic sound as he slapped the side of the plane with his open palm. "I flew this little baby during the war. In Europe."

"I know," said Mike—a little irritably, perhaps. He still wasn't quite sure what it was all about.

"Picked her up for a pittance. Well, Grandma didn't think so. The government was auctioning them off. Back in the '50s. It was a deal I couldn't pass up."

"Uh-huh."

"I used to take her up every once in a while. Later, your dad made her into a kind of clubhouse. 'Headquarters' for all his adventures and explorations and so on. Stocked with everything he needed: food, water, bedding, extra clothes, camping gear, shovels, maps, books. He could've *lived* out here if he'd wanted to!" Pop chuckled. "Sometimes he did, too. I've kept it all pretty much the way he had it." He smiled—a sad, mellow smile. "Until a few days ago, it was years since I'd had a look inside. I hope I've got her cleaned up enough for you."

A light began to dawn inside Mike's head. "For *me*? Do you mean . . . ?" He stopped and stared up into Pop's blue eyes in disbelief. "Are you saying . . . ?"

"That's right," Pop nodded. "She's yours now. I had a feeling you could use a place of your own. A thinking place. A 'laughing place.' That's important for a *young man* of your age." His eyes twinkled. "So," he concluded, turning to go, "I'll leave you to it."

For a moment, Mike just stood there, sweeping the beam of his flashlight over the cockpit's shiny black and silver instrument panel, the 50 caliber Browning machine guns, and the antiquated radio equipment. Then, coming to himself all at once, he suddenly leaped to the door, gripped its sides, and leaned out. "*Thanks*, Pop!" he shouted.

Pop, who was halfway across the parking lot, turned and waved. Mike could see him smiling in the glow of the diner's green and white neon lights. A puff of unseasonably warm air blew off the desert and ruffled his silvery hair.

"Oh, I almost forgot your *other* present!" he called. "You're now an *official* employee of the Last Chance Gas and Diner: part-time in the kitchen, part-time at the pumps! Two hours every day after school. First payday is next Friday!" Then he turned and started walking back toward the diner.

Mike gaped after him. Then, "Just a minute!" he shouted, jumping from the plane. "Wait!" He sprinted across the parking lot and didn't stop until he was standing straight in front of Pop, looking up into his broad, wrinkled face.

"Here," he said sheepishly, reaching into his jacket pocket and pulling out the cell phone. "Just tell Mom that I won't be needing this tonight after all. Too much else to do right now."

Pop nodded. Then he pocketed the phone and disappeared back inside the diner.

3

Treasures

"That's it, Mom!" said Mike, glancing up at the clock and tossing his sponge into the sink. It was 4:30 in the afternoon and his shift at the diner was up. "I'm done for the day!"

Quickly he slipped out of his blue apron and hung it on the hook beside the dishwasher. Then, wriggling into his leather aviator's jacket and slinging his green backpack over one shoulder, he leaned over toward the kitchen window, where Gail was clipping up a new round of orders from the counter.

"I'll be out in the B-17," he said.

Almost overnight, Mike's world had changed. No longer was it the narrow, restrictive, suffocating world he'd known ever since coming to Ambrosia—a world fenced in on every side by the barren open spaces of the desert and the sky. Now it was a world of unfathomed mystery and adventure, a world of hopes, dreams, and endless possibilities: an entire universe within a thin, silver tube with shining wings. Inside the B-17, Mike felt, lay answers to the questions he'd been asking ever since he was six years old. Answers to questions about his dad. And he was determined to find them.

"All right, Mike," said his mom, without looking up. "Thanks. You've worked hard today."

"Sure have!" chimed in Grandma, sliding a couple of her famous apple pies out of the big stainless steel oven and turning to wave a red quilted pot holder at him.

Mike turned and went swinging out through the kitchen's double door. He crossed the black-and-white checkered floor and headed for the diner's front entrance. Even now he could see the Flying Fortress through the window, gleaming in the late afternoon sun.

Grimly, he smiled. *I'll get out of Ambrosia someday*, he thought. *That should be easy now, with all the money I'm earning.* But for the time being, there could be no question of going anywhere. For the time being, the pathway of his search lay within the walls of the World War II bomber. Ever since the night of his birthday *this* had been his all-consuming passion. It had eclipsed his desire to escape from Ambrosia. It had driven Jamie Fletcher from his mind.

"Any homework?" Gail called as he touched the doorknob. It was her perennial parting shot.

"I'll do it *out there!*" he answered.

A lone customer sitting at a table near the entrance looked up at the sound of Mike's voice—a tall, athletic-looking man with strong, chiseled features, sky-blue eyes, and a clear complexion. His brown hair was cut short on top and shaved close to the head on the sides and in the back. He wore blue jeans, a faded red cotton shirt, a short denim jacket, and dusty hiking boots.

Strangers were common at the Last Chance Diner, but something about this one's face stopped Mike in his tracks. The firm mouth, the proud chin, the military posture, the confident look in the eyes. Mike was completely taken off guard.

It was odd, but everything about this person reminded him of his dad. He knew it *wasn't* his dad. There could be no question about that. He'd be sure to recognize his dad if he ever saw him. And yet there was something about this man . . . something inviting and appealing and reassuring. Something that made Mike want to sit down alongside him and ask him where he was from and what he was doing in Ambrosia. *This* man, Mike felt certain, would understand his inner struggles. He'd connect immediately with his feelings about the desert and the dry emptiness of life in this dilapidated little town. He'd know what to do.

The stranger lowered his newspaper and smiled as Mike passed. Mike returned the smile with a friendly nod. He wanted to speak, to blurt out his feelings and ask the man whether he knew John Fowler. He wanted to ask for his help. But the words stuck in his throat. With a nervous grin, Mike turned away, shoved the door open, and emerged into the lavender twilight.

"Quitting time?" grinned Pop from the brightly illumined door of the gas station as Mike set off at a run across the dirt-and-gravel parking lot.

"Yeah," he shouted back. "Call me when dinner's ready. I'll be out in the B-17."

Trotting around to the far side of the Flying Fortress, he came to a halt just in front of the crew entry hatch—the small rectangular door on the right rear side of the aircraft—and thrust his hand into the front pocket of his jeans. A smile tugged at the corners of his mouth when his fingers touched the cool smoothness of the lanyard. Out flew the key, flashing like a silver star at the end of a sky-blue leash. He fitted it into the hole and snapped off the padlock. With one last glance at the fading light in the desert sky, he yanked the door open and ducked inside.

A broad smile spread across Mike's face as he switched on a light and surveyed his new kingdom. *The Flying Fortress*, he thought with a sense of deep satisfaction. Yes. And now it was his own *personal* fortress—a place miles away from Ambrosia in the heart of Ambrosia itself. A place where nobody could find him if he didn't want to be found. A place where he could begin his search in earnest.

Slowly, he let his gaze sweep from the cockpit to the old bomb bay, over the ball turret, and past the guns and Plexiglas windows in the waist. As he did so, once again he felt strongly that the B-17 was something more than an empty old airplane. Something much more. It was a long corridor stretching away into the future and the past . . . a hallway lined with tantalizingly mysterious doors—doors that might conceal answers to some of his deepest and most pressing questions about his dad.

How could a dry, forsaken hole like Ambrosia have produced a hero like John Fowler? For a hero was what Mike firmly believed his dad to be. A hero mysteriously snatched away in the prime of life. A hero who would nevertheless return someday. Mike just *knew* that he would.

How had *he*—John Fowler—found ways to grow and thrive in this wasteland at the edge of civilization? What was it that had enabled *him* to go from Ambrosia to the United States Air Force Academy, and to emerge as the man Mike pictured in his mind's eye every night when he prayed by himself in his bed: a tall, strong, clear-eyed man; courageous, kind, and wise; quick to listen and slow to speak? A man like the one he'd just seen sitting in the diner. Maybe—just maybe—if he could discover answers to these questions, they might help him form some idea of what had happened to John Fowler in the Middle East. Perhaps they'd even supply the clues that would enable him to find his dad. Someday he would. He just knew it.

Mike dropped his backpack and plopped himself down in a straight-backed wooden chair. In just a few days he had already discovered a great deal—things Pop and Grandma and Mom had never told him. Things about his dad's fascination with the heavens and his love for astronomy. Even now Mike was working on a theory that astronomy might somehow be the key to the riddle he was hoping to solve.

Thoughtfully, he chewed his tongue and scanned the aircraft's tubular cabin. Here and there its ribbed walls were adorned with star charts and sky maps. A small telescope, covered with an old brown woolen Boy Scout blanket, stood on the radio operator's table. Above it, alongside several topographical maps of the Arizona desert, was a picture of the Lowell Observatory's 24-inch Clark Refracting Telescope. There were posters, too, depicting details of the surrounding countryside—the Painted Desert, the Navajo and Hopi Reservations, the Cliff Dwellings, Sunset Crater, Ives Mesa, Flagstaff, Humphreys Peak—and a map of the moon, and a faded photograph of Neil Armstrong taking his historic "small step for a man." Mike stared long and hard at an old hand-drawn picture of some planet or other—a reddish globe with a white cap, crisscrossed by a network of fine lines. He wondered whether his dad had made it.

In Mike's mind, all of this gave his dad's enthusiasm for planes and flying a whole new significance. He began to see John Fowler's choice of an Air Force career in an unexpected light. *Maybe he had ideas of becoming an astronaut*, he thought. *Maybe he wanted to see the stars.*

A glance at the pine shelving Pop and his dad had installed appeared to confirm this suspicion. There, in a conspicuous place, stood a soiled blue copy of *The First Men in the Moon*, by H. G. Wells. Apparently John

Fowler had been an avid fan of Wells's writing; several other volumes bearing the author's name stood alongside this one: *The Invisible Man, The Time Machine, The Secret Island of Dr. Moreau, In the Days of the Comet.* Mike drew one of them, *The War of the Worlds,* off the shelf and opened it to the first page, where he read:

> *No one would have believed in the last years of the nineteenth century that this world was being watched keenly and closely by intelligences greater than man's. . . .*

Mike scratched his head, closed the book, and returned it to its place. Then he stood up to examine the contents of the shelf more closely. It was filled with all kinds of books, magazines, and atlases. Carefully he ran his forefinger down the row: *Treasure Island* and *Kidnapped,* by Robert Louis Stevenson; *King Arthur and His Knights of the Table Round; The Merry Adventures of Robin Hood,* retold and illustrated by Howard Pyle; *The Story of the Grail;* Jules Verne's *Journey to the Center of the Earth;* Mark Twain's *Huckleberry Finn* and *A Connecticut Yankee in King Arthur's Court; Mars As the Abode of Life,* by astronomer Percival Lowell. They were all there, along with others: *The Anasazi Mysteries, Legends of the Navajo, Desert Hikes and Trips on Twos, Wilderness Survival,* and an extensive collection of old *National Geographics.*

Mike selected one of the *Geographics* and slowly turned its brightly colored pages. New Zealand, Mozambique, "Undersea Life in the Arctic"—marvels greeted his eyes on every page. He sat down again, enchanted with a panoramic shot of thick white mists over Kenya's great Rift Valley. But in a moment—why, he wasn't sure—something caused him to look up at the shelf again.

Immediately his eyes locked on a dark spot between two of the yellow-spined *Geographic*s. His heart jumped into his throat. Why hadn't he noticed it before?

There, alongside the empty space the *National Geographic* had occupied, stood a small, inconspicuous volume bound in worn black leather. Mike jumped up to get a closer look.

Was it possible? He rubbed his eyes and looked again. No—he hadn't been mistaken.

Along the edge of the leather cover, in faded silver ink and hand-written characters, ran the following title:

John Edward Fowler. Private Journal.

4

The Journal

Mike dropped the *National Geographic*. With tingling fingertips, he reached up and touched the little book's dusky leather cover.

His brain raced. John Fowler's journal? Filled with his dad's own words, thoughts, and recollections? With firsthand descriptions of his expeditions and adventures in the desert? With details of his everyday life in Ambrosia? Containing perhaps even a few meaningful clues as to the sort of people he might turn to, the kinds of places he might seek out if hard-pressed by desperate circumstances—circumstances like those that had led to his disappearance in the Middle East? This was too good to be true! Trembling, he tipped the journal off the shelf and blew the dust from its upper edge.

Eagerly Mike flipped through the yellowing blue-ruled pages, stopping here and there to read a snatch or two. The entries were done in bold, block-style print letters—all caps—rather than in cursive script. For the most part, the hand was clearly legible, except where it became obvious that his dad had been writing in a hurry.

Some of these entries were disappointingly mundane. For instance,

> September 23. Pop quiz in calculus today. Guess I blew it. Oh, well. The day would have been a loss except for Mr. Anderson's lecture in Ancient Civ. Knossos and the Minoans. Fascinating stuff . . .

Or,

> November 6. Borrowed Pop's car to go to the game last night. Fender bender over by the Galaxy. Mom was pretty worried and upset. Pop says no car for the next two weeks.

But others really did contain some fascinating descriptions of John Fowler's camping trips, science projects, athletic endeavors, and other interesting tidbits about his life as a teenager. Such as:

> December 18. Made it to the arch and the fork off the hidden canyon today. Signs of a new Anasazi site. Big find. Lasiloo thinks so, too. Anxious to get back. But no time for further explorations for a couple of weeks. Geographic article has drawn a lot of attention. Trying to keep things under wraps for the time being.

But Mike's heart sank when he realized that relatively little of the journal was written in plain English. Much of it seemed to have been recorded in some kind of code. Either that, or a very strange foreign language—one he'd never seen or heard of before. In fact, the English portion of the December 18 entry—the one about the Anasazi cache—broke off abruptly and gave way to the following:

Belasana dah lhacha'e wollachi glo'ih tsah thanzi lin ahnah dibeh shida neshchi jeha tlochin d'zeh klesh be ne'asjah glo'ih achin awoh akha glo'ih tsegah d'zeh gah ahjah thanzi cha ahnah dah ahlosz d'zeh tsenil dibeh noda'ih dahnestsa dibeh-yazzi t'kin ahnah klesh.
Thanzi cha dzeh jadholoni tsah t'kin ma'e ahnah . . .

This kind of thing went on for pages. He leafed to the middle of the book, then all the way to the back. It was the same no matter where he looked. Fairly short sections in English were always followed by long passages of this strange verbal gobbledygook.

"Great!" said Mike angrily. He slammed the book shut and dropped it on the radio operator's table, raising a cloud of dust. "A lot of good this is gonna do me." He slumped back into the chair and sat for a long time with his chin on his knuckles, staring straight through the Neil Armstrong poster on the wall.

Unless . . .

Pop was out on the airstrip behind the gas station when Mike found him. The lights were out at Last

Chance Gas, and the proprietor was taking advantage of the hour before dinner to work on his latest pet project—the restoration of an old Cessna biplane.

"Pop!" yelled Mike when he saw him. "You gotta see this!"

"What is it?" Pop responded, climbing out from under the plane's landing gear as Mike came tearing into the hangar.

It was a couple of minutes before Mike could catch his breath. As soon as he did, he yanked the journal from his backpack, shoved it up under Pop's nose, and blurted the whole story just as fast as he could get the words to tumble out of his mouth.

"Well," said Pop slowly, wiping his hands on a rag. He reached into his shirt pocket, drew out his spectacles, and settled them on his nose before accepting the journal from Mike. Carefully he examined one page, then another. At last he let out a long, low whistle. "Well, I'll be! I had no idea!" he said.

"So you haven't seen this before?"

"Me? No. Like I told you," Pop answered, glancing up with a sad smile, "it's been years since I took a look inside the B-17. Just couldn't bring myself to do it. That's part of the reason I've kept her locked up all this time."

"But do you know how to read it? Do you know what it says? What language is that?"

"I'm no scholar, Mike," said Pop after a brief pause. "But you can't spend as much time on the edge of the reservation as I have without learning a thing or two about Native American culture. This is Diné—the language of the Navajo. That much I know. You see this word here"—he pointed to the page—"*lhacha'e*—that means *dog*. I've heard that one used quite a bit. And this one—*dibeh*—that's *sheep*. Mainstay of the Navajo economy. But then that's about as much as I can make of it."

"My dad knew how to speak Navajo?"

"It's news to me, Mike. Though it doesn't really come as a surprise. He probably learned it from Lasiloo."

"Lasiloo? I saw that name in the journal! Who's Lasiloo?"

"Harrison Lasiloo. He was your dad's best friend. A full-blooded Diné. Those two went everywhere together. They knew every inch of this desert and all the country to the north: Humphreys Peak, the Petrified Forest, the Observatory, the Pink Cliffs. Practically inseparable."

"*Lowell* Observatory?" said Mike, brightening.

"Oh, sure. They spent a lot of time there. Over at the Vernon County Cliff Dwellings, too." He stopped and smiled. "Those two!" he said. "Why, once they found a cache of Anasazi artifacts up in Coconino Canyon that actually got them into *National Geographic*!"

"That's mentioned in the journal, too!" said Mike, his sense of wonder growing.

"Really? Well, I'm not surprised."

"But what did my dad care about dogs and sheep? I mean, why go to the trouble of learning Diné just to write about something like *that*?"

Pop closed the journal and handed it back to Mike.

He rubbed his jaw thoughtfully. "That's hard to say. Your dad was into all kinds of . . . *interesting* things. The only way to find out for sure would be to find someone who can translate the journal. A native speaker of Diné. Like Harrison."

"Well, let's go see him! Do you know where he lives?"

"Harrison Lasiloo." Pop ran his fingers through his thinning white hair. "I lost track of him about the time John left for the Academy. Last I heard, he'd gone off to the Mediterranean—Crete, I think—on an archaeological dig."

Mike was at a loss. "Well, there's got to be *somebody* around here who can read this. I mean, this is Navajo country, isn't it? Can't you take me over to the reservation to . . . well, to look for some help?"

Pop took off his spectacles. "I know what you're thinking, Mike," he said presently. "And I understand. I don't blame you for wanting to find out as much as you can about your dad. But sometimes we just have to let the past stay in the past. Some things that are hidden just have to *stay* hidden for a while . . . until the Good Lord sees fit to bring them to light. Besides, what you're proposing wouldn't be as easy as you think."

"Why not?"

"Well, for one thing, there aren't many towns of any size inside the reservation. There's Indian Wells and Tuba City, but they don't amount to much, and they're pretty far away. The Navajo Nation is almost completely rural. You'd have to hike from ranch to ranch, settlement to settlement, and hogan to hogan. And even if you found someone who was willing to help, I doubt that they'd actually be able to *read* this. Traditionally, Diné isn't a *written* language—only spoken. Educated Navajo have worked out a system for putting it down on paper, but I doubt that the average rancher or farmer would know much about that."

"But Pop! Don't you realize how important it could be to find out what this journal says? It could—well, it might help us *find* him! Don't you see?" He looked up at Pop with pleading eyes. "Can't you just drive me over to the reservation on Saturday?"

Pop smiled indulgently, though Mike couldn't help thinking that there was a sad look in his eyes. "Mike," he said slowly, "my Saturdays are booked solid at least until after Christmas. I'm sorry." He picked up a wrench and turned back to the Cessna.

For a moment Mike just stared after him, his jaw tense, his hands clenched tightly around the leather-bound book. Then he pursed his lips and let out a long breath through his nostrils.

"Okay, then! Fine!" he said at last. "I guess I'll just have to get to the reservation by myself somehow!"

And with that, he thrust the journal back into his pack and ran out into the clear darkness of the early evening.

5

Thanksgiving

"For the food we are about to receive," prayed Pop in his soothingly resonant voice, "and for the many rich blessings You have poured out upon us, O Lord, we give You thanks . . ."

Mike squirmed a little in his chair. It was Thanksgiving, and the rich, warm smells of the hot turkey and gravy on the table in front of him were almost unbearably tantalizing. He was hungry. He wished they could get on with dinner.

". . . For our being, our reason, and all other endowments and faculties of soul and body . . ."

His own hand felt uncomfortably hot and clammy against the coolness of his mother's smooth palm. He shifted his weight and twitched his nose. He was feeling . . . well, *antsy*. It wasn't that he had anything against thanking God. Or that he didn't think the Fowler household had plenty to be grateful for. He did. Still, with all that he had on his mind, it was hard to *feel* thankful. Restless—yes. Frustrated—yes. Agitated, confined, confused, angry—absolutely. But thankful? Not this time around.

". . . For our health, friends, food, and clothing, and all the other comforts and conveniences of life . . ."

Praying was all well and good. Prayer was fine. But Pop *did* have a tendency to go on—especially at times like this. On Sunday mornings, too. And at Wednesday night prayer meetings. Mike had been to plenty of those—in the little storefront room that the Ambrosia Fellowship used for its informal church gatherings.

He sighed inwardly. Opening one eye a tiny crack, he stole a sideways glance at his mother.

Gail was sitting with her chin bowed upon her chest. Her eyes were shut tight, and her lips were moving in rapid but silent speech. Mike closed his own eye again and tried to listen to Pop's prayer.

"Even when things don't work out as we'd planned or expected," Pop was saying, "—even when the very worst thing we can imagine has come upon us—even *then*, Father, we know that *You* still have a plan for us. We know that You will reveal that plan to us in Your own good time, if only we'll trust and obey and be patient."

Be patient. Again Mike's nose began to itch, and he stifled a sneeze. He crossed and recrossed his feet under the table.

The very worst thing has happened, he thought. *And every time I come up with a plan, somebody or something gets in my way!*

His mind wandered. His thoughts went back to Jamie Fletcher and the bus schedule. A vision of his friend's freckled face and reddish-brown hair rose before him. He remembered that his $53.83 had now grown to a couple of hundred dollars—more than enough to make that trip back home.

But no! It was impossible! Somehow, he knew that he could never seriously consider that option again. Not since the night of his birthday. Not since the B-17 and the journal. He couldn't leave Ambrosia until he'd followed these clues to their logical end. Strangely enough, he realized now that as long as he remained in Ambrosia, there was hope. Hope of finding someone who could translate Diné. Hope of breaking the code. Hope of getting inside John Fowler's mind.

He couldn't go back now. He had to move forward.

But there was another point on which he was equally clear. He'd never *really* be thankful again until his dad was back at this table. That's what he was holding out for. And it *would* happen one day—he *knew* it! If only he could get started on the search . . .

". . . and so, our God, just as surely as we know that You work all things together for good for those who love You—as surely as we believe that 'they who wait upon the Lord shall mount up with wings as eagles'—even so, Father, we entrust ourselves to You completely, leaning wholly upon Your grace, and thanking You from the bottom of our hearts for all Your manifold blessings. In Jesus' name we pray. Amen."

"Amen," said Grandma Fowler with quiet conviction. "Amen."

"Amen," assented Gail just under her breath, giving Mike's hand a firm squeeze before letting it go. Mike wiped his sweaty palm on the front of his shirt and looked at his mom out of the corner of his eye. She was smiling.

"Hungry, Mike?" she said, reaching for the steaming tureen of mashed potatoes.

Mike tried to smile back. "Sure am," he answered.

"Well, then," said Grandma, getting up to fetch the holiday bean dish from the oak sideboard, "looks like the Good Lord has already worked all things together. You've got the appetite and we've got the food!"

That, of course, was an understatement. Beneath Pop's and Grandma's bountiful hands each plate was soon filled to overflowing. Pop carved, Grandma dished, Gail passed, and Mike ate. Besides the turkey and gravy there was cornbread stuffing, green beans and crisped onions in a cream-of-mushroom sauce, mashed potatoes, potatoes au gratin, baked yams, cranberry sauce (jellied and whole), buttered corn and peas, whole wheat rolls (hot from the oven), and, for dessert, the inevitable pumpkin and mince pies.

Mike ate silently, staring at a gravy spot on Grandma's linen tablecloth. Meanwhile the conversation of the adults buzzed around his head. The atmosphere inside the little ranch-style house was hot and close. Through the window Mike could see the desert stars blinking in between the black, bare branches of the big cottonwood tree outside the dining room. From time to time the lace curtains stirred in the intermittent breeze; the evening was warm and the windows had been left open.

When the meal was nearly finished, Mike saw Pop suddenly straighten in his chair. He heard him clear his throat and saw the twinkle in his eye as he looked intently at the faces gathered around the table. Mike hunched down in his chair and winced. He knew what was coming. It happened every year in just this same way.

"Well," said Pop, leaning back with a smile. "Why don't we go around the table and each take a turn telling what we're thankful for this year?"

Gail's yellow curls bounced as she nodded in agreement.

"Good idea," said Grandma. "And since I think so, I'll go first. *I'm* thankful for a man who can carve a turkey just as neat and slick as he tunes an engine"—she reached over and laid her hand on Pop's—"and who never forgets to come home for dinner!"

Mike looked down and played with his fork. Gail spoke up next.

"I'm grateful for a good son," she said, touching Mike on the shoulder. "A fine boy who is growing into an even better man."

"Thanks, Mom." Mike couldn't help feeling irritated. His face flushed hot and red.

"*And* for a family that's always there to help—no matter what," Gail added. Mike thought he could see a glint of moisture in the corner of her eye.

Pop beamed. "What about you, Mike?" he said after a short pause. "Do you want to tell us what you're thankful for this year?"

For a long moment Mike couldn't find the courage to lift his eyes. They were glued to the gravy spot for what seemed like ages. Drops of sweat formed on the back of his neck. The room felt unbearably hot. He could feel the stares of the others focused on the top of his head. Then, so suddenly that it took him by surprise, he felt the blood drain away from his face. An inexplicable rush of cold rage burst over him. He clenched his napkin in his fist and looked up at Pop.

"No, I *don't*," he said in a very low voice. "Because I'm *not*." With that, he pushed back his chair, threw the napkin down on his plate, and ran from the table.

He was sitting on the edge of his bed, staring down at the white rubber toes of his tennis shoes, when his mom found him.

"I know what you're feeling," she said, sitting down alongside him and smoothing her blue gingham jumper over her knees. "I—well, I can't forget, either. Not *ever*. But what's done is done, Mike. And we—you and I—we just have to keep going somehow. You've got your whole life ahead of you!"

He turned and saw her put a hand to her eye. "What were you praying at the table, Mom?" he asked.

She tried to smile, but her lip trembled. "I was asking God to bring him back. It's what I always pray. You know that. But—"

"But we've got to do *more* than pray!" Mike interrupted fiercely. "We've got to go out and look! We've got to *make* the prayers come true! At least that's what *I'm* going to do!"

Gail looked stunned. For a moment, an expression of blank bewilderment smoothed the lines of grief from her face. Then, just as suddenly, it seemed to Mike that the pain flooded back into it with redoubled force. A furrow crossed her forehead—the same little crease that appeared whenever she was worried or angry. He watched her mouth harden into a straight line. She dabbed the corner of her eye with a handkerchief and looked him in the face.

"Life has to go on, Mike. There's Pop and Grandma. There's the gas station and the diner. There's church and school and—well, you need to find some friends. I've *always* felt that way."

Mike stood up and looked down at her. "You've always felt that way!" he said. "What about *my* feelings? I don't want any friends. I don't need any friends. I want my dad back. I'm going to find him. And until I do, I don't have *time* for friends." Then he turned on his heel and left the room.

He was trying to slip out through the back door—on his way to the B-17—when he felt a large and heavy hand on his shoulder.

"Old or young," said Pop, "a man has to do what a man has to do. Nobody knows that better than I. And now I'm seeing it all over again—in you."

Mike turned and looked up at him.

"I'm not sure where this path will lead you," Pop continued. "But *whatever* happens, just remember to keep your eyes on the Lord and hold tight to the truth. Remember what your mom and your grandma and I . . . *and* your dad . . . have taught you ever since you were knee-high to a grasshopper. If you do, you won't go wrong."

"What are you trying to say, Pop?"

"I'm sorry, Mike. I'm sorry if you feel that I've been standing in your way."

Mike stared, not sure how to respond.

"Oh, I wasn't kidding when I told you I was busy," Pop added with a little smile. "Unfortunately, *that* situation doesn't seem to be improving. Bill Carothers brought in a twin-engine Piper today—cutest little thing you ever saw. Wants it overhauled by the first of the year. And that's on top of the Cessna and everything else I'm doing out back on the airstrip. You've been a big help, of course—working at the diner and manning the pumps. Still, it'll probably be several weeks before I can get away . . . to take you over to the Navajo reservation, I mean."

"Oh," said Mike, looking down. "Well, I guess that's okay."

"As long as we understand each other, then," said Pop, standing back and sticking his hands down into his pockets. "I just want you to know that I'm on your side . . . and that I'll do my best to help you. As soon as I can."

"Thanks, Pop," said Mike, reaching for the door. "I'll be out in the B-17."

6

The Sheriff

The Saturday after Thanksgiving dawned dark, gray, and wet. It was a strange day—a quiet, muffled kind of day. A day when one of Arizona's rare winter rainstorms almost made Mike forget that he was living in a dry and desolate desert.

The iron sky pressed down on the tops of the red buttes and bluffs. Away near the horizon black and greenish-blue veils of rain stretched themselves between heaven and earth. Every so often a bolt of lightning split the air like a jagged kachina lance, followed by a confused and distant tumble of thunder. The wind was knife-edged.

Mike sat watching all of this through the window of the gas station office. Every time he had to step out into it to attend a customer, he retreated inside just as quickly as he could, convinced that Arizona must be the coldest place on the face of the earth.

He was just finishing his morning shift at the pumps and looking forward to making good use of the afternoon, when a blue Chevy pickup pulled into the station. Mike shivered and drew the hood of his yellow poncho up over his head. The sound of the bell, deadened by the steady rainfall, dropped away into silence as he hurried out to the pumps.

"Fill 'er up, sir?"

The driver rolled down his window and leaned out. Mike's jaw dropped. It was the man he'd seen that afternoon in the diner—the one who reminded him so strongly of his dad.

"Where's your self-serve island?" asked the customer.

"Oh, we don't do self-serve here," Mike answered—not without a touch of pride. "My grandpa—he owns this place—he believes that every customer deserves full service."

The man frowned. His jaw, the slight downward curve of the lips, the weathered creases across the tanned forehead—it was all so much like his dad . . . at least as he remembered him. True, there was something hard-edged about the lines that extended from the nostrils to the corners of the mouth. And the look in the eyes wasn't quite the same—not as warm and engaging. But that wasn't enough to destroy the resemblance. The close-cropped hair, the strong, sunburnt neck, the air of silent toughness. The disciplined toughness of a trained military man. All of it stirred something deep inside of Mike. He moved closer to the window of the truck cab.

"That's very nice," said the man at last. "I can respect that. But I was really looking for a self-serve island."

Mike fumbled for words. "Well, I—I'll be happy to fill 'er up for you, sir," he said. "It's no extra cost. I'll check your oil, too, and—"

"Don't bother with that," said the stranger curtly. "Just the gas. And make it quick as you can. I'm on a schedule."

"Yes, sir!"

Mike tried to engage him in conversation while the pump was running. He jawed about Ambrosia, about the unusual weather, about work and school. He asked where the driver was coming from and where he was headed. But he never succeeded in getting more than a one-word answer. The *click* of the pump shutting off struck him with an odd sense of disappointment. Why, he didn't know, but for some reason he had a strong desire to go on talking to this mysterious stranger. If only he could get him to listen. He felt sure that he'd be sympathetic. He'd understand all about the search for his dad. Mike just knew it.

When it came time to pay, the man reached into his back pocket, pulled out his wallet, and handed Mike a $50 bill. "Keep the change," he said. "I don't have time for it now."

Mike was speechless. All he could do was stare down at the faded, rumpled portrait of U. S. Grant. When he looked up, the truck was out on the road, roaring back through Ambrosia in a cloud of exhaust and spray, headed for Interstate 40.

"What was that all about?" asked Pop, coming up

alongside Mike as he stood there staring after the stranger through the rain.

"I'm not exactly sure," Mike answered, feeling a little bewildered. "Just a satisfied customer, I guess."

⟹

The weather had already ruled out any attempt at visiting the reservation that afternoon. Hitchhiking—his original idea—was out of the question. But Mike knew the value of a good Plan B. So as soon as he was finished with his last customer, he slung his backpack over his shoulder, pulled the hood of his poncho up over his head, and set out for Sheriff Smitty's.

The Vernon County and Ambrosia City sheriff's office was about a half-mile walk from the Last Chance Gas and Diner—straight down the main street of town, not far from the Indian Trading Post and the concrete wigwams of the Teepee Motor Lodge. That was far enough for Mike's tennis shoes and the lower part of his jeans to be completely soaked by the time he got to the door.

"Is that Mike Fowler?" mumbled Arlene through a mouthful of raspberry Danish as he came squelching into the room. She frowned and regarded him with a look of distaste. "You look like a drowned rat!"

Mike smiled apologetically. He drew off his dripping poncho and hung it on the coat-and-hat tree beside the door. Then he stood for a moment surveying the room: the two old wooden desks shoved together under the west window, flanked by a couple of tall gray filing cabinets; a coffeemaker on a folding table; the obligatory jail cell in the corner (empty as usual); the cork board bristling with posters and notices; a small shelf crowded with several police coffee cups and a bronzed donut; the pale and dirty green walls bearing two or three framed photos of a much younger Smitty in the uniform of the Army Rangers; the dusty venetian blinds. He wrinkled up his nose at the odd mix of scents in the air—a combination of stale coffee, Arlene's *Eau de Toilette* perfume, and the lingering odor of strong industrial detergents.

Arlene waved the half-eaten pastry at him, holding it delicately between the thumb and pudgy index finger of her right hand. "What reason could you *possibly* have for coming down here on a day like this, Mike?" she scolded good-naturedly. Her headset wobbled and the red bow on top of her knot of blond hair bobbed in sympathy.

"I've got my reasons," Mike answered, involuntarily marking how the lacy frills around the collar of her pink sweater reminded him of a Valentine's Day card. "Is Smitty around?"

Arlene's eyes narrowed suspiciously. "There's some kind of trouble, isn't there? Don't tell me—a robbery at the gas station!"

"No," sighed Mike, taking off one of his shoes and thinking that a robbery might have been exciting. He dumped the water from the shoe into a potted plant. "Nothing like that. Just a really generous customer—a stranger—at the pumps this morning."

"Really?" said Arlene, her eyebrows arching upward

and her mouth drawing into a tight little circle. "Was he—good-looking?"

Mike looked up at her and frowned. Then he sat down on the edge of a wooden chair and slipped his foot back into his shoe. "I didn't come here about that, Arlene. I came for *information*."

Arlene brightened. "Information?" she lisped with a dimpled smile. "Oh, we *specialize* in information! What do you want to know?"

"Can I talk to Sheriff Smitty?" Mike asked again, getting to his feet and glancing around the office.

"Out on a call. But *I* can pretty much tell you anything about everything that goes on in this town." Mike could almost see her round little body swelling with pride as she said it.

"Well, I . . ." Mike began, wondering how much he should tell. But then he stopped short as a rack of tourist literature and guides to local attractions caught his eye. There were street maps of Ambrosia. Road maps tracing the route of Interstate 40 across California, Arizona, and New Mexico. Colorful brochures describing the Petrified Forest, the Cliff Dwellings, Sunset Crater Volcano National Monument. Mike crossed the room to get a closer look.

Two of these brochures captured his attention so entirely that he didn't even notice Arlene's continued babbling. One was a bright, multicolored *Guide to the Navajo Country*. The other was an informational pamphlet about the Lowell Observatory in Flagstaff. On the cover it sported an old black-and-white photo of a distinguished-looking gentleman with calm, piercing eyes, a high, clear forehead, and a handlebar mustache. Below the picture was a caption: *Percival Lowell.*

"How much for these?" he asked, pulling them off the rack and looking back over his shoulder at Arlene.

"Those?" she said with a quizzical look. "They're yours if you really want them. Hardly anybody ever does. But then hardly anybody ever comes in here. Except to pay a parking ticket or report a missing dog."

A sudden burst of static and distortion crackled over Arlene's radio receiver. Looking flustered, she fumbled to resettle her headset. "Ambrosia dispatch," she said. "Arlene here."

More static. Then a snatch of a man's voice: "*. . . State Police and the FBI . . .*"

"FBI?" exclaimed Mike. He laid the brochures on the desk and leaned closer.

"Sshh!" shushed Arlene. "This seems to be coming in from a distance. The weather doesn't help."

"*. . . coyote operating in the area . . .*" resumed the voice as the signal momentarily gained strength. "*10-20 last verified as north Vernon County . . . Hopi Buttes and . . . near the ruins of . . .*" The transmission faded.

"Oh, fiddlesticks!" puffed Arlene. "And that sounded like a *good* one!"

Mike frowned. "The FBI's chasing coyotes?" he asked doubtfully.

"That's police talk!" said Arlene, making a note of

the call with one hand and reclaiming the raspberry Danish with the other. "*Coyote* is code . . . for a 'wetback runner'—a guy who smuggles illegal aliens across the Mexican border and into the cities and farm towns up north. They're usually drug dealers, too."

At that moment the front door flew open. Sheriff Smitty stood there, filling the rectangular space with the bulk of his imposing frame. The sheer size of the man was enough to inspire a 12-year-old boy with an involuntary feeling of awe. Though he stood all the way across the room from him, Mike couldn't help giving way before the sheriff's advancing presence. Unconsciously, he backed into the rack of tourist brochures as Smitty, like a vision out of the old West, his wide-brimmed gray hat cocked determinedly forward on his head, his black poncho fluttering wildly around his broad shoulders, stepped into the office, followed by a gust of wind and rain.

"Whew!" he whistled, throwing off the hat and poncho and sitting down heavily on the chair. "This is *some* kind of storm for December! I reckon they'll get some serious snow out of this north of Albuquerque. How's it going here, Arlene?"

"Smitty," she said, "did you hear that call about a 'coyote'?"

"Sure did," he answered. Without looking up, he pulled a big red bandana from his back pocket and began wiping the rain and mud from his boots. "Everything's under control. Hello there, Mike," he added abruptly, as if noticing the boy's presence for the first time. "To what do we owe the pleasure of this unexpected visit?"

"Sheriff," said Mike, without preface or explanation, "what's the quickest way onto the Navajo reservation?"

Smitty gave him a sharp glance and stroked his unruly salt-and-pepper mustache. "Who wants to know?"

"I do. I'm—well, I'm looking for some Navajo people. I mean, I'd like to meet some."

"Would you now?" Smitty's forehead contracted over his bushy gray eyebrows. Something about his expression made Mike feel that he was in for an inter-rogation.

"Yeah. I'm trying to learn as much as I can about their language," he faltered. "You know—Diné."

Smitty raised an eyebrow. "Is this for a school project?"

"Not exactly." Mike hesitated. "Do *you* know any-thing about the Navajo language, Sheriff Smitty? You speak Spanish pretty well, don't you?"

"*Me?*" Smitty laughed. "No, I'm afraid Spanish and Diné don't have much in common! I don't know a whole lot about Navajo talk . . . except that the Marines once used it as the basis of some kind of code."

"A code?" said Arlene, polishing off the raspberry Danish with a flourish. "How do you mean?"

"Military business, Arlene," said Smitty, getting to his feet and crossing the room to the coffeemaker. He poured himself a cup of the steaming black liquid and took a sip. "World War II. Hardly *anybody* knows any-thing about it. But it must have been something like the code we use around here. You know, 'coyote' for 'drug-runner' and 'smuggler of illegal aliens.' '10-20' for 'location.' That kind of thing. Except that it was based on Navajo words."

Mike thought about the strange words in the journal. *Belasana dah lhacha'e . . . Thanzi cha dzeh jadholoni . . .* Could his dad have known anything about military codes? Even when he was a teenager? It seemed like a stretch. Still, he supposed it was possible. He shifted his weight and watched the sheriff swirl his coffee with a plastic stirring stick. He still wasn't sure how much he should tell.

"Well, anyway," he said at last, "it seems my dad knew a little bit of the Diné language."

Smitty put down his cup. "*John* spoke Navajo?" He leaned back against the table, smiled, and ran his fingers through his graying hair. "Well—can't really say it surprises me! Him and that Harrison Lasiloo!"

Mike tried to smile back. "Yeah. At least I think so. And it's because of my dad that I'd like to learn something about it, too. But that's hard when you don't know anyone who speaks it. I asked Pop if he could take me over to the reservation sometime . . . just to ask around. He's too busy right now. So I just thought that if I . . ."

Smitty's eye fell on the colorful *Navajo Country* brochure Mike had dropped on Arlene's desk. He picked it up, studied it a moment, then took another long sip of coffee. "In that case," he said, "I'd suggest that you just wait a bit . . . until he *isn't* quite so busy."

Mike stared. Arlene cocked an ear in Smitty's direction and sat forward on the edge of her chair.

"What do you mean?" said Mike.

"I mean," Smitty answered quietly, "that the Navajo reservation is no place for a kid like you to go snooping around. Not by himself. Not right now, anyway. That's my considered *professional* opinion."

"But why not?"

"Ambrosia," came another crackling call over the transmitter. *"Come in, Ambrosia."*

Smitty motioned to Arlene to take the call. Then, putting an arm around Mike's shoulder, he hastily ushered the boy to the door.

"Mike," he said, handing him his poncho, his backpack, and the two brochures from the rack, "take my advice and forget about the Navajo reservation for a while. Okay? Now if you'll just excuse us, we've got some official business to attend to. I'll see you at the diner sometime."

A moment later, Mike stood on the pavement, watching as the wind tore a gaping blue hole in the gray sky and sent a detachment of shredded black clouds scudding out eastward. The rain had stopped and the clouds to the west were fringed with fiery gold.

"No place for a kid to go snooping around," he thought bitterly. *"Not by himself"*! Well—we'll just see about that!

7

Ben

*Now it came to pass when Percival's father, the noble
Gahmuret, had been slain in battle in the service of the
Baruc of Baghdad, that then his mother Herzeloyde for-
sook her three kingdoms and all her possessions and
withdrew with her son to the wilds of the Desolate Forest. And there in secret, away from the eyes of men, she
cherished young Percival, and cosseted him, and made a
solemn vow that never should he come to any knowledge
of knighthood or weapons or horsemanship or feats of
arms. For she feared to lose him as she had lost his
father.*

*Now it chanced upon a day that the boy, who was
proud and handsome and unacquainted with fear, jour-
neyed at his pleasure through the open vales of the Desolate Forest. It was at that fair season of the year when
trees bud, bushes leaf, and meadows turn to green. And
as he went along, it happened that a great clamor came
to his ears through the eaves of the wood: the jingling of
hauberk and spurs, the clash of sword and shield, the*

knocking of spear-beam against the boughs of the hemlocks, the thunder of hoof-beats upon the turf.

Then, as he stood all amazed, a wondrous portent broke through the leaves and branches of the oaks and stood before him upon the greensward: a man, brighter than the sun, clad all in shining steel, and seated upon the back of a great stamping horse.

"Are you an angel?" asked the boy.

"By my troth," answered the man, "no!"

"Are you God?"

"Foolish youth! I am not!"

"Then who are you?"

"I am a knight."

"I never knew a knight before," said the boy, "and never saw one or heard talk of one. But I trow you are more beautiful than any angel. I wish I were like you, so sparkling and so formed."

Young Percival went home and told his mother that he had seen a knight. Then was she wroth and faint of heart. And she cried out, "Alas, wretch that I am! For I had thought, my darling son, to protect you from all knowledge of knighthood and deeds of arms. For sure it was in the service of chivalry that your father, my beloved husband Gahmuret, forfeited his life and left me desolate. And now what shall I do?"

But Percival comforted her, saying, "Nothing now will serve, Mother, but that I go to King Arthur's court and become a knight myself. For I have seen the glory of the Office of the Shield, and so must Arthur's kingly

power guide me till I have achieved that place of honor,
if it so please God. . . ."

Mike glanced up from the book he'd been reading—
his father's old worn copy of *King Arthur and His Knights
of the Table Round.* The shafts of sunlight angling in
through the windows on the south side of the B-17 hurt
his eyes. He glanced down at his watch and yawned.
2:23—almost time to start work in the diner kitchen.

There had been no school that day; the teachers
were busy with bookkeeping and parent conferences.
So Mike had spent the morning in the Flying Fortress,
seated at the radio operator's table, staring diligently at
the strange words on the pages of the journal, randomly
dipping into the books that lined the shelves. And as he
read, the shifting beams of the sun, bright with dancing
dust motes, had marked the passage of time like the
shadow that marches across the face of the sundial.

He got up and stretched his arms and legs. *Nothing
now will serve.* He let the words play over in his mind.
Nothing now will serve, but that I go . . . if it so please God.
He stared at the picture in the book—a yellow-haired boy
looking up at a knight on horseback, all in silver and scarlet armor. Suddenly the sheriff's words came back to him:
No place for a kid like you to go snooping around.

Mike slammed the book shut, sending a puff of glittering dust into the air. He replaced it on the shelf and
stood there for a moment, studying the yellow spines of
the *National Geographic*s.

All at once it hit him—what Pop had said about his dad and Harrison Lasiloo: that their exploits had actually been written up in an old issue of the *Geographic*. *Why didn't I think of it earlier?* he wondered. In a few moments he had pulled the entire collection down from the shelf and spread it out across the floor of the B-17.

"Dad!" he exclaimed when at length he had found it.

There could be no mistake about it. He knew that face! Picking up the yellow-bordered magazine, he blew off the dust and laid it on the table. The cover bore what he recognized as a photograph of a very young John Fowler, perhaps 15 or 16 years old, standing alongside a lanky Native American of about the same age. Both boys were heavily armed with picks, shovels, and camping equipment. They were standing in front of a sheer cliff of red sandstone, 50 or 60 feet high. At the top of the cliff, nestled in a deep alcove, stood the ruin of an ancient cliff dwelling—a regular apartment block of square stone houses, two or three stories high, punctured here and there with black rectangular windows.

"Desert Treasure," read the title of the feature article. The subcaption continued: "Harrison Lasiloo and John Fowler of Ambrosia, Arizona: Two local boys uncover the biggest Anasazi cache of the past 20 years."

"*Wow!*" breathed Mike. This was just the kind of thing he'd been looking for! Eagerly he flipped open the magazine, intending to bury himself in the article. But then something about the angle of the light through the windows caused him to glance down at his watch again.

3:05! Already past time to report for work!

Without taking time to zip up his backpack, Mike flung it over his shoulder, shoved the crew door open, and bounded from the B-17, stopping briefly to lock the door.

Outside, the day was mild and bright. The cloudless sky was a clean and piercing blue. Mike tore across the parking lot and hit the diner door at full speed.

"I'm here, Mom!" he called, bursting into the room. "Sorry about being late!"

Gail looked up from the roll of dimes she was holding poised over the cash drawer.

"That's okay, honey," she said, cracking the roll open and dumping the coins into the drawer in a clattering heap. "Slow time of day, anyway—in between the lunch and dinner crowds."

"Right," said Mike. Then, scraping together his courage, he added, "Oh, by the way, Mom—I was sort of wondering if you could . . . well, take me somewhere this weekend."

"Somewhere?" said Gail with a skeptical frown. He saw the little crease appear on her forehead.

"Yeah. Like the Navajo reservation. Or the Cliff Dwellings."

His mother crossed her arms and gave him a searching look. "Struck out with Pop, so you're giving me a try —is that it?"

Mike said nothing.

"I don't know, Mike. I've already told you how I feel about this 'quest' of yours. It worries me. I don't want you getting into trouble. Anyway, you know how hard it can be for me to get away. When I'm not waitressing and cashiering, I'm doing the books or catching up on housework. Do you understand?"

"Yeah. Sure."

"Now you'd better get back there. Grandma's waiting."

"Right, Mom."

Mike *didn't* understand. But then he wasn't really surprised. He'd known it was a long shot when he tried it. Shouldering his backpack, he hurried back toward the kitchen.

His mom was right. The place was unusually quiet this afternoon. Deserted, in fact. Completely empty of a single soul.

Except one.

Ping! Chk-chkk! Ping! Ping! Chk!

Mike turned at the sound. It was a sound that had become increasingly familiar—and irritating—to him over the past few days.

"Oh, no!" he groaned. "Not again."

"All *right*!" came an excited shriek from the back corner of the room. "Another 500 points!"

Mike shook his head. There, standing in front of the vintage Space Invaders pinball machine—a brightly painted early '50s model, complete with bells and flashing lights—was a short, stout boy in a green-and-blue striped T-shirt. A boy not much younger than Mike himself. Certainly no older. His placid round face was the very picture of ecstasy. A strange, distant light danced in his wide blue eyes. His curly hair formed a wild, dark, reddish-brown halo around his wagging head as he plied the levers and handles with abandon and enthusiasm, completely lost in the game.

It had been this way almost every afternoon since Mike began working in the kitchen. Gail and Grandma Fowler called the boy a "regular." Mike just called him "annoying."

Ping! Chk-chkk! Ping!

"Gotcha, you gross, disgusting alien! *Whoopeee!*"

Again the lights flashed and the bells clanged. Mike rolled his eyes. "Do you *mind*?" he demanded, turning and regarding the source of the ruckus with an expression of absolute intolerance.

The boy swung his head around. There was a look of innocent bewilderment on his pudgy face. "Mind what?"

"Just tone it down, okay?"

"Hey, I've just racked up a total of 7,693 points!" The boy released the controls and waved both hands over his head. "Do you realize what that means?"

"No." Mike backed away as the boy took a step closer to him. He had an uncomfortable feeling that this pinball wizard wasn't entirely rational. "Should I?"

"It means the Martians are practically beaten! It means they'll never make it to London after all—not at this rate! The way I've got it figured, I've pushed 'em all the way back to Weybridge! I've got my own system worked out— it's all based on points! See? You wanna play?"

"Weybridge?" said Mike, still edging away. "What are you talking about?"

"This!" The boy drew a rolled-up comic book from his back pocket and spread it out just under Mike's nose. "I put *this* together with a point system based on Space Invaders. I invented a game of my own. When I miss a shot, the Martians advance a mile. When I score, they're forced to retreat. Get it?"

Mike was about to shove the comic book away when he noticed the title on the cover: *Illustrated Classics: The War of the Worlds,* by H. G. Wells. He stood gaping at it for a moment.

"Where'd you get this?" he asked, eyeing the boy closely.

"Bert's Comics and Fanzines. Over on Buckley Street. It's worth a *lot* of money. See the date? *1968!* I'm Ben Jones, by the way. Do you collect comics? I'm going over there later this afternoon. Wanna come?"

"Look, kid," said Mike, taking another quick step backward, "I've got work to—"

Crash! Before he knew what had happened, Mike had fallen over a chair, struck his shoulder on a table, and rolled to the floor. His unzipped backpack slid across the newly waxed floor, plowed violently into the base of the counter, and burst open, spilling its contents halfway across the diner.

"Whoa!" said Ben. His jaw dropped and his blue eyes popped wide. "Sorry about that! Lemme help!" With an embarrassed little-boy look, he scurried to pick up the books and papers that lay scattered on the floor. "I didn't mean to—hey! Whatcha got here?"

Painfully, Mike raised his head and looked over at Ben. The boy had a happy, knowing look on his face. He was holding up a piece of paper bearing an old black-and-white photo of a distinguished, mustachioed gentleman.

"Oh," said Mike, sitting up with a groan. "That's just a brochure about the Lowell Observatory."

"I know *that!*" said Ben. "I know a lot about Percival Lowell. He believed in life on Mars. Seriously! He even wrote a book about it!"

Mike stared.

"When *I* talk about the Martians, people think I'm nuts. But *this* guy had proof! Scientific evidence! *He* knew the truth! He studied Mars through his big telescope and drew maps of the canals and the polar ice caps and everything. I'm telling you—what was your name?"

"Mike," said Mike, groaning again.

"I'm telling you, Mike, this is for real! The government's been covering it up. My dad says so! And guess what? He's taking me to Lowell Observatory to check it out. On Saturday! I've got this theory. I think the Martians have been here before! Right here in Ambrosia!"

"Wait a minute! What did you just say?"

"They've *been* here! There's all kinds of evidence. They've left their marks all over the place!"

"No, I meant what did you just say about *Saturday*?"

"Oh, just that my dad's taking me to Flagstaff. To the observatory. To check it out. You wanna come?"

Mike gave the boy a skeptical look. "Are you serious?" he asked after a pause.

"Why not? We can pick you up here—sometime after breakfast. It'll take all day."

"Lowell Observatory?" Mike took the brochure from Ben and examined the picture of the gentleman with the mustache.

"That's the one."

The wheels of Mike's mind raced. He'd been so focused on the journal and the Navajo reservation and the Diné language that he hadn't given his dad's astronomical interests a single thought. The possibility of taking a trip to the observatory—the same observatory his dad had apparently loved so much as a kid—had never entered his mind. He wondered . . .

"You really want *me* to come along?" he asked.

"Sure!" said Ben. "It'll be fun!"

Maybe, Mike thought, *just maybe . . .*

But no. He wasn't looking for a partner. Definitely not *this* partner. His quest was too secret. And too important. A kid like this could mess everything up.

Then again, if Ben were really offering him a ride to Lowell Observatory . . . a *free* ride . . .

"So what do you think?" asked Ben, shoving the last of the books and papers down into the backpack and handing the whole disorganized mess back to Mike.

Mike took the proffered backpack, stood up, and eyed Ben up and down.

"I'll see you here Saturday," he said at last. "Nine o' clock."

8

Spence

"Are you sure we're still in Arizona?"

Mike's face was pressed up against the back window of Mr. Jones's 1989 Plymouth Voyager. Outside, the ponderosa pines marched by in stately procession along the edge of Mars Hill Road. After nearly two hours of driving they were finally winding their way out of Flagstaff and climbing the last curving mile to the Lowell Observatory.

It was just past noon on a bright and cloudless day. Here and there clear beams of sunlight sloped northward through the pillared distances of the forest. There was a thin layer of light snow on the ground. Clumps of snow clung sparkling and white to the dark green needles of the trees. The air outside was chill; Mike could tell by the plume of steamy exhaust streaming from the van's tailpipe.

"What was that, son?" asked Mr. Jones glancing back over his shoulder.

"I was just saying," Mike answered, "that I didn't know they had mountains like these in Arizona! I mean, the Superstitions are one thing. But *this*! And the trees! They're incredible!"

"Mountains?" answered Mr. Jones. He waved a hand carelessly into the rearview mirror. "Oh, sure, we got mountains!" He had to shout to make himself heard above the blare of the music. He'd been raising his voice ever since plugging a Garth Brooks tape into the cassette player back in Winslow. Apparently he wasn't aware that it came equipped with a volume control knob.

"Did I ever tell you how I invented karaoke back in the 70s?" he added. "Back when I was dating Charo?"

Ben leaned over the back of his seat and rolled his eyes while his dad shoved another tape into the slot—Baha Men's *Who Let the Dogs Out?*—and began singing along at the top of his lungs. This sort of thing had been going on for at least the last 60 miles. Mike might have started screaming by the time they got to Winona if he hadn't been so enchanted by the changing landscape. He simply couldn't believe what he was seeing.

Ben turned around, jammed his chin down into the torn upholstery on the top of his seat, and grinned. "I toldja," he said. "I toldja it'd be great! Just wait! They've got a gift shop and everything. And pictures of the Martian canals!"

But Mike wasn't thinking about gift shops or Martian canals. He was gazing out over the top of Mr. Jones's bobbing bald spot at the fresh, frosted greenness of the pines. He was remembering hikes with his dad through the woods back home.

At the top of the drive, Mr. Jones pulled into a paved parking lot among the overarching trees. The boys piled out while the engine was still running and shuffled through the powdery snow to a sign that stood at the edge of a sidewalk:

Lowell Observatory: Steele Visitor Center. Daily Tours, November to March: 1 P.M. and 3 P.M.

Below were brief directions to other points of interest: Slipher Building Rotunda, Clark Telescope and Dome, Pluto Walk, Pluto Discovery Telescope and Dome.

"This is it!" said Ben, pointing up the walk to a long, low building with thick stone walls. The sun gleamed sharply off the thin stripes of snow that lay along the ridges and in the corners and crevices of its rust-red steel roof. Beyond, in the bright distance, a high silver dome flashed through the canopy of trees in the daylight. Ben's face was rosy with the cold and with excitement.

"Over there," he added, pointing through the woods, "is the big telescope they used to get their first good look at the Martians. You'll see!"

Mike zipped his brown leather aviator's jacket up to the chin and blew out a cloud of white breath into the frosty air. "Great," he said, kicking the toe of his sneaker into the dusty snow at his feet. He still wasn't quite sure how to talk to this pudgy-faced, wild-eyed maniac.

"So—where to first, guys?" asked Mr. Jones, stepping up alongside them. He drew the hood of his blue nylon windbreaker up over his balding head and stuck his hands down into his pockets. "Brrr! Kinda cold up here, isn't it?" He smiled pleasantly and stroked the reddish whiskers that grew along the edge of his upper lip. He had a way of reaching up to touch this sparse excuse for a mustache—as if to reassure himself that it was still there—every time he spoke.

"Are we going to take a tour?" asked Mike, glancing up at the sign. Now that he was here, he wasn't exactly sure what he was looking for, and he had no idea where to begin. A tour, he thought, might be a good way to find out.

"A *tour*?" sneered Ben. "No way! Tours are for old people! *That's* where *I'm* going!" He pointed to the silver dome beyond the visitor center. "To the rotunda. That's where they keep the Mars globes!"

"Whatever you say, son," said Mr. Jones with an indulgent laugh.

"Then we'll come back here," Ben continued, "to the interactive exhibit hall—the *Tools of the Astronomer.* It's really cool. Did I tell you they've got a gift shop?"

Mike bit his lip and fumed inwardly as they climbed the broad steps to the Slipher Rotunda, an impressive round building of reddish-gray stone under an imposing silver dome. He hadn't come here to play interactive games or spend money on souvenirs. He certainly wasn't interested in hanging around with pinball Ben and his karaoke dad. He was groping for something—anything—that might connect him with his dad.

Pop said he spent a lot of time here, he thought as the

Rotunda's massive oak door swung open on its iron hinges. *Maybe he left some trace of himself behind— carved his initials on the bathroom wall or something.*

He had expected to find a telescope inside the Rotunda. Instead, he found himself standing in what felt like a library or a museum. There was a kind of hush about the place; a quiet, muffled smell of books and aged wood and other musty old things. Their shuffling footsteps echoed softly around the walls and up into the high, rounded, dark-beamed hollow of the ceiling as they moved almost reverently about the room. Above their heads hung something that looked like a model of the planet Saturn—a big coppery ball encircled by a series of flat, silvery rings. Rows of shelves and glass-covered display cases, filled with brassy antique-looking optical instruments, lined the walls and extended out into the center of the open space under the dome.

Distancing himself from Ben, Mike gravitated toward a plaque on the wall that bore a portrait of the same formal-looking gentleman he'd first seen on the cover of the observatory brochure. *Lowell Observatory*, read the title under the photograph. *A Distinguished History*.

Lowell Observatory was the first astronomical observatory in Arizona. In 1894, Dr. Percival Lowell, a mathematician and amateur astronomer from Massachusetts, was one of several astronomers in search of clearer skies through which to observe the planets and stars. Flagstaff, with its dark skies and high elevation, was an ideal location. Dr. Lowell founded the Observatory primarily to explore the possibility that intelligent life might exist on Mars. Spurring him on was the knowledge that Mars would soon be at its closest point to the earth. . . .

"Did you boys see this?"

Mike's thoughts were interrupted by the voice of Mr. Jones, who was stroking his mustache and standing alongside one of the oddest of the many odd astronomical curiosities that filled the room—a large, black camera-like contraption with a protruding eyepiece and a flipping shutter.

"This is the Blink-Comparator. With this little device, an astronomer can capture images of different views of the night sky, line them up them side by side, and *compare* them in rapid sequence—*click, click, click!*"—he flipped the shutter back and forth several times—"You see? Clyde Tombaugh used it to discover 'Planet X' back in 1930. 'Planet X'—that's Pluto. The ninth planet. Did you know that Pluto was discovered right here at Lowell, Ben?"

"Sure, Dad," Ben answered flatly.

Mike could tell that Ben hadn't been listening to his father at all. Instead, he was staring intently at a display case containing a series of antiquated drawings on brittle yellow paper: pictures of reddish globes, each crisscrossed by a series of thin black lines in intricate geometric patterns and capped with a splotch of white.

Ben spread his hands out on the top of the glass case and raised his eyebrows. "Whoa!" he said.

Mike walked over and glanced down into the case. He caught his breath. These pictures were almost identical to the one that hung on the wall of the B-17!

"What are they?" he asked.

"Mars globes!" Ben answered. "Percival Lowell made them. After hours of studying Mars through the big telescope. See these lines? Canals! Dug by the Martians to carry water from the melting polar cap down to their big cities! Pretty amazing, huh?"

Mike squinted at the drawings. He had to agree that the lines, straight and neat and marked with dark spots at intersecting points, looked very much like the work of intelligent beings.

"And you know what else?" There was a strange and intense light in Ben's blue eyes. "I think they've been *here* and done the same thing! Just like in *The War of the Worlds*! A long time ago, maybe. Remember how they found that 'Mars Rock' in Antarctica a few years ago?"

"You're crazy, Ben!" sneered Mike, turning away.

"No, really!" objected Ben. "Think about it! What about all those canyons up north of Ambrosia? Up in the Navajo country? Where do you think *they* came from, huh? What about the *Grand* Canyon?"

"It's possible," observed Mr. Jones, who was already pulling his hood up over his roundish head and waddling toward the door. "These things get covered up by the government, you know. I don't doubt that for a minute."

They're both nuts, thought Mike.

⎯⎯✦⎯⎯

By the time they had left the Rotunda and were wandering back under the pines to the Steele Visitor Center, Mike was kicking himself for ever having decided to come. He dawdled along behind Ben and Mr. Jones, his hands in his pockets and his chin on his chest. The Mars globes *were* sort of interesting, he supposed. But on the whole, this day was turning out to be a waste of time.

Gift shop! he thought, stopping to pick up a small stone that lay in the snow beside the path. *Charo! Blink-Comparator! What's any of that got to do with me and my dad?* He reared back and heaved the stone into the depths of the forest. It rebounded off the trunk of a distant tree with a lonely, hollow, wooden sound.

Mike shuffled dejectedly through the *Tools of the Astronomer* exhibition hall, checking his watch from time to time. He wondered how long it would be before they could go back to the car and get started on the two-hour drive back to Ambrosia. Not that he couldn't appreciate the marvels of astronomy or the glories of the heavens as they were represented in the various displays. He *could* and he *did*—if only because he knew how much John Fowler had loved these things. But for all its brightness and color and interest, there wasn't anything in this place that could give him what he was *really* looking for: a feeling of some kind of *direct* connection with his dad. He saw all of it as if from a distance, or through a veil of thick mist.

Listlessly he cast his eyes around at the star charts, the sky maps, the models of the solar system that crowded the aisles of the hall. On every side were interactive games that demonstrated optical principles and the properties of lenses and parabolic mirrors. Mike walked past all of them without feeling even the slightest twinge of a desire to play. There were small telescopes like the one he'd found sitting atop the radio operator's table in the Flying Fortress, and detailed cutaway mock-ups of the large, powerful refractors and reflectors used by astronomers to study Uranus, Neptune, and Pluto. He stared at them with an odd feeling of disinterest.

Dimly he sensed something of the joy his dad must have known in coming to this place, but it had no power to stir him. It affected him like a news report of events in a foreign country. As he stood there in the midst of the planetary globes and sparkling simulations of the sky, a sort of cold, clinical realization overtook him: an awareness of the profound mystery of immeasurable distance, the allure of the vast unknown, the siren call of deep space. *No wonder he wanted to fly,* he thought sadly.

Mike was standing in front of a series of displays on "Blind Spots" and "Limitations of the Eye" when he realized that he had lost track of the Joneses altogether. He had no idea where Ben had gone. Probably to the gift shop. Not that he cared. All he wanted out of *them* was a ride home.

He looked up and noticed a boy he hadn't seen before. A small, slightly built African-American boy in beige dockers and a short-sleeved, button-down-collar, blue plaid shirt. His dark brown, tightly curled hair was cropped close to his head, and he had a large pair of thick, dark-rimmed glasses perched on the bridge of his nose. There was a calm, perceptive, intelligent expression on his clear young face as he stared intently at a model of a reflecting telescope—a large, shiny white tube that stretched from floor to ceiling just in front of a multicolored mural depicting the orbits of the planets. Every so often the boy would stop and jot something down on a yellow pad that he held poised on a big, clear plastic clipboard.

Though he couldn't have said why, something about this boy struck Mike to the heart. Perhaps he was thinking of what his dad must have been like when *he* was 10 or 11 years old—tinkering with telescopes, building model airplanes, shooting homemade rockets into the coral-colored desert evening sky. Perhaps the purity and intensity of the boy's devotion to the object of his attention made Mike think of young Sir Percival and his desire to become a knight. Whatever it was, he found himself slowly gravitating toward this young scholar.

Mike sidled over to the telescope display. Silently, unobtrusively, nonchalantly, he took up a position alongside the boy. He leaned against the railing with his forearms and pretended to concentrate on the white tube. For several minutes the two of them stood there staring straight ahead, as if neither was aware of the other's presence. At last the boy stuck his pen into his pocket and turned to Mike.

"Are you interested in parabolas too?" he said.

"Parabolas?"

There was something about the boy's manner, at once so self-assured and so completely unassuming, that Mike suddenly found a bit intimidating.

"Is that like *parables*?" he asked, in an attempt to appear as knowledgeable as possible. He'd heard a message on the parable of the prodigal son at Ambrosia Christian Fellowship the previous Sunday.

"As a matter of fact, the two words *do* come from the same Greek root," the boy answered matter-of-factly, "though for different reasons. *Paraballo* means to place one thing alongside another; so that, in the one case, a *parable* is a *comparison* or an *analogy*, whereas a *parabola* is a geometric curve whose axis runs parallel to the side of a cone."

"Oh. Right."

"But the two have something important in common: a *focal point*."

"Really?" Mike straightened up and finger-combed his sandy hair out of his staring blue eyes. He felt big, cloddy, and stupid somehow.

"Yes. You see, the mirror of a reflecting telescope"— the boy pointed to a sketch he'd made; it looked like a large block-style capital letter "I," except that its left side was straight and its right side curved inward—"the mirror gathers up parallel light rays from distant objects and bends them back into a focal point somewhere just above the surface of the mirror. I'm going to be grinding my own mirror soon," he added, "so I'm here gathering all the information I can. By the way, my name is Spence—Spence Martin. From Ambrosia." He stuck out his hand and smiled.

Mike stood staring down at the extended hand. *"Ambrosia?"* he said. "That's where *I'm* from!"

"Are you? It's a long drive," observed Spence, the glare of the fluorescent lights reflecting off his glasses. "Lucky my dad's been doing some geological research out here lately. At the base of Woody Mountain. He takes me with him every Saturday. Some weekdays, too—I'm home schooled. Drops me off here in the morning and picks me up in the afternoon."

"Oh. Great," said Mike.

"So what brings *you* to Lowell?"

Just then Ben ran up.

"Mike! Look what I got in the gift shop! Mars globe postcards! Cool, huh?"

Spence retreated a step and eyed the newcomer carefully. "Mars globes?" he said in the same unruffled tone. "Interesting." Mike was beginning to think that he didn't like this young scientist. *Talks like a know-it-all,* he thought.

"What do *you* know about Mars globes?" asked Ben with a scowl.

"A little," said Spence. "I've been interested in astronomy since I was about eight. I had a chance to browse through Lowell's *Mars As the Abode of Life* a couple of weeks ago. They have an old copy over in the Rotunda. It's fascinating—even if a bit quaint and outdated."

"*I* have a copy of that book," said Mike, seeing an opportunity to demonstrate his own knowledge. "At home. In my B-17."

"Seriously?" said Spence, giving him a searching look. "Do you think I could borrow it sometime?"

"Sure," said Mike, turning around and lounging against the railing. "That's not all I've got. I've got one of those Mars globe things, too. Only *mine's* an original."

"No way!" said Ben. "You're kidding me!"

"Nope," said Mike.

"Wait a minute," said Ben, backing away and holding up both hands as if to ward off the inevitable letdown. "*You* have a copy of *Mars As the Abode of Life*? And your own *B-17*?"

"That's what I said."

"Well, hey! We should all get together sometime!" said Ben, his excitement growing visibly. He turned to Spence. "So what's your name?"

"It's Spence," offered Mike. "And he lives in Ambrosia."

"No *possible* way!" shouted Ben.

A few of the other visitors turned and gave the boys unfriendly looks.

"So how come I've never seen you at school?" Ben continued in a lower tone.

"Like I was telling your friend—" Spence glanced over at Mike.

"Oh—I'm Mike," Mike said, a little apologetically. "Mike Fowler."

"Well, like I was telling Mike, I'm home schooled. I've got lots of projects going. Right now, I'm working on building my own telescope—an eight-inch Dobsonian reflector. I'm here picking up all the information I can get."

"Awesome!" enthused Ben. "Are you gonna use it to study Mars?"

"Possibly," answered Spence. "But first I want to check out a theory of my own—about the possible existence of a *10th* planet. I'll use the Dobsonian to make my initial observations when it's finished. Then I have plans to build a homemade version of Tombaugh's Blink-Comparator."

"Cool!" said Ben.

"Anyway," said Spence, turning back to Mike, "you never answered my question. What brings *you* all the way to Lowell?"

"Me?" Mike responded. He hesitated. "I'm—looking for my dad."

Ben stared.

"Is your dad lost?" Spence asked.

"Lost," said Mike. "Yeah. Since I was little. So little that I can hardly remember anything about him anymore. I came here because Pop—that's my grandpa; he owns the Last Chance Gas and Diner—Pop told me that my dad used to love this place. He was really into astronomy and flight and space travel and all that. In fact, he left behind a whole bunch of astronomical books and stuff—out in the B-17. Maybe you guys would like to see it sometime."

"Would we!" said Ben.

Mike wasn't sure if this was a smart move or not. He still found Ben irritating. He definitely would have preferred to pursue the quest for his dad alone and unassisted. And yet he couldn't help thinking that even a stuck-up snob like Spence, if he was really as smart as he seemed, might be able to help somehow—especially if he was knowledgeable about astronomy and the writings of Percival Lowell.

"I *would* like that," said Spence in response to Mike's offer. "Very much."

"Sure!" said Ben. "I mean, why not? If we work together, I'm *positive* we can find out exactly how the Martians got here, and why they dug those canals up in the Navajo country, and what happened to them!"

Spence gave Ben a blank look.

"Well!" said Mr. Jones cheerfully, coming up from behind them. "Ready to move on, guys? There's still the Pluto walk and Dr. Lowell's mausoleum to see!"

Mike and Spence exchanged phone numbers before parting ways.

"It's interesting," said Spence, as Mike was turning to follow the Joneses to the exit. "I was just thinking."

"Thinking?" said Mike, a little irritably.

"In the *parable*," observed Spence, before pulling out his pen and returning to his notes, "it was the *father* who was watching out for the *son*. Wasn't it?"

9

The Quads

So it befell that the raw youth went away to Arthur's court and was made knight. But he knew not that it broke his mother's heart.

Now when he had passed through many trials and divers adventures in the service of King Arthur, it happened at the feast of Pentecost that the King and the Lady Guinevere and all the fair fellowship of the Table Round sat at meat together in the great hall at Camelot. Then anon they heard a cracking and crying of thunder, so that they thought the whole place should be riven all to sunder. And in the midst of that blast entered a sunbeam clearer by seven times than any ever they had seen.

Then there entered into the hall the Holy Grail covered with white samite. But there was none that might see it, nor could any tell who bore it. And the hall was filled with sweet odors, and every knight had such meats and drinks as he loved best in the world. Then the Holy Grail departed suddenly, so that they wist not where it had gone.

"Now," said Sir Gawain, "but one thing has beguiled us: we have not seen the Holy Grail. Wherefore I will make here a vow that tomorrow morning, without delay, I shall labor in the quest of it, and I shall hold me out a twelvemonth and a day, or more if need be, and never shall I return till I have seen it."

Then rose up Sir Galahad and Sir Launcelot, and the most part of the knights of the Table Round, and made such vows as Sir Gawain had made. And young Sir Percival also rose up amongst them, and right heartily did he assent thereto.

But King Arthur was sore aggrieved; "for," said he, "my heart forewarns me that when they depart from hence, they all shall never meet more in this world. For many shall die in the quest. . . ."

"Whoa! Check it out! You mean you can actually get down inside this thing?"

Mike looked up from his book, annoyed. It was the week after Christmas, and school was still out. Ben and Spence had taken it upon themselves to pay him an unannounced visit at the Last Chance Gas and Diner. After that, Mike had kept the promise he made to them at the observatory: He took them out to the B-17 and gave them the grand tour. Naturally, he made sure to flourish the silver key at the end of the blue lanyard all the way across the gravel parking lot.

Spence had immediately taken a keen interest in the radio equipment. He sat at the operator's table, trying on the headphones, flipping switches, and turning dials. Ben, meanwhile, got busy at once exploring every cubic inch of the Flying Fortress's interior. He sat in the cockpit. He climbed down into the bomb bay. He pretended to fire the Browning machine guns. He swung himself in and out of the cockpit hatch.

After a while, Mike had grown bored and picked up the old copy of *King Arthur*. Now he was inwardly fuming at Ben for interrupting him . . . just when the story was getting interesting.

"Could I try it?"

Ben's voice was strident and persistent. He was standing in the waist of the plane, gawking at the ball turret mechanism—a big, gray, round thing like a large metal volleyball or a miniature space capsule, set down into the floor and hooked up to a lot of pipes, wires, and hoses.

"Sure," said Mike with a sigh, getting to his feet and reshelving the book.

"What's it for?"

"That's where the turret gunner used to sit. In battle, he'd fire at the enemy from the underbelly of the plane. See?"

Mike flipped a switch, and the ball began to roll forward with a whirring sound. "I just bring the hatch up into the plane—like this . . ."—he opened the hatch—"off with the lid . . . and in you go."

"Awesome!" said Ben, his brown eyes wide. "You mean it's really okay?"

By way of answer, Mike gave him a little shove. *He*

can sit down there till his parents call for all I care, he thought as Ben squeezed himself into the turret. *That way I won't have to listen to him.*

"Just for a couple of minutes. Okay, Mike? I get claustrophobic."

"Right."

Mike closed and secured the hatch. As the ball rotated back into position, he glanced over at the radio operator's table. Spence was still there, peering intently at the tubes and wires inside the old black radio.

"So," he said—a little coldly and standoffishly, per-haps—"what do you think?" He still couldn't help feel-ing a bit intimidated by the younger boy's vast intellect and quiet self-confidence.

"As a matter of fact, I think it might be possible to get this thing working," Spence answered, looking up at him. He picked up the headphones, put them on, and began fiddling with the dials and knobs again.

"You're kidding. For real?"

"Just a guess. Do we have a power source?"

We? thought Mike. Aloud he said, "We will. Soon. Pop's working on it. He wants to run a line out here from the gas station."

"Excellent," said Spence, almost as if talking to him-self. He took off the headphones and turned his dark eyes on Mike. "You really have something special here, Mike. Your own Flying Fortress!"

Mike felt a swelling in his chest. But he answered matter-of-factly. "Yeah. I know."

"I mean, the potential is incredible. The things you could do! I was just thinking . . ."

Something deep down inside of Mike leapt at the compliment, but he said nothing. He didn't want to encourage Spence unnecessarily. He'd been hoping that his visitors would get bored and decide to go home soon. Then he could get back to more important things. Like *King Arthur*. Or the business of his *own* quest.

In the momentary silence, they could hear Ben down inside the ball turret, making battle noises with his mouth—the *errrrrrr* of roaring engines, the *rrrowwwww* of diving fighters, the *t-t-t-t-t-t* of rattling machine guns, the descending scream of disabled bombers. Mike shook his head and rolled his eyes.

"Anyway, what I was thinking," Spence continued, "not that I want to impose—but, well, that little spot back there, behind the two guns, would be a *great* place to grind my mirror."

"Your *mirror*?"

"Yes. For my telescope. You remember I was telling you that I'm building a Dobsonian reflector?"

"Oh. Right. I forgot."

"Anyway, this would be perfect. Enclosed. Dust-free. Away from distractions. And in return, I've got some stuff I could add to your collection." Spence stood up and admired the star charts, the Neil Armstrong poster, and the Mars globe that hung along the plane's concave wall. "Maps and things. And some great books. I could help you make this place even better than it is."

Mike hemmed and hawed. "Well, I'll have to ask Pop," he said lamely, fingering the blue lanyard and the silver key in his pocket. "We can talk about it later. Do you want to see the cockpit?"

"Of course!" said Spence, bending to retrieve the notebook he'd left lying on the radio table.

Mike was turning to lead the way when he saw Spence stop and pick up something that lay beside the radio: a small, leather-bound book with well-thumbed pages and silver letters on the binding.

"Hang on!" said Spence. "This wouldn't be the radio operator's log, would it?"

"No!" said Mike. He hadn't intended to speak so sharply; he was angry with himself for having left the book lying out in the open. "It's my dad's journal. Here—I'll take it."

But Spence had already flipped the journal open and was examining the pages intently. "Incredible!" he breathed, looking up at Mike. "Can you read this?"

"Can *you*?"

"Would you expect me to?" Spence studied the page more closely. "I know some Spanish—"

"Me too," put in Mike.

"—and a little bit of French, but—well, I've never seen anything like *this* before! *Jad'holoni t'kin akehdiglini . . .*" —he pronounced the words very slowly—"what is it?"

A satisfied smile tugged at the corners of Mike's mouth. At last! Something Spence *didn't* know!

"I'm not exactly sure what the words mean," he

admitted. "But I *do* know that they're Diné—the language of the Navajo. Sheriff Smitty thought it might have something to do with a World War II military code. That's about all I can tell you. I've been trying for weeks to get over to the reservation to talk to someone about it."

The look on Spence's face was one of complete wonder. "Well, when you *do* go, do you think I could come along?" he asked. "This is fascinating! Besides, I've been meaning to take a look around that area myself—to scope out some good dark-sky locations. For my observatory."

Mike frowned. "Not unless your dad wants to give us a ride. I've got no transportation. Pop's been too busy to take me. If I only had some other way to get there . . ."

At that moment there came a knock at the rear of the plane.

"What's going on in there, Mike?" came Pop's good-natured voice. He shoved the crew door open and ducked his silver-gray head inside.

"Hi, Pop," answered Mike. "Nothing, really. We're just messing around, that's all. This is Spence—"

Pop nodded a greeting. "Good to see you, Spence!" Then, with a mysterious little smile, he added, "I just dropped by to see if you'd like to come and take a look at what I've got over in the garage. You might find it interesting." He raised his bushy eyebrows, then turned and ducked back out the way he'd come.

Mike and Spence exchanged looks.

Within minutes they were standing with Pop alongside the gas pumps with the desert wind in their hair, staring at a collection of small, one-seater, all-terrain vehicles—four altogether—that sat parked in the shadows just inside the Last Chance gas station's garage. They were immaculate, brightly painted, newly refurbished, and equipped with big, black deep-tread tires. Mike scrunched up his nose and scratched his head.

"*Quads?*" he said, glancing at Pop, whose wrinkled face was beaming.

"That's right," said Pop. "Just your size, too."

Mike saw Spence give him a quizzical look. "I don't get it, Pop. I mean, what . . . who . . . ?"

Pop chuckled. "Remember that Cessna I was working on? Well, Carothers wanted it. Bad. Only he didn't have the money—not enough, anyway. We talked about working out some kind of payment plan. But then he offered to barter with these. Call me an old fool—I *know* Grandma will!—but I took him up on it."

Mike looked at the quads. Quickly he put two and two together. *Transportation*, he was thinking. *Navajo country*.

"So," said Pop at last, "do you think you can find a use for them? You and your friends?"

Friends? thought Mike, staring at the quads. *Well . . . maybe.*

When Pop had gone back inside the office, Mike turned to Spence and gripped him by the arm.

"This is incredible!" he said in a low, intense voice. "This is great! We've got wheels now! We can go!"

Spence nodded. Mike noticed an odd, preoccupied look in the boy's dark eyes, but he was too excited to stop.

"Tomorrow," he said. "We'll go tomorrow."

"Sure, Mike," said Spence. "That's great, but—"

"Navajo country!" said Mike. "We can go to the reservation! We've got wheels! We'll take these quads across Interstate 40 and over into the reservation. Don't you want to go?" he asked irritably, noticing that Spence was looking over his shoulder at the B-17. He thought he could hear the muffled sound of distant screams coming from that direction.

"Yes!" said Spence. "I already *told* you I want to go. It's just that Ben—"

Ben.

Mike squeezed Spence's elbow. Their eyes met. All at once they laughed. And then both of them shouted it at once.

"We left him in the ball turret!"

10

The Tunnel

Smitty was already there, gulping black coffee at the counter, when the three boys gathered at the diner early next morning. Mike's plan was to get a good breakfast and pick up the makings of some sandwiches from the kitchen before setting out. Outside, the darkness of the star-spattered late December sky was just beginning to give way before a faint but rising glow on the eastern horizon.

"I'd like to get going before the sun comes up—if we can," Mike said as they sat down across from the sheriff.

"Shouldn't be a problem," observed Spence, taking off his thick glasses and wiping them on the sleeve of his blue hooded sweatshirt. He pulled a small pocket almanac from his backpack and flipped it open. "Sunrise isn't until 7:16 today."

"Great," said Mike dryly. *Does he have to be so exact about everything?*

"Well, boys," drawled Smitty, setting down his coffee cup. He smiled, and his coffee-stained teeth glittered with silver behind the bushy gray shroud of his mustache. "Off on adventures?"

"Uh-huh." Mike glanced up nervously. The memory of that afternoon conversation in Smitty's office was still fresh in his mind. *Not a place for a kid your age to go snooping around.* Smitty was the *last* person he wanted to find out about this foray into Navajo country! "Just sort of a desert picnic," he said. "Before we have to go back to school."

"I see," said Smitty. "Sounds like fun."

"More coffee, Smitty?" asked Gail, setting a plate of steaming buttermilk pancakes in front of the sheriff.

"Yes, ma'am!" Smitty was always enthusiastic about breakfast. "And one of those donuts, too—if you don't mind." He grinned and poured a stream of amber syrup over the top of his pancakes.

"Can we order now, Mom?" said Mike, eager to deflect the conversation away from the subject of their plans for the day.

"Sure, honey." Gail pulled out her order pad and tossed her hair away from her face. "What'll it be?"

"Something quick. How about corn flakes all around?"

"Corn flakes!" objected Ben. "C'mon! I gotta have more than that! How about bacon, eggs, a side order of French toast, *and* a donut?"

"Ben Jones!" laughed Smitty. "The only kid I know who can out-eat *me!*"

"All right," said Gail, taking it all down. "And for you?" she smiled up at Spence.

"Granola, please," he answered with conviction. "I like the fiber."

"And, Mom," Mike said as she was turning away, "did you ask Grandma about the sandwich stuff?"

"Yes, Mike," she answered in a tone of pretended longsuffering. "I'm on the case!"

"Great!" said Ben. " 'Cause I know I'm gonna get good and hungry ridin' that quad up through those canyons!"

Gail disappeared into the kitchen. Smitty put down his fork and looked up at Ben. Mike hunched down in his seat and cringed.

"And what canyons would those be?" asked the sheriff, wiping his mustache with a napkin.

"That's just it, Sheriff Smitty!" said Ben, warming to the subject. "They're not really canyons at all. They're *canals*—dug by Martians a long time ago. I'm gonna show these guys!"

Smitty took another sip of coffee and glanced over at Mike. Mike could feel the blood rushing into his cheeks. "Ben's got a big imagination," he said, forcing a quick smile. "We're just going over to Chaquito Canyon—to the Vernon County Cliff Dwellings. The state park. Pop says my dad used to spend a lot of time there."

Gail, who had returned with Mike's corn flakes and Spence's granola, gave her son a searching look. "I didn't know you were planning to go to the Cliff Dwellings today."

"Well—sure," said Mike, glancing over at Spence. Spence lifted his eyebrows in return. "I mean, why not?

We've got the quads, and we've got all day. It'll be fun. Right, guys?"

He gave Ben a kick under the counter. Ben glared back at him.

"Are my pancakes ready yet, Mrs. Fowler?" asked Ben.

"Patience," said Gail with a puckish smile as she turned to go back to the kitchen. "All in good time, dear Ben."

Smitty rubbed his chin with the back of his hand. "Well, I suppose you'll be fine over at the Cliff Dwellings," he observed slowly. "As long as you stay in the park, stick to the trails, and cooperate with the rangers." He set the cup down and looked straight at Mike. "I think I've already told you to be careful about wandering into Navajo territory."

Mike was about to respond when the front door opened. He turned and saw a face come through the opening and into the light. A face he had seen before: square-jawed, clean-shaven, young, strong. As on the first occasion he'd seen it, something about the set of the firm mouth stirred memories long-buried in his mind. The cold light of the steel-blue eyes beckoned to him. Everything about the man—even his clothing: blue jeans, denim jacket, cotton T-shirt, hiking boots—reminded him of his dad.

It's him, Mike thought. *I wonder . . . I wonder if he'd go with us . . .*

He jumped up from his stool. Then, stumbling toward the door, he raised a hand and opened his mouth to speak. But the face, as if suddenly alarmed at something it had seen, withdrew into the darkness outside. The door shut quietly behind it.

Mike ran to the window, drew back the yellow curtains, and peered out. But the face and its owner were gone. There was nothing to see but the gas pumps and the sleek outline of the B-17 silhouetted against the lightening sky. Mike turned around to see Ben and Spence staring at him strangely.

"What's wrong, Mike?" said Gail, returning with Ben's breakfast. She put the plate down and hurried out from behind the counter. He could see the little worry-crease on her brow.

"Nothing," said Mike. "I just thought I saw someone, that's all. But I guess it was nothing."

"This half-light can fool your eyes," observed Spence, sitting down to his granola.

—≫—

The Vernon County Cliff Dwellings State Park lay just inside the boundary of the Navajo land, at the end of Chaquito Canyon, a narrow, winding gorge cut deep into the layered red sandstone deposits at the base of the Superstition Mountains. From Ambrosia, Mike, Ben, and Spence crossed Interstate 40 and drove the quads out across the open desert, over outcroppings of rock and clumps of gray-green yucca, until they struck the black ribbon of paved road that snaked into the canyon itself and down to the stone-and-timber ranger station and visitor center. The morning air grew warm as the sun rode up the clean blue sky, slanting down over red and yellow knife-edged peaks, jagged cliff walls, and castellated buttes, sucking the moisture out of the bare earth and coaxing the scent of sage and cedar from the canyon floor.

"Why *here*?" asked Ben as they pulled up to the visitor center in a cloud of sand and pinkish dust. The sun glinted from his helmet as he yanked it off and screwed up his face in a look of disgust. "I must've been here like about a thousand times before! I've already seen the basket and sandal exhibit! I thought we were gonna go exploring . . . for Martian evidence!"

"For one thing," said Mike as he swung off his quad and tied his helmet to the saddlebag, "I told my mom and Smitty that we were going to the Cliff Dwellings. You don't want me to lie, do you? Besides," he added, catching Spence's skeptical frown out of the corner of his eye, "there may be something that we can use."

"What?" asked Ben, as the boys stepped over the visitor center's rough-hewn pine threshold.

"Maps."

There were, in fact, two maps for sale inside the center that Mike thought might turn out to be useful: a plan of the park and a topographic diagram of the surrounding canyon country. He stood at the counter under the eyes of the grizzled ranger and shelled out $4.79 for them while Spence and Ben went sauntering slowly among the historical and archeological displays.

The place was filled with the fragrance of the bare pine paneling and lavender-scented candle wax. Along the walls ran shelves stocked with all kinds of touristy gifts: baskets, sandstone sculptures, red clay pottery, crystal rocks, Native American "dream catchers," and welded-iron representations of the "Flute Player"—in all sizes.

"Enjoy the park," smiled the ranger as he bagged the maps and handed them to Mike. "And remember to stay on the trails."

"Look at this!" said Ben when Mike caught up with him. Since there was no gum or candy for sale, Ben had had to content himself with examining a dioramic representation of the ancient cliff houses: row upon row of little rectangular rooms built one on top of the other within a shallow recess of a paint-and-plaster cliffside. Below the model was a short description of the life and culture of the cliff dwellers. *Mysteries of the Anasazi,* read the title.

" 'The Kiva,' " read Ben, pointing to a deep, cylindrical well-like chamber cut into the courtyard of the toy-like village. "It says they'd climb down into this thing by this long ladder. Sometimes kivas were connected with other kivas by underground tunnels. There was a fire pit down there. And this little hole in the floor—the *sipapu*—they thought it was like a door to another world. Can you believe that? Sounds kind of far-fetched to me! If you ask me, it looks a lot more like a rocket launching pad. See the scorch marks on the floor? It says they built these cliff dwellings, stayed here about 50 years, and then went away and left it all—just like that! Kind of fishy, huh?"

"It's not fishy at all," said Spence with a smirk, stepping over to join them. "There are all kinds of ideas about why the pueblos were abandoned. But tree ring studies indicate that it may have had something to do with drought. My dad's partial to the theory that Diné raiders drove them out. Others think there were religious reasons."

Ben looked at Spence out of narrowed eyes. "*That's* not why they left," he said. "*I* can tell you why they left! *They went back to Mars!*"

———◆———

After some discussion, the boys decided to have a look at the Cliff Dwellings before attempting to cross over to the reservation. Ben wanted a closer look at the *real* ruins—he had a vague idea that there might be a few Martians still lurking around amongst the rocks. Spence thought it would be an educational experience. And Mike, after examining the maps he'd bought, came to the conclusion that there just *might* be a shortcut into Navajo land through Chaquito Canyon. From what he could see, Dinétah House, the largest ruin in the park, was set into a cliff that backed right up to the border of the Navajo Nation.

No Motorized Vehicles read the sign at the head of the trail, so they had to shoulder their backpacks and leave the quads behind. It was a mile hike down the rocky, root-bound canyon—longer than Mike had anticipated—to Dinétah House, the first of the Vernon County ruins. The sun was high by the time they got there, and Ben was huffing, muttering, and whimpering with the growing heat and the exertion of their trek.

"Why didn't you tell me this was gonna be such hard work?" he complained as they halted in a shady spot beneath a lone bristlecone pine. He moaned and leaned his back against the crumbling canyon wall to rest. "I thought we came out here to ride the quads!"

Mike didn't answer. Irritating as he found Ben's babbling, he didn't have time to bother with it just now. At the moment, he was staring up at the face of the cliff on the north side of the canyon, spellbound and lost in another place and time.

There, under the cool and shadowy arch of a gigantic cavelike niche in the rock, rose the terraced splendor of Dinétah House: tower upon tower and room upon room of perfectly angled, square-cut blocks, enclosed within a low, curving wall. The stonework was the color of autumn leaves; pale red and yellow it glowed in the hazy midmorning light. From this distance, the ruin looked exactly like the diorama at the visitor center: a still, silent, toy-sized city, perched among the swallows halfway up the side of the vast red cliff.

Before his mind's eye rose the picture he'd seen in the old *National Geographic*: his father and Harrison

Lasiloo, laden with picks and shovels, standing in front of the ancient block of apartment houses. Suddenly it occurred to him that he'd never had a chance to read the rest of that article. He made a mental note to get back to it at the first opportunity.

"Whoa!" said Ben. His jaw dropped as his eyes followed Mike's gaze up the sheer wall of the canyon. "Check it out!"

"Spence," said Mike, without moving his eyes from the vision, "do you think there's a way to get up there?"

"These places were usually accessed by steps of some kind," Spence answered. "Sometimes not much more than handholds and footholds cut into the cliff. Often cleverly concealed. These people were good rock climbers."

"Concealed?" asked Mike, turning and rubbing his neck.

"Hidden from view."

"I know what the word means," said Mike testily. "But why?"

"Threat of attack."

"Attack!" said Ben. "Attack from *whom*? That's what *I'd* like to know!"

Suddenly, almost inexplicably, Mike was possessed by the thought that his dad may have visited this place. That maybe he'd even left his initials—*J. F.*—scrawled on the rock somewhere. "Well, let's see if we can find those handholds," he said. "I'd love to take a look around up there."

Spence gave him a questioning look. "What about staying on the trails?" he said.

"You worry too much," said Mike. "Come on!"

"Aren't we going to stop for lunch first?" Ben pleaded.

"No. It's too early. Spence, you lead the way."

Together they crossed the canyon floor. At its lowest point it was as smooth and sandy as a beach, punctuated here and there with clumps of dry grass or little prickly pear cactus. Everywhere the earth glittered with bits of quartz and obsidian as if with a million bright jewels. Closer to the north side, the ground began to climb, growing rockier and rougher. Against the base of the cliff, directly below Dinétah House, their view was obscured by a grove of trees, bare and dormant, but dense and orderly in their arrangement.

"What's this?" asked Mike, licking his lips and wiping the sweat from his forehead as they drew closer. "These trees don't look natural somehow. It's as if someone planted them here."

"I think you're right," said Spence, stepping up and touching the bark of the nearest trunk. "They're peach trees. It's an orchard. Probably Navajo work. Very old. Probably hasn't been cultivated for a long time."

"Peaches?" asked Ben eagerly, laboring up from behind.

"Sorry, Ben," said Mike. "You'll have to wait till summer."

They pushed their way through the trunks and

branches, crunching dry twigs and squashing the remains of rotted fruit, moving in the direction of the cliff. But on the far side of the orchard, their approach was completely blocked by a thick growth of live oak and tall, spiny ocotillo.

Spence stopped, drew his water bottle from his pack, and took a swig. "I still say we should have followed the sheriff's advice," he said.

"What advice?"

"Stick to the trails," Spence answered, replacing the bottle and wiping his chin.

Mike's face burned. "Stop obsessing," he said. "We'll get back to the trail. *After* we've visited the ruin. Right now, we've got to find some way around these trees. That's all."

Emerging again on the nearer side of the orchard, they followed its edge down toward the end of the canyon. At last the trees thinned and stopped, just at the point where a sharp spur of rock jutted southward from the cliff.

"This way," said Mike. "Between the orchard and the rock!" He pushed ahead of Spence and led the way through the narrow passage toward the cliff face.

He hadn't gone 50 feet before he felt Spence's hand on his shoulder. "Mike! Wait a minute! This can't be right! Look up!"

Spence was right. They had entered a place of deep shadow. There were no steps or handholds anywhere to be seen—only walls of vertical rock. Their view of

Dinétah House was now completely obscured. Over their heads, like a high-vaulted red-orange canopy, was a large overhang of smooth, rounded sandstone. And just ahead, where the outcrop met the cliff, was a narrow opening in the shape of an inverted V. Mike ran ahead and peered inside.

His heart fluttered in his chest as he pulled out his maps and consulted them once again. *Yes*, he thought. *It could be a passage to the other side!*

"C'mere, you guys!" he said. "It's a cave . . . or a tunnel! I can see light on the other side!"

Spence held back. "I'm not so sure," he said.

"Hey! Look at this!" Ben was standing at the right side of the opening, pointing at something on the wall of the cliff. "Pictures!"

Mike leaned over Ben's shoulder and studied the rock. Sure enough, a row of stiff, sticklike figures were marching across the wall toward the narrow opening, carefully and meticulously chipped into the sandstone. There were three bighorn sheep, another horned shape that walked on two legs, and a manlike figure on a horse with an odd-looking hat or helmet on its head.

"What'd I tell you?" said Ben, puffing excitedly. "Is that evidence or what?"

"They're petroglyphs," said Spence. "Navajo or Anasazi."

"Whoever heard of a Navajo with antennae?" said Ben, pointing to the horned figure. "Or a space helmet?"

"Come on!" said Mike, feeling that he didn't have

time for Ben's nonsense just now. "Let's see what's on the other side. Maybe there'll be *more* pictures, or . . . well, *other* things."

He led the way into the opening. Spence followed reluctantly. Ben took up the rear, gabbling in the dark about underground tunnels, spaceports, and craters formed by falling cylinders. The passage was dry, cool, stony, and about 20 yards long. At the further end, Mike had to squeeze his way out between the wall of the tunnel and the trunk of a young piñon tree that had taken root in the opening.

"I'm through!" he said. "Come on, Spence!"

In a moment the two of them were standing in the open air again, staring up at a sheer wall of crumbling sandstone. They appeared to have found their way into an entirely different canyon. Shoots of piñon, scrub oak, and yucca clung to the cliff face wherever they could find a foothold. Far above, a sharp, bladelike pinnacle of stone, gleaming dull red against the sunswept blue of the sky, leaned out over their heads. Strata of varying shades—maroon-reds, brown-reds, yellow-oranges, bone-white—showed plainly in the rock. Spence knelt in the chilled shadows to examine the base of the cliff.

"Shale," he said, "under a layer of Coconino sandstone. Very unstable."

Meanwhile, Ben was still inside the tunnel, struggling to push his way out between the sapling and the stone.

"I'm stuck, you guys!" he wailed. "You gotta get me out of here! Or else come back with me!"

"Stuck?" Mike groaned. *Only Ben,* he thought. He didn't want to go back. Not for Ben, not for anybody else. Somehow, he had a strong feeling that he was on the verge of some great discovery. That he was about to find something he'd been looking for. A clue. A sign. A piece of evidence. He scanned the new, unexplored canyon and then looked back at Ben. Suddenly he grabbed Spence by the arm.

"Here!" he said, gripping the piñon with his other hand. "If we can just—*unnhhh*—yank this out of the way . . ."—he tugged at the tree—"see what I mean? Grab hold, Spence. We can do it!"

Spence looked at him skeptically. Then, with a shrug, he stepped up beside him and wrapped his hands around the slim, rough-skinned trunk. Together they pulled and strained. For a moment nothing happened.

"Harder!" yelled Ben. "Harder! I'm getting claustrophobic again!"

Suddenly the soil at the base of the tree bulged. The trunk bent and swayed like a slender wand. Then, in an explosion of dirt, pebbles, and sand, the root ball burst from the earth. Mike and Spence tumbled backward and fell with the tree on top of them. Ben rolled out of the tunnel and sprawled at their side.

"Thanks, guys!" he said. "That was awesome!"

Mike couldn't repress a grin. He brushed the dirt out of his face and pushed himself up on one elbow. "It was easy—right, Spence?"

Spence's eyes were wide behind the gleaming lenses

of his glasses. He opened his mouth and pointed up. "Look out!" he yelled. "Rock slide!"

In a sudden burst of energy, Spence thrust the young tree off of them and rolled down the bed of shale that lay at the foot of the cliff. Without thinking, Mike grabbed Ben by the arm. "Get up!" he yelled. "Run!"

There was a *crash!* of falling rock, a cloud of choking dust. They dashed down into the canyon about 50 feet and threw themselves on their faces. A barrage of flying pebbles and clods pelted them where they lay with their hands over their heads. Slowly the din subsided and ebbed away.

When it was over, Mike lifted his head and looked back in the direction of the tunnel.

It was gone.

11

The Hidden Canyon

"What happened?" said Ben, sitting up and brushing the dust and sand from his curly reddish-brown hair.

Instead of answering, Mike rolled over and groaned. He opened his eyes. The air was filled with clouds of settling dust.

Spence got up and stumbled over mounds of broken rock and sand to the cliff. Then he knelt and began scrabbling in the pile of rubble—a wide-fanned spray of gravel, shale, and broken sandstone—that covered the mouth of the tunnel.

"It's blocked," he said at last. "We might be able to dig it out, but that'll take time. Especially with our bare hands."

"In other words, we're trapped!" said Ben. "Great! Just call us 'Martian fodder.' "

Mike looked over at the pudgy boy as he sat there whimpering and muttering to himself, hunched over in a round-shouldered heap. The voices of Smitty and the ranger played over and over again in his head: *Stay on the trails.*

"Don't worry, Ben," he said, trying to be encouraging. "It's not a big deal. We'll be through in no time."

Ben laughed—a short, grim, dry laugh. Then, suddenly, he looked up. "Hey! Wait!" he said. Zipping open his backpack, he began rummaging furiously through its contents. Out came *The War of the Worlds* comic book, a few Mars globe postcards, two Snickers bars, and a bag of corn chips. "Here!" he concluded triumphantly, producing a small garden trowel. "I brought this for digging up Martian artifacts!"

"It's better than nothing," called Spence. "Bring it over here."

Ben scuttled over to the rock slide. Immediately the two of them set to work clearing away the debris. Mike stared at them gloomily, propping himself on one elbow and thinking that he should probably get up and lend a hand. The sun, now high in the sky, glared unmercifully in his eyes. He flung out his right hand and pushed himself up into a sitting position.

But what was this? His fingers had touched something—something cold, hard, and smooth in amongst the grit, sand, and rough-edged stones . . . something man-made. He felt for it again. Then he turned, knelt in the rubble, and picked it up.

It was a pocketknife. A big one. About four-and-a-half inches long folded up, with three blades, a pair of miniscissors, and a corkscrew. Mike brushed away the dust, pulled out the longest blade, and held it up, gleaming in the sunlight.

The casing was of white pearl, secured at either end with a silver stud. It was obviously very valuable—a pocketknife any 12-year-old boy would have been proud to own. But Mike wasn't thinking about its cost or its possible uses as he stared down at the knife with his heart in his throat. What made him catch his breath were the initials that were inlaid into the pearl in turquoise and silver:

J. F.

His heart was pounding. Was it possible? Quickly he glanced back over his shoulder. Spence and Ben were still digging furiously. They hadn't seen him pick up the knife. Closing the blade, he dropped the precious treasure into the inside pocket of his jacket—next to the compass and the Bible. He patted it gently and smiled to himself. Then he got up and trotted over to the cliff.

"Gimme some room," he said, coming up behind the other two and pushing his way in between them. He grabbed up a big, flat piece of slate that lay on the side of the heap and began scooping the dirt and sand away with it.

"This is what I call an adventure!" he said, an irrepressible glow rising inside him. "Exciting, huh?"

Ben and Spence grunted in reply.

They worked together for about half an hour. Even though the soil was so loose—possibly *because* it was so loose—they found it very difficult to make any headway. Every stroke of the shovel seemed to bring another tiny avalanche of rocks and sand tumbling down the cliff to fill the space they'd already cleared. They dug until the sweat was pouring down their noses and into their eyes. Eventually they had to stop, shed their jackets and sweatshirts, and rest a while. After that, Mike and Spence went at it again.

Figures! thought Mike when he saw that Ben, instead of joining them, had remained sitting on a pile of rock, puffing and wheezing heavily. The boy's round, red face was glistening with perspiration as he produced a Snickers bar from his backpack and took a long pull at his water bottle. Mike sighed and let his piece of slate fall to the ground.

"Come on, Spence," he said. "Maybe Ben has the right idea."

The two of them stumbled over to Ben and began raiding their own food supplies.

"I don't know," said Spence, taking a bite of a chicken sandwich. "The slide seems to have filled it in pretty deep. There's no telling how deep. I've got a feeling we're in trouble."

Mike sat listening with his chin in his hands. He couldn't help feeling that there was a lecturing, *I-told-you-so* tone in Spence's voice. But he said nothing. Instead, he unwrapped his own sandwich—a ham and Swiss—and ate it in silence.

After eating, Mike took another look at his maps. Oddly enough, the canyon they'd stumbled into didn't appear to be marked on either one of them . . . though the topo map *did* seem to indicate the presence of a

Y-shaped gorge diverging northwest and northeast.

He stood up, pulled out his compass, and flipped open the brass case. According to the silver-blue needle, he was facing north. The sun had passed the meridian and was leaning over toward the southwest. The long, black shadow of the sharp rock formation at the top of the cliff fell straight through a natural archway on the other side of the canyon—a small opening about 30 feet high, like the eye of a needle in the face of the salmon-colored rock. This arch, as far as Mike could tell, opened into the right-hand branch of the Y—a narrow, meandering, rough-floored tributary off the main canyon. *Interesting*, he thought, *but it looks like hard going. Besides, it might just lead to more trouble.*

Northwest, to Mike's left, lay a relatively broad, flat-bottomed valley, hemmed in on either side by sheer rock walls. He was tired of digging and he didn't want to commit himself to a difficult hike—especially not with Ben. More than that, he was determined to explore this hidden valley. His father had been here. He felt certain of that now. The pocketknife was all the evidence he wanted.

"I think we're wasting our time here. Let's see what we can find down this way," he said, pointing to the left. "There's just *got* to be another passage back to the other side. Don't you think so, Spence?"

Spence stuffed his blue sweatshirt into his backpack and wiped his glasses on his sleeve. "The parable says to take the *narrow* way," he said with a wry expression. "Doesn't it?"

Mike clucked his tongue. "How do you know so much about parables? Come on—I'm going *this* way!"

As it happened, the valley wasn't as short as it looked. Instead of ending where it seemed to end, it bent gradually northwards, then made a sharp turn back to the south. After that it narrowed and wandered this way and that, almost like a maze or a winding riverbed, until Mike was no longer sure where they were or how far they had walked.

"Those Martians!" wheezed Ben, wiping his forehead with his sleeve. "Why couldn't they have built *straight* canals—like the ones they made on Mars?"

By now they were all tired, dusty, thirsty. Mike's tongue was sticking to the roof of his mouth. If he'd thought about it, he would have realized that he was ready to drop in his tracks. But he wasn't really aware of his discomfort. There was too much else to occupy his attention: the fierce beauty of the place, so severe, so overwhelming— the glowing red and orange streaks in the rocks, the ever-varied shapes of the formations, the contrasting deep greens of the few evergreen trees, the spotless white of the puffy little clouds riding overhead. *So this, too, is Arizona,* he mused as he trudged ahead. *To think that you can find something like this so close to Ambrosia!*

At last the eastern sky took on a purplish tinge, barred with thin pinkish clouds. The sun sank lower toward the western horizon. The day was wearing away, and Mike knew it. For the first time, he felt an anxious flutter in his chest.

"So where are we going?" Spence wanted to know. "Any ideas?"

"Give me a minute to think," Mike answered testily.

Streams of golden light were throwing long, blue-black shadows rippling up and over the flaming pinnacles of rock. With every passing minute the air was growing colder. Mike led Ben and Spence up a short rise to a large, flat stone beneath a dead cottonwood tree. Then, as the other two sat down to rest, he reached inside his jacket and felt for the pocketknife.

It was still there, alongside the compass and the Bible. That was good. That, at least, was something. It was a great deal indeed. And yet, so far, he hadn't found a single trace of anything else that might be even remotely connected with his dad. What was worse, he was responsible for getting them all lost. He wondered what Pop would say. He wondered what would happen if Smitty found out. He could see his mom's face with that little worry-wrinkle across the forehead. He sighed and shook his head.

Ben's voice, shrill and excited, broke in upon his thoughts. "Check it out, guys!" After another Snickers bar, Ben had been the first to get up and take a closer look at their immediate surroundings.

"What now?" Mike heaved himself up and trudged over to see what it was that Ben was examining on the ground.

"Footprints!" said Spence, coming up alongside him. He scratched his head and knelt down in the dust.

"Yeah!" said Ben. "How do you explain that?"

"How do I explain that?" laughed Mike. "Some-body's been walking around down here! *That's* how I explain that!"

"Ha ha! Very funny!" said Ben bitterly. "You know that's not what I meant! Think about it! *We* had to get lost to find this place! There's no one else around! No tourists—nobody at all!"

"He's right," observed Spence. "And look—these aren't the prints of conventional modern shoes. They're . . . well, rather odd-looking if you ask me. Kind of primitive or . . . alien."

"See?" beamed Ben. "You see what I mean?"

"He means 'foreign,' Ben," said Mike. "I wish you'd just get off this Martian thing!" He bent down to examine the prints, then straightened up with a laugh. "They're *moccasin* prints! This *is* Navajo country after all—remember? Anyway, we've got more important things to think about right now. Like finding a way back to our quads!"

"I'm telling you, Mike," said Ben, with a pleading, lost puppy dog look in his eyes. "This is serious! I told you these canyons aren't just an accident! I told you somebody's been here before!"

"Forget about it, Ben!"

"Hold on!" said Spence, who had taken a pair of binoculars from his pack and was scanning the opposite cliff.

"What is it?" asked Mike.

"Here—take a look!"

Mike took the binoculars and swept them over the upper part of the cliff. There, at the very top of the sheer wall of rock, where the sharp edge of the bluff was silhouetted against the blaze of the setting sun, he saw something. Something he hadn't expected to see. Something that sent a shock of cold fear and desperate hope through his body, from the top of his head to the tips of his toes.

"What do *you* make of it, Spence?" he asked, returning the binoculars.

"What? Let *me* see!" pleaded Ben, pushing his way forward.

"It's a person," Spence responded, passing the binoculars to Ben. "On horseback. Coming down a track in the cliff face. Coming this way."

He was right. As they watched, the dark figure descended out of the fading glory of the sun and rapidly dropped down into the canyon along a zigzagged path, a cloud of reddish dust rising into the pale air behind it. Ben retreated to the cottonwood. Spence stood still, monitoring the visitor's approach through the binoculars. But Mike, with a strange, fluttering sense of impending destiny rising in his throat, ran forward to meet the rider in the dusk.

It was a girl. A girl just about his age, in denim overalls. She had long, glossy brown hair, dark, shining eyes, and high, distinct cheekbones. A Native American girl. She reined in her roan pony, stopped directly in front of Mike, and peered down at him with a look of disdain.

"Ben! Spence! It's okay!" he laughed, motioning for the others to join him. "It's *just a girl!*"

The girl lifted her chin, narrowed her eyes, and curled her lip.

"Try having a little more respect," she said. "You're talking to a full-blooded Diné!"

12

Winnie

Mike stood staring up at the bold young rider. *A full-blooded Diné?* His thoughts flew to the journal. But once again his inward ruminations were shattered by the sound of Ben's voice.

"Oh, no! Not *her*! You gotta be kidding!"

The girl leaned forward along her horse's sleek brown foam-flecked neck and peered at the boy who stood under the cottonwood tree.

"Ben Jones?" she said, wrinkling up her nose in an expression of distaste. "How in the world did *you* get down here?"

That's when Mike was hit by a sudden realization. The glare of the sunset . . . the sense of awe inspired by her dramatic descent from the cliff . . . her towering presence on horseback—all of this had blinded him to it at first. But now it came home to him in a flash.

Mike had seen this girl before. Not that he *knew* her. But he *did* know who she was. He'd seen her at the Indian Trading Post in town, where she worked most weekends.

She was a year behind him at Ambrosia Middle School—same grade as Ben. He'd run into her time and time again during his years in Ambrosia, though never once had they spoken. In fact, now that he thought about it, she'd always had a way of averting her eyes whenever he got close enough to see her face. *Just another snob*—that was his general opinion of her.

"How do you think I got here, Winnie?" said Ben, trotting up and standing at Mike's side. "I came with these guys. You got a problem with that?"

She smirked. "Did they carry you in on their backs? Like a *papoose*?"

"Actually, Ben's done a pretty good job of pulling his own weight," said Mike. Ben gave him a grateful look. "I'm Mike. Mike Fowler. From the Last Chance Gas and Diner. And this is Spence."

He saw her eyes grow wide as if she, too, had been hit with a sudden realization. It lasted only a split second. Then she regained her composure and said:

"I'm Wynona Whitefeather. Winnie to my friends. Of the Cliff Dwelling Clan. Do you have any idea where you are?"

"Not exactly. We got in through the park—you know, the Vernon County Cliff Dwellings. But then there was sort of an accident, and now we have to find another way back. It's been a long day. Our quads are still parked back at the—"

"You shouldn't be here!" she snapped, cutting him

short. "This valley is dangerous. It's haunted. My people say that the *Hisatsinom* once lived here."

"You mean the Anasazi," said Spence, stepping forward.

"I mean the Ancient Enemies—the ones they sometimes call the Little People. If you ask me, they're still living here *now*. Watching us with dark eyes." She looked around and shuddered.

Mike felt something poking him in the ribs. It was Ben's elbow. He turned and saw Ben raising his eyebrows with an expression that said, *What did I tell you?*

"I've seen their lights at night," she continued. "Lots of them lately. They come and go in the darkness. You'd better follow me—now! The sun has already set, and there won't be any moon until almost morning. Come on!"

Mike couldn't argue. Wearily, but thankfully, he and the others shouldered their packs and followed the girl up the cliff trail. It was a steep track, full of loose, crumbling rock—more like a rain-cut gully than a path at some points—and Mike found it extremely hard going at the end of such an exhausting day. But Winnie's horse footed it with firm and sure steps, and at length they found themselves standing beside her on the rim of the canyon, looking out over a wide, blue plateau. The red-purples of the fading rock formations had sunk to violet and indigo, and the once sharp outlines of their imposing shapes had dissolved to indistinct shadows hovering on the edge of the gathering darkness. A steady, cold breeze touched Mike's perspiring forehead and sent Winnie's long hair streaming out behind her.

Mike reached into his jacket and pulled out the compass. It gleamed softly in the dark. He opened the case and peered down at the markings on the dial. According to the needle, they were facing west-northwest. Just to his left, a faint greenish glow still lingered between the horizon and the emerging stars. Winnie glanced down from the back of her roan and laughed.

"You can put that thing away," she said. "You don't need it out here in the desert, where the light and the stars and the wind are enough to show you the way. Besides," she added, "it can't tell you anything about *up* and *down*."

"Up and down?" said Mike.

"The Diné say there are *six* points of direction: east, west, north, south, above, and below. *Up* and *down* are very important out here."

"I can see why," said Mike, looking back over his shoulder into the black gulf out of which they had just climbed. "But I think I'm going to hang on to my compass anyway." He closed the case and returned the instrument to its place beside the Bible and the pocketknife.

Winnie led the way on her horse. They followed her for a long while, through the darkness and over the rocky ground. At last lights appeared in the distance.

"That's where I live," said Winnie. "Come on."

It was only a short distance now, but there were plenty of steep "ups and downs" to negotiate, and they had to go slowly and carefully in the dark. Fox and rabbit holes, clumps of yucca and tamarisk, sand pits, and oddly eroded knobs of rock had to be avoided at almost every step. Deep cuts and arroyos had to be crossed and gravelly slopes ascended and descended. The scent of sage and jimsonweed passed over them in waves, wafted on the wind. As they went along the stars gathered courage and shone out bravely.

What touched Mike most profoundly was the silence. It was deep and curiously soothing. From time to time he heard the thin wailing of birds or the cries of beasts on the air. It was all so strange, he thought. Nothing like the lush green beauty of the place he still called home. And yet it *was* beautiful nonetheless. Beautiful in an enchanting, unearthly way. No wonder it made Ben think of visitors from other planets.

At last they could see the tiny settlement just ahead: three small modern tract homes, situated at some distance from one another; some sheep and a few horses snuffling and stamping in a common pole corral, flanked by a couple of unpainted wood-frame stables; and directly behind the nearest house, a dome-shaped, earth-covered, six-sided hut, made of logs, bark, sand, willow branches, and clay mortar. Like a heap of earth and rock it appeared in the dim light that streamed from the windows of the modern house—a natural outcrop of the desert floor rather than a man-made structure.

"This is it," said Winnie, swinging herself down from the horse and pointing to the contemporary dwelling. "My house." She looked at Mike, then glanced quickly away. "You better come inside while I ask my mom what we should do with you." Then she turned and led the way toward the house.

"*Do* with us?" said Ben in a concerned voice. "What does she mean by that?"

"Don't worry," grinned Spence. "The Navajo eat sheep. Not people."

Mike quickened his pace and came up alongside the girl just as she reached the door of the house.

"Um . . . Wynona?" he said.

"You can call me Winnie."

"Do you have a phone? So I can call home?"

She cocked her head at him, tucked a strand of dark brown hair behind her ear, and smiled. "We're not *that* primitive. Come on. I'll show you where it is."

Mike called his mom from the Whitefeathers' neat, whitewashed kitchen, perched on a three-legged stool in the corner. He cast his eyes around the room as he held the phone to his ear and waited for an answer. The windows were bright with blue curtains, and the electric range was white and immaculately clean. The house was equipped with electric lights, indoor plumbing, heating and air conditioning—in short, with all the modern amenities Mike had always assumed the Navajo did without. Along the counters stood handmade baskets full of dried corn, onions, carrots, and other foodstuffs. Off the kitchen there was a pantry and a small refrigerator, and in another corner a very large basket full of rough, yellowy, uncarded wool. On the wall beside it hung a handwoven blanket, done in bands and diamonds and zigzags of red, brown, orange, yellow, and dark green. Mike had seen the tall loom standing in the yard outside.

Across the room Mike could see Winnie sitting at the green formica-topped table, explaining the boys' situation to her mother. Mrs. Whitefeather was a young but stern-faced and sturdy-looking Diné woman. Her dark, shoulder-length hair was parted in the middle and braided behind her head, and she wore a white sweater over a knee-length yellow print cotton dress. She smiled up at Ben and Spence as they hung back meekly in the doorway.

"Mom?" said Mike once he heard Gail's voice at the other end of the line. "You're not gonna believe this . . . but we're out here somewhere on the Navajo reservation . . ."

"You're *where*?" Mike pulled the phone away from his ear. He could hear the anxiety—and irritation—in his mom's voice.

"It's a long story," he said. "Anyway, do you think Pop could bring the truck and pick us up?"

Winnie's father, who had been listening from the other room, put his head around the corner and raised a hand. Mike glanced up at him in surprise. He was a small, lean man, trim and fit, but with a deeply lined, dark brown face and longish graying hair. He wore faded blue jeans, a red flannel shirt, and cowboy boots.

"They needn't bother," he said quietly. He glanced

over at Winnie. "My daughter and I will take you back to town."

Mike responded with a grateful nod. "Mom?" he said into the phone. "Don't worry. Looks like we've got a ride."

Mike hung up the phone and stretched his aching legs. The tone of his mother's voice had brought a disturbing picture before his mind's eye: her face, with worried eyes and that little crease across the forehead. He didn't like to think about the reception he was likely to get at home. Grounding was a serious possibility. He knew he ought to be thinking his way through a carefully worded explanation.

And yet . . . In another way, things couldn't be better. *A full-blooded Diné!* Even as he sat there pondering this piece of good luck, he could hear Winnie's parents talking softly together in the strange, unhurried language of the Navajo. It was the chance he'd been looking for; he couldn't have planned it more perfectly. Here he sat, in the home of a real, live, authentic Navajo family! The blood rushed to his head and his fingertips tingled. He stood up, set his backpack on the stool, zipped it open, and drew out the little leather-covered journal.

"Winnie," he said going over to the kitchen table and sitting down beside the girl.

Winnie's neck and cheeks flushed darkly. She turned her dark brown eyes on him—shyly, almost hesitantly, he thought.

"We owe you," Mike went on. "*And* your family. Big time. I just want to say thanks."

"Ditto," echoed Spence with a nod.

Ben stood leaning against the wall with his hands behind his back. He said nothing.

"She helped us out of a really bad spot, Mrs. White-feather," Mike explained, turning to Winnie's mother. "I don't know where we'd be right now if it hadn't been for her."

The woman responded with a smile. "It's what we've always taught her," she said.

Mike cleared his throat. "Right. And Winnie, after all that—not to mention your dad offering to drive us home and all—I hate to ask another favor but . . . well, I've just got to!"

He turned his head slightly and saw Ben and Spence giving him strange looks. Then, pressing his lips together in an expression of grim determination, he slapped the journal down on the table and flipped it open.

"Can you tell me what this says?" he asked. "It's written in Diné."

Mr. Whitefeather strode over to the table and stood looking down at the little book. A boy of about six—Winnie's little brother, Mike guessed—came into the kitchen and peered impishly at him from behind his father's back.

"We don't read or write Diné," said the man solemnly. "Diné is not written. It is not a dead thing. It cannot be confined to a piece of paper like a sheep in a pen. It lives in the mouths of the people who speak it."

"Well, *I* can read it," said Winnie, studying the writing on the page. She took the journal from Mike and drew it to herself. "*Thanzi cha dzeh*," she began slowly. "*Jadholoni tsah t'kin ma'e ahnah . . .*"

The little boy laughed. Winnie screwed up her nose and glanced sideways at her father.

"What is this book?" asked Winnie's mother. "Are these student exercises? Just words and words and no meaning at all!" She, too, laughed.

"*Turkey-hat-elk-kettle-needle!*" shouted the little boy. He sat down on the floor and laughed hilariously.

"*Turkey-hat-elk-kettle-needle?*" repeated Ben. "Weird!"

"It's my father's journal," explained Mike, reddening. "I've just *got* to find out what it says! My grandpa told me someone on the reservation might be able to help."

He felt a heavy hand on his shoulder and turned to see Mr. Whitefeather's stony, deeply creased face staring intently down into his own.

"Say no more," said the man in a low voice. "Perhaps the words *do* have a meaning. If so, it is beyond my knowledge. But I can take you to someone who *may* be able to tell you what it is."

"You can?" said Mike.

"Really?" exclaimed Winnie.

"Yes. But to meet him, you will have to come with me. To the Grandfather House. To the hogan."

13

The Hogan

"Where are we going?" whispered Mike as they shut the door behind them and walked out into the shadowy yard.

Ahead of them, across a gravelly stretch of ground, loomed the miniature hill of earth and logs they had seen earlier. Sheep bleated gently in the darkness. Far off in the silent night Mike could hear the lonely *yip-yip* of the wild coyotes. The air was cold and still. Mr. White-feather led the way. Mike walked beside Winnie, followed by Spence and Ben.

"This," said Winnie, pointing to the hut, "is the hogan. The house of my *sechai*—my grandfather. He and my grandmother live here. My dad seems to think he might know something about your father's journal."

Mr. Whitefeather put up a hand, signaling silence, as they came up to the hogan's large wood-frame door—the little house's only point of communication with the outside world. Without a word, he pushed it open and ducked inside, motioning for them to follow.

Mike felt that he had never come across a scene as strange or as enchanting as the one that met his eyes inside the hut. It was as if, in passing beneath the wide-timbered lintel of the hogan, he had traveled back in time or stepped into an entirely new and different world. Shadows danced and shimmered along the rough log walls, cast by the red-orange light of an open fire that burned in the center of the room, its smoke escaping by a hole in the middle of the roof. On each side of the fire, squatting on colorful handwoven woolen rugs, sat a group of three gray-headed old men—six old men in all. All of them were dressed in traditional Navajo costume: blousy shirts of blue, maroon, or green velveteen, loose-fitting white pants, moccasins, and red or white cotton headbands. Belts, necklaces, and bracelets of silver and turquoise flashed in the firelight. Over against one of the six facets of the inner wall sat an old woman in a flowing dress of blue-green cotton print. Her face, as intricately lined as a raisin, crinkled up in a smile as they entered. Mike had seen *her* before, too: Winnie's grandmother owned and operated the Indian Trading Post where Winnie helped out on weekends.

"They are playing *Keshjee'*," Winnie's father explained in a low voice as they arranged themselves in a line with their backs to the wall just inside the door. "The Moccasin Game. We must not interrupt. Not yet."

"Moccasin Game?" said Ben, wrinkling up his nose. "What's that?"

Winnie glowered at him. "You don't have to show off your ignorance, Ben."

Mr. Whitefeather hushed his daughter, laying a hand upon her shoulder. Then he explained: "Our people say that the beasts played the Moccasin Game at the beginning of time. They played to determine whether day or night, darkness or light, should rule the world. My father and his friends are taking the part of the animals. The team on the left represent the nighttime animals. The others are the day animals. Sometimes men play *Keshjee'* all night long. And they sing the old songs of the tribal chantways as they play."

"So who's supposed to win?" Ben wanted to know.

"Ssshhh!"

Again Mr. Whitefeather raised a hand for silence. After this, no one spoke at all for what seemed to Mike like a very long time.

He watched the old men carefully. Each group of players sat facing two pairs of leather moccasins that were buried in the dirt floor of the hogan. Only the tops of the shoes stuck out above the ground. As he looked, two men from the "day" team stood up and held a blanket in front of the buried moccasins, hiding them from the members of the "night" team. Then the third man reached into the folds of the blanket in which he was wrapped and produced a ball, about the size of a walnut, made of the dried fibers of the yucca plant. Carefully, secretly, he pushed this ball deep down into the toe of one of the shoes.

In the meantime, the men on the other side of the

room began to sing, chanting rhythmically in the Diné language with deep, resonant, otherworldly voices. And as they chanted, light and darkness mixed and mingled, shifting and tossing backwards and forwards across the chamber like the lights and shadows in an aquarium.

"What are they saying?" whispered Spence, his eyes wide with wonder.

Mr. Whitefeather crouched in front of them.

"It is the Origin Legend," he explained. "They are telling how Begochiddy, the Great God, created all things. How he made the four worlds, black, blue, yellow, and white, and the Four Sacred Mountains, *Tsisnaajini*, *Tsoodzil*, *Doko'oosliid*, and *Dibe'ntsaa'a*. He created ants, red, black, yellow, and gray, and fertile soil, and cotton and corn and reeds and other plants. He made bees and many kinds of insects. He made the figures of a man and a woman, the *Ethkay-nah-ashi*, and breathed his spirit into them. And Begochiddy smiled as he made them, because all of it was very, very good."

When the singing ceased, the two men drew the blanket aside and sat down again. Then one of the men from the other side of the fire picked up a short stick. Solemnly, almost reverently, he reached out and touched one of the moccasins with it.

"He's trying to guess where they've hidden the ball," said Winnie. "Watch."

Slowly, the man who had done the hiding folded his

arms and shook his head. The silver bracelets he wore flashed red in the firelight. Then he drew a sliver of yucca leaf from a pile that lay on the floor and placed it on the floor in front of the fire.

After this, the man on the "night" side passed the stick to one of his teammates. He in his turn also reached out and touched a moccasin. This time the guess was correct. Then he, too, picked a strip of yucca from the pile and laid it on the ground.

"Huh! Lucky!" said Ben.

"Ssshh!" hissed Winnie.

Now it was the "night" team's turn to hide the ball. Again two men rose and held up a brightly striped blanket while, behind this screen, the third took the little wad of yucca fiber and thrust it down inside one of the moccasins. Again the chanting was taken up, this time by the members of the "day" team. Only now the music was slow and sad.

"But Coyote, the child of Dawn Light, was ever a troubler and a trickster," said Mr. Whitefeather, picking up the interpretation. "He discovered the child of the Water-Monster, a baby with long black hair, floating in the whirlpool. And so he stole it and hid it within the folds of his blanket. Then he unleashed great monsters upon the earth to devour it. Storms and floods arose, and all was shaken—a black storm from the East, a blue storm from the South, a yellow storm from the West, and a white storm from the North. And the people were stricken with terror, and Begochiddy looked down on the world in sadness."

At this, Winnie's father began chanting himself, in English:

Earth, for it I am ashamed,
Sky, for it I am ashamed,
Evening, for it I am ashamed,
Blue sky, for it I am ashamed,
Darkness, for it I am ashamed,
Sun, for it I am ashamed,
In me it stands, with me it talks,
For it I am ashamed.

Mike stood and stared as the blanket was drawn aside a second time. Once again the guessing began. When at last the ball had been discovered and the strips of yucca laid out neatly on the floor—Mike assumed this was their way of keeping score—the "day" team had another chance to do the hiding.

The veil of the blanket was raised. Again the sounds of singing filled the room. Mr. Whitefeather resumed his translation.

"Then Begochiddy blew upon the monsters, and they became strange rocks—huge, majestic, and wondrously beautiful. Their evil powers were stilled, locked within the stone. And all was well with the world again. All was beautiful as before. And yet this beauty was won only at great cost.

Restore all for me in beauty.
Make beautiful all that is before me.
Make beautiful all that is behind me.
Make beautiful my words.
It is done in beauty.
It is done in beauty.

"That's the Prayer of the Mountaintop Way," whispered Winnie. But even as she said it, the singing abruptly ceased.

"Does your friend wish to play the part of Coyote?" said the grandfather, slowly lifting his dark, leathery face in the silence. His expression was grave. Webs of wrinkles emanated from the circles around the deep sockets of his eyes.

"*Me?*" Mike mouthed the word voicelessly, turning to Winnie with a feeling of helplessness. Beads of cold sweat broke out on his forehead.

"Odd man always takes the part of Coyote," explained Winnie's father. "He belongs to neither team. He joins the winning side in the end. It is a hospitable offer."

Mike fumbled for words. "That's okay. I didn't really come to—"

But Mr. Whitefeather did him the favor of cutting him short. "He is here for another reason, Father," he explained. Then he turned to Mike and said very softly:

"Show him the book."

14

The Ancient Enemies

Hesitantly, Mike drew the journal from his backpack and approached the old man. Fear and hope competed for first place in his feelings. He took a few steps forward and stood trembling in the presence of the *sechai*.

Opening the book to the page they'd been examining in the kitchen, he laid it out in front of the grandfather.

"This was my dad's," he explained, feeling as if his voice sounded very small and distant. "He's an Air Force pilot—missing in action. I'm trying to find out what happened to him. My grandpa said that someone here might know how to read it. That's why my friends and I"—he pointed to Ben and Spence—"came looking for a way into the Navajo country."

"We did?" interjected Ben. "I thought we were searching for Martians."

Mike ignored him. "We found our way into a hidden canyon," he said. "I've got—well, a *feeling* that my dad has been there, too. Anyway, that's where your granddaughter met us." He paused. "Do you think you can help me?"

The old man's eyebrows lifted. Slowly, the corners of his mouth turned downward ever so slightly. He looked up, not at Mike but into the glow of the fire. He said nothing.

"Winnie read some of the words of the journal to us," Mr. Whitefeather ventured after a few moments. "She has learned to read writing at the school in the town. But the words make no sense. Do you know what it is, Father? Do you think it might . . ."

The *sechai* lifted his hand. He glanced quickly at the old men seated around the fire, gazing intently from face to wrinkled face. Mike saw them exchange silent nods.

"We will not speak of it," Winnie's grandfather said at last. "Not now. But of another matter something *must* be said. You tell me that my granddaughter found you in a hidden canyon?" he asked, giving Mike a piercing look. Mike felt as if the old man's black eyes were burning a hole in his soul.

"Well, yeah," he answered.

"Is this true, Granddaughter?" said the old man, turning to Winnie.

"Yes, Grandfather." Mike could see that she, too, squirmed under the old man's gaze. But Winnie pushed ahead bravely. "I was out riding Roan," she explained. "I saw them from the cliff. Otherwise, I wouldn't have gone down there at all. They needed help. It was getting dark."

The *sechai* grunted. "The hidden valley is hidden for a reason," he said, turning back to Mike. "The land belongs to the people of the Diné, yet we do not set foot there, nor do we allow outsiders to see it. Did my grand-daughter tell you that the place is very dangerous?"

"Yes, sir," Mike answered meekly.

"According to the traditions of our people, none may go to that place without running a grave risk—the risk of angering the inhabitants. Many who take that risk never return to the fires of their own hogans."

"Inhabitants!" Mike heard Ben say in a loud whisper. Spence shushed him.

"Our legends say that the *Hisatsinom* once lived there," continued the old man. "The Little People. The Ancient Enemies. The Anasazi. Many believe that they live there still."

"I knew it!" said Ben under his breath.

"Once they filled this land as the grass fills the valley after the summer rains. They were a powerful people, and none could stand before them. They built great cities of stone on the tops of the mesas and in the clefts of the rocks. Many beautiful things they made of clay and stone and the fibers of the *tsa'adzoh* plant. They grew white and yellow corn on the floors of the canyons and ground it into meal with *metates*. They hunted with the *atlatl*. They lived long and grew strong.

"But Coyote deceived them. He told them that they had achieved all these things by their own godlike wisdom and might—that they had not received them as gifts. Soon they became proud and enamored of themselves and the works of their own hands. Their pride angered the rain gods, so that they withheld the rain, and the little fields of corn and squash dried up. The wild animals they used to hunt fled far away to the valleys of the great river, because the water holes in the rocks were empty. Many of the people fled too, to the land of the Hopi and the Kachinas in the south.

"Then the rainmakers and the elders of the *Hisatsinom* gathered in the greatest of the great round underground kivas. They took counsel together. The oldest medicine man said that the people must bring offerings of prayer-sticks to the rain gods. With feathers and paints and sinew they made them, and laid them on the altar of the great round kiva. And the elders and the rain-makers lit their long clay pipes, and they puffed and blew out smoke until the kiva was filled with it. Thus they made a cloud offering to appease Begochiddy and the gods who send the rain.

"And as they sat puffing, there came a flash of lightning and a crash of thunder. They looked up and saw Coyote standing in their midst in the very center of the kiva, over the *sipapu*, the tiny hole that leads to the worlds below. And Coyote laughed and said, 'Your cloud offering is too small, fools! The rain gods are angry. If you want to see any rain at all this summer, you had better hurry up and make a bigger cloud somehow.'

" 'A bigger cloud?' answered the elders. 'But how are we to do this?'

"Coyote smiled. 'My suggestion,' he said, 'is that you burn the roof of the kiva!'

"Then the elders and the rainmakers lifted their eyes

to the ceiling of the great circular chamber. It was made of logs that rested first upon the six stone pilasters of the kiva, and then were built up, rank upon rank, until they formed a high dome with a smoke-hole in the center. The old men told themselves that Coyote's counsel was good. And so it happened that they built a huge fire in the middle of the kiva floor. Then they climbed up the ladder and began to sing and dance with the people in the courtyard above, until the dry logs of the kiva's roof caught fire. The flames licked upwards to a great height and a huge cloud offering of black smoke went roaring up into the sky."

"So did it start raining after that?" blurted Ben.

"No. The rain did *not* come. Instead, the great fire killed the elders and rainmakers. Then it spread to many of the houses of the city. The people were driven from their homes. They fled thirsting, hungering, and nursing the pain of their wounds and burns, howling and wailing all down the length of the hidden canyon. Some died. Some escaped and joined their kinsmen in the south. But a few remained in the valley, hiding among the sharp red rocks, living in old stone cliff dwellings that none have yet discovered, cursing the gods and hating men. Most especially do they hate the people of the Diné, for it was to them that Begochiddy gave the land that had once belonged to the *Hisatsinom*. This is the *Dinétah*, home of the Diné—all the land that lies between the four sacred mountains.

"But Coyote went his way, laughing at his trick, and hid himself in the waterless wastes beyond the *Dinétah*.

"All of this," concluded the old man with a grave nod, "is why the Diné have determined that the valley must remain nameless and unknown. And why you, my children"—slowly he looked from Winnie to Mike and from Mike to Ben and Spence—"must not return to that place. Of late many of us have seen signs that the Ancient Enemies have returned to strength, that they are becoming more active and powerful than ever: lights and smokes, thunder and lightning, the comings and goings of great birds, whirlwinds in the valley.

"Of all this we have now said perhaps more than was needful. Let us return to our game of *Keshjee'*."

As Mike, Spence, Ben, and Winnie followed Mr. Whitefeather out into the starlit night, they heard the old men take up their chanting once again:

The voice that beautifies the land;
The voice above,
The voice of thunder
Within the dark cloud,
Again and again it sounds,
The voice that beautifies the land. . . .

"My truck is this way," said Winnie's father as they crossed the yard and came around behind the modern house. "Believe it or not, you're almost close enough to Ambrosia to go the rest of the way on foot. *That's* how far you traveled down that hidden canyon this afternoon. But we won't make you walk in the dark alone."

15

Truth

Then rode out young Percival, bravely armed and clad all in scarlet, in quest of the Holy Vessel. And in his journeyings he came at length to a broad lake of shining waters, and one sat a-fishing thereon in a boat. And Sir Percival cried out upon him, asking him in God's name and of his courtesy to tell him where he might seek lodging for the night.

"Nearby stands a lone castle," answered the fisher. "I urge you to go there."

Now when Percival had come up to the castle, he found the drawbridge lowered of its own accord. Then he rode in and crossed a spacious courtyard. And when he had dismounted, he was led by seven fair maidens into a hall where a hundred chandeliers burned with many bright candles.

In the midst of the hall, in a sling bed beside the fire, lay the lord of that castle, the Fisher King, a handsome man with graying hair in a robe of sable, black as mulberry. And he moaned at divers times as if with the pain of a great wound.

*Then was Sir Percival seated beside that lord upon
a couch spread with rich quilts and coverlets. And
anon there came a page into the hall bearing a shining
lance by the middle of its shaft. And from the tip of the
lance fell a drop of blood, so that it ran all the way
down to the page's hand. And he carried the lance four
times around the walls, and then ran out again.*

*After this came fourteen maidens of surpassing
fairness, clad in samite of Azagouc greener than grass,
each bearing two large candles of yellow wax and
crowned with a dainty garland of flowers above her
hair. And behind them followed a lady in a gown of
cloth-of-gold. In her hands she carried the Holy Grail
itself; yet were young Percival's eyes so dazzled with
the light of the vessel's wondrous splendor that he
might not rightly discern it. Then it too passed four
times about the hall and departed.*

*Then did Percival's heart burn sore within him to
see the Grail and know the meaning of these strange
portents. But, for good or ill, he asked no question. . . .*

"So explain to me again what we're doing?" said Ben,
pushing his stubby fingers through the thick growth of
hair on the top of his head.

Mike looked up and realized that he'd been day-
dreaming. He shoved the old copy of *King Arthur* aside,
rubbed his eyes, and turned back to Winnie and the
journal.

Ben drew a short wooden stool up to the carom

board that Mike and Winnie were using as a table and
plopped down between them. It was late afternoon—
they'd had to wait until Mike was finished with his shift
at the pumps—and there was a hazy, orange tint to the
light that filtered in through the windows of the B-17.

"Do you always have to be so slow, Ben Jones?" complained Winnie. "How many times have we taken you
through it? I'm helping Mike translate the Navajo words
in his dad's journal. To see if we can discover any special
meaning in them."

"It's okay, Winnie," said Mike, smoothing down the
pages of the journal and trying to make his voice sound
as mature and even-tempered as possible. "Don't be so
hard on him."

Mike was tired of having to play diplomat and baby-
sitter. He'd been finding out the hard way how much
work it was to keep the peace between those two. He
sighed and wondered if Percival had ever had to put up
with people like Winnie and Ben. Questing, he thought,
wasn't all it was cracked up to be.

This was the third time the task of translating the
little book's contents had brought them together since
the night at the *sechai's* hogan. Much as Mike would
have preferred to keep the journal to himself, he realized
that he couldn't possibly decipher it without Winnie. So
they'd been spending a lot of time together. Mike wasn't
sure how he felt about that.

Ben came along because no one could figure out
how to keep him away. There was one thing you could

say in Ben's favor—he was persistent. He brought all of his comic books and spread them out on the floor of the B-17, waxing poetic over his collections of *Silver Surfer*, *Batman*, *The Mighty Thor*, and *Illustrated Classics* by turns. He expounded his theory of the Martian excavation of northern Vernon County several times over. He filled up the empty spaces on the plane's inside walls with his Mars globe drawings, his superhero trading cards, and his sci-fi posters.

It was odd, thought Mike, shaking his head over the journal—as quirky and odd as Ben himself. Never once had the boy asked permission to do any of this; somehow, he just assumed that he'd been given carte blanche to decorate the B-17 as he liked.

Even stranger than this was the fact that Mike didn't really mind. Somehow, he accepted Ben's presumption and even felt flattered by it. It was nice to have something that other people found exciting and attractive. And Ben really did like the B-17—even more than pinball. That was obvious. And that made Mike, as the "proprietor" of the classic Flying Fortress, feel like somebody special. After all, *he* was the possessor of the silver key at end of the sky-blue lanyard.

Spence was there too, but for an entirely different reason. As the others pored over the pages of John Fowler's journal, Spence stood in a small space near the tail of the plane behind an old wooden barrel. On top of the barrel he had placed a thick slab of oak, and on top of the slab a circular piece of glass, eight inches in diameter, covered in a pasty solution of water and grit. Over this, slowly, carefully, and rhythmically, he was stroking a second piece of glass of exactly the same dimensions. Ten strokes in one direction, then 10 in the other. After that, Spence would shift position—90 degrees to the right around the circumference of the barrel—before beginning the process all over again.

"Okay, let's get back to work, Winnie," Mike was saying. "How about we try a new tack? We'll read each Navajo word together. You give me the English meaning and I'll write it down. When we've got a lot of words written down, we'll go back and see if there's any way to make sense of them."

"All right," said Winnie. "But how?"

"I suggest you look for patterns," said Spence from behind his barrel. "Or ways to rearrange the words. Maybe it's like Scrabble or something."

"Good idea," said Mike, wishing he'd thought of it first. "Okay. The first word is *mo . . . mo . . .*"

"*Moasi,*" said Winnie. "That's *cat.*"

"*Cat,*" said Mike. He wrote the word CAT in large block letters on a sheet of yellow paper. "All right. Next word." He sucked his pen thoughtfully. "*Tsennel.*"

"*Tse-NILL,*" corrected Winnie.

Mike gave her a less-than-grateful look. "Whatever. What's it mean?"

"*Axe,*" she said.

Carefully, Mike printed AXE alongside CAT.

"After that comes . . . *tsah*—"

"*Needle*."

"—and . . ." he hesitated, "*tsa'adzoh*."

"That's *yucca*," said Winnie with an encouraging smile.

Ben scratched his head again. "Doesn't mean anything to *me*."

"Me neither," said Mike with a sigh. He laid down his pen, ran his fingers through his hair, and looked up at them. "Now listen," he said. "What we're looking for is some indication of exactly *where* my dad and his friend Lasiloo had been. What they were looking for. How they expected to find it. More than that, I'm wondering if the journal might contain any clues as to where my dad might go if—well, if he were ever pressed to look for a good hiding place . . . for some reason or other."

"Right," said Winnie. "I think we've got that."

"The English part of this entry says they were hoping to discover a 'new Anasazi site' . . . 'off the hidden canyon.' I've got reasons of my own for believing that they must have been searching close to that tunnel where we caused the rock slide. Just north of the Vernon County Cliff Dwellings. But *where* exactly? It must be a very *secret* kind of place."

"What's the big secret?" asked Spence. "Didn't you say that their finds got written up in *National Geographic*?"

"That's just it!" Mike answered. "I think that was something different! I've read that article. It was published in *September*. But the journal entry is dated *December 18* of the same year! It looks like they were on the point of making a whole *new* discovery. But I don't know if they ever did. Otherwise, there would have been a *second* article. Don't you think so?"

"Hmm," said Spence, shifting positions again. "I suppose you're right."

"I *know* I'm right," said Mike. "The frustrating thing is that the English section breaks off without giving any details. Then it goes into this Navajo stuff!"

Winnie rubbed the back of her neck and looked skeptical. "I don't know, Mike," she said. "Excuse me for saying so, but the whole thing sounds pretty far-fetched. Even if you could find that 'Anasazi site,' there's absolutely no reason to believe that it has anything to do with where your dad is right *now*. I mean, give me a break!"

Mike glared. Silently, he reached into his pocket and fingered the pocketknife. But he thought it better to keep his evidence to himself . . . at least for the time being.

"Anyway," Winnie continued, "my grandfather already told us to stay away from that hidden canyon. And I think he's right. My people say it's haunted. They say the *Hisatsinom* live there."

"Maybe," interjected Ben. "Or maybe someone else. Is it dinnertime yet?"

Winnie let out an exasperated groan. "Oh, go on, Ben!" she said. "Go find a few burgers and eat to your heart's content—as long as you do it somewhere else! And take your stupid comic books with you!"

"They're *not* stupid," said Ben, standing up with a hurt and offended look on his face. "Especially not *this* one." From his back pocket he pulled out the worn *Illustrated Classics* version of *The War of the Worlds* and unrolled it in front of her face. Immediately an inspired light appeared in his eyes. "It's based on the book by H. G. Wells. Written over a hundred years ago. He was a *real* writer, from England and everything! See?"—he pointed to the bookshelf—"Mike's dad had *all* his books. *He* knew the truth!"

"Yeah, right!" scoffed Winnie with a sarcastic curl of the lip.

"I've told Mike all about it! Spence, too! Right, Spence?"

"Sorry, didn't catch that," said Spence, making another quarter-turn around the barrel. "I'm concentrating. Mirror-grinding is a very precise art."

"I showed them the evidence down in that canyon," Ben continued, nothing fazed. "Didn't I, Mike? There were pictures of guys in space helmets on the walls and weird footprints in the dirt and a spaceship landing pad and everything! The Martians made those canyons! I'm telling you, Winnie! Just like the canals they built on Mars!"

"And you call *that* the *truth*?" laughed Winnie.

"Hey! It's truer than those old stories your grandpa told us!" shouted Ben, his round face reddening. "About 'Begochiddy' and water monsters and talking coyotes!"

Winnie set her jaw and clenched her fists. She rose to her full height and glared at Ben with eyes like fire. "Those songs are part of my people's sacred chantways," she said in a cold, dignified voice. "I won't stay in the same room with a—a *boy* who doesn't know any better than to make fun of the Origin Legend! Good-*bye*!"

Oh no! thought Mike. He laid a hand on her arm as she turned to go. To his surprise, she stopped and looked down at him.

"You can't leave now, Winnie!" he pleaded. "We're just getting to the good part! And I—well, I can't finish the translation without you." He lowered his voice. "I *really* need your help."

A strange, softened look came into her dark eyes. She brushed a strand of brown hair away from her face and sat down again. He thought he saw a tinge of red in her neck and cheeks. "You're right," she said. "I shouldn't let him get to me like that."

"Exactly," agreed Mike. "Besides—you don't really *believe* all those stories anyway, do you?"

Immediately she was on her feet again. "Oh, I don't, don't I? And just what do *you* believe, Mike Fowler?"

Mike could feel tiny beads of perspiration popping out on his forehead. *Wrong thing to say.* She was so touchy, so hot-tempered . . . just like Donald Duck! *It's like walking on eggshells, talking to this girl!*

Just what do you believe, Mike Fowler? What kind of a question was that, anyway? She couldn't talk to him like that! What right did *she* have to question *his* beliefs?

He thought of his mom and his dad and everything they'd taught him ever since he was little. He thought of Pop's wise words and Grandma's loving ways. He thought of the pocket Bible that lay hidden inside his jacket next to the compass and the knife. And suddenly, as he thought of all these things, a feeling of deep pride welled up within him, like a flow of hot lava bursting up from the heart of the earth and blasting through the side of a mountain.

"What do *I* believe?" he said at last, calmly, quietly, and yet with a tremor in his voice. "I'm a Christian. I believe in *the truth.*"

For a moment there was silence in the B-17. Then Spence, picking up his mirror and angling it toward Mike, so as to eye the texture of the surface more carefully in the light from the windows, said casually, "Do you really?"

Winnie made a move toward the rear of the plane.

"I think I'd better be going now," she said. "Roan's waiting outside. My parents will be expecting me for supper." With that she turned, opened the crew door, and leapt from the B-17.

Mike sat watching her go. Then he turned back to the journal, put his chin in his hands, and groaned.

"What was *that* supposed to mean, Spence?" he asked, his voice strained with irritation.

Spence looked up with the light reflecting off his glasses. There was an expression of clueless innocence on his face.

"I just didn't know," he said. "That's all."

16

The Telescope

Mike closed the journal and stood up. *Now what?* he wondered. Without the girl and her knowledge of the Navajo language, he was stuck. Sunk. At a dead end.

He stared down at the words he'd written across the yellow pad: *cat, axe, needle, yucca* . . . He thought about the knife and the hidden valley. Somewhere in that canyon lay the thing he was seeking. He was certain of it. Not that he knew exactly what that thing was—that was something he tried not to think about too much, since the more he thought, the more confused he became. Maybe he was hoping to uncover the Anasazi treasure mentioned in the journal. Maybe he was expecting to find something else that had belonged to his dad. Maybe John Fowler was down in that canyon himself. *Crazy idea!* And yet . . .

He reached into his pocket and fingered the knife. Yes—it was still there. It was solid and real. He pulled it out and looked at it. No—it wasn't a dream. The initials in silver and turquoise—*J. F.*—were as plain and clear as they'd ever been. And the knife was just a promise of bigger things to come . . . what Pop would have called an "earnest." It was all part of a plan. *God's plan.*

Yes. It had to be so. Everything had fallen into place with such precision. Every step had led him to this point: first the discovery of the journal; then Ben and Lowell Observatory and the meeting with Spence; after that the trip to the Cliff Dwellings and the accidental discovery of the hidden canyon; and finally Winnie and the hogan and her knowledge of Diné. It was all there. It all made sense.

So why did she have to run out on him *now*? Mike tore the yellow sheet from the pad, crumpled it in his fist, and threw it down into the plane's old bomb bay. He'd had a feeling that this girl would be trouble from the moment he'd laid eyes on her.

By now the sun was very low in the west, and the light inside the B-17 had turned a dusky red. Mike leaned over to the radio operator's table and switched on the lights.

"I really *am* getting hungry," said Ben. "That wasn't a joke. I think I'd better head home."

"Just a minute," said Spence. He lifted the two circular pieces of glass from the barrelhead, dipped them in a pail of water, and wiped them dry with a towel. "Before you go, do you think the two of you could help me with something? I need to check the curvature and focus of my mirror. This would be a good time to do it—just before the sun goes down." Carefully, almost tenderly, he wrapped one of the glass disks in a soft woolen cloth and held it to his chest.

"How do we do that?" asked Mike sulkily. He was still smarting from Spence's pointed question and Winnie's sudden retreat.

"Here." Spence took a large sheet of white paper from a portfolio on the floor beside him. "Mike, you hold this. And *you*," he added, handing a tape measure to Ben, "can do the measuring."

"Aw, I don't know," said Ben. "I really gotta get home!"

"It won't take long," said Spence. "Come on! In a few minutes it'll be too late!"

Together they walked out into the brilliant glow of the sunset. The sun itself was a bright, flaming red-gold ball, quivering and shimmering just above the horizon. The sky above it was a steep scree of pink and purple cirrus, fading to limitless blue at the zenith. A chill wind was rising off the eastern desert.

"Quick!" said Spence, placing his free hand on Mike's shoulder and pushing him into position.

I wish he wouldn't touch me like that! thought Mike.

"Hold up the paper—like this. Facing me, with your back to the sun."

Reluctantly, Mike took the sheet of paper in both hands and held it up toward Spence. He saw his own shadow, long, thin, and black, stretching out across the rocks and gravel toward the diner.

"That's right! Good! Ready with the tape measure, Ben?"

Ben nodded, his eyes wide. "Sure. What do I do?"

"I'm going to uncover this piece of glass—it's my tele-scope mirror—and point it at the sun. The reflection will bounce back and hit the paper. Whatever you do, Mike, don't look at the mirror! Close your eyes if you have to! Ben, you've got to measure the distance at which the image of the sun comes into focus on the paper. It's got to be perfect, with a sharp, clear outline. That should be at about 64 inches. At least I hope so. Ready?"

Mike looked at Ben. Ben looked back and shrugged.

With great care, Spence drew off the woolen cloth and held the mirror up toward the light. A blinding glare suddenly burst from the circular surface of the mirror. Mike dropped his eyes and fixed them upon the paper, where a bright but fuzzy projection of the sun's fiery disc now appeared.

"Pull out the tape, Ben!" said Spence. "Hand the end to me—good! Now go stand next to Mike."

Ben obeyed without a word, slowly reeling out the tape. Spence held the end of the tape in one hand and the mirror in the other. Then he took a step forward.

"Okay. What are we at now?" he asked.

"Um . . . about 73 inches, I guess," Ben answered.

"Still looks pretty fuzzy to me," said Mike.

Spence nodded. Taking tiny tiptoe steps, he advanced a little further. "Now?"

"Seventy," said Ben, staring down at the tape meas-ure. "Sixty-eight."

Mike kept his eyes glued to the orange disc on the

paper, watching its edges grow sharper and sharper as the image itself slowly shrunk and contracted. He could feel the heat increasing at his fingertips.

"Sixty-seven," said Ben slowly. "Sixty-five . . ."

"Hey!"

All at once the orange spot in the center of the paper burst into flame. With a yell, Mike let the sheet drop to the ground and jumped backwards, stumbling over a large stone and falling to the ground.

"That's it!" shouted Spence in great excitement. "That's *it!*" He covered the mirror again and stowed it gently inside his jacket. "We did it! It focuses at 64 inches exactly! An eight-inch mirror with an F-8 focus! It's perfect! It's ready to mount in the tube!"

The sun dipped below the horizon. Dusk fell. Mike got up and brushed himself off, staring down at the piece of paper as it burned to ash.

"You're crazy, Spence," he said.

Spence looked a little hurt. "No, I'm not. I just wanted to get the focus right."

"Were you trying to kill me, or what?"

Ben stood staring down at the little smoldering heap. "That was *cool!*" he said. "Howdja do it?"

Spence laughed. "It's the parabolic curve I told you about, Mike," he said. "The mirror is concave. See?"

"It's got something to do with a *cave?*" said Ben, his eyes growing ever wider.

"Well, in a way. The surface of the mirror curves

inward—like a cave does. The grinding and polishing I've been doing—rubbing one circular piece of glass over the top of another, again and again and again—automatically creates a curve that's a cross section of a *parabola*. 'Parabolizing' takes hours and hours. But when it's finished—bingo! This mirror will gather up parallel rays from a light source hundreds or thousands or millions or billions of miles away, and bend them back to a focal point 64 inches above its surface. What you get is a tiny but perfect image of the thing you're looking at. Everything comes into focus in a flash! Like in a *parable*. It's a beautiful concept, really."

"Great, Spence," said Mike wearily. "So now what?"

"Now what?" said Spence. "Well, since you've asked, I had some stuff delivered to the Last Chance garage today. Your grandpa told me it would be okay to have it brought here instead of to my house—since I'm going to be building it here anyway."

"Building what?" said Ben.

"The telescope, of course," Spence answered. "My eight-inch Dobsonian. I've been working on the Blink-Comparator at home. At this point I'm ready to mount the mirror in the tube and put the tube on the rocker box. The hardest part is done.

"You mean we'll be able to see Mars?" asked Ben, a look of disbelieving wonder on his face. "The canals and the polar caps and everything?"

Spence grinned. "Mars and beyond. I told you about

my theory, didn't I? About a *10th* planet? I can't wait to test it out with the Dobsonian and a version of the Blink-Comparator that Clyde Tombaugh used up at Lowell. I'm going to discover what I call 'Planet Y'! Just wait! Maybe I'll get an article in *National Geographic* too!"

———

Pop, who'd had to drive out to the Vernon County Cliff Dwellings to pick up the quads in his truck, told Mike that he didn't want them used for any more trips into Navajo country—at least not for the time being.

"I'm sorry, Mike," he said as they stood together a few days later alongside the gas pumps, looking out for customers and watching Spence at work in the garage. "I wanted you and the other boys to have free rein with the quads, but—well, I can't help feeling that you abused the privilege your first time out."

"How, Pop?" said Mike. "We only took them over to the Cliff Dwellings."

"But you didn't bring them back. *I* did. And some-how or other, you ended up in a place where you weren't supposed to be—where Smitty specifically told you *not* to go."

"But it wasn't our fault! There was an accident, and . . . well, we got lost. It's a good thing we got back home at all!"

Pop rubbed his chin. "Apparently there's more to this story than you're telling me. I know the Cliff Dwellings, and I don't see any reason to have an accident or get lost as long as you stick to the trails. They're clearly marked and maintained by the rangers." He raised a bushy eyebrow. "*Did* you stay on the trails?"

Mike looked down and kicked at the curb with the toe of his tennis shoe.

"I don't want to be unfair with you, Mike," Pop continued. "But I think it might be a good idea to stay off the quads for a while."

Mike jammed his hands down into the pockets of his jeans. "Yes, sir," he said sulkily.

"Hey, Mike! Can you help me with this?"

Mike looked up. It was Spence. He was standing just inside the garage door, and he had both of his thin but wiry little arms wrapped around a large, heavy-duty cardboard tube—the kind of tube commonly used for casting concrete pillars. Mike couldn't help but laugh. The tube was bigger than the boy, and Spence was struggling to guide one end of the long, unwieldy thing into an open-ended square wooden box.

Mike glanced up at Pop. Pop smiled back. "Go ahead," he said. "I can handle the customers. Looks like you're needed in the astronomy lab!"

"This is the tube-box," Spence explained as Mike helped him slip the cardboard tube through the wooden square so that about 10 inches stuck out on the other side. "It's the thing that lets me move the telescope tube up and down. The two round pieces of plywood on either side—they're called the *side bearings*—fit down into the cradle on top of the rocker box. Like this."

Together, the boys set the circular bearings into two notched boards that projected upward from the top of another, slightly larger wooden box. This larger box, in turn, swiveled on a square wooden base.

"Good!" said Spence, taking off his glasses and wiping them on his sleeve. "It's almost finished! Once I've mounted the mirror and inserted the eyepiece, she'll be ready to go!"

At that moment Ben rode up on his bike.

"Hey, guys!" he said. "Whoa! What's that? A cannon?" He eyed the tube-and-box structure curiously.

"It's Spence's telescope," Mike explained. "But you're right. It *does* look like a cannon!"

Spence replaced his glasses on his nose and crossed his arms. "It's no cannon," he said. "It's my gateway to the heavens!" Lovingly, he touched the tube and rocked it up and down in its cradle. "With this little baby I'm going to discover that new planet I've been looking for. All my calculations lead me to believe that it's out there. All I need now is some tangible proof."

"Cool!" shouted Ben, jumping off his bike and letting it drop to the ground. "And we can look at the Martian canals, too!"

Mike gave Spence a skeptical look. "And exactly *how* are you planning to do this?" he asked. "I mean, where are you going to put the thing? On top of the B-17?"

"Well, since you've asked," Spence replied confidently, "I've been scouting around, and I think I've found the perfect spot. Away from town. Out where the

sky is darker. It's everything Percival Lowell was looking
for when *he* built *his* observatory in Flagstaff. There's
even a tower—a sort of a tower, anyway—where I can
keep the Dobsonian."

"Really?" said Ben. "Where?"

"The old McCracken mine," Spence replied.

The McCracken mine! thought Mike. *That's right on
the edge of the reservation! It can't be far from the hidden
canyon!*

He looked at the telescope and smiled.

"That's great, Spence!" he said. "We'll help you get
set up!"

*And maybe we'll find out what's going on down in that
canyon. Maybe I'll discover something about my dad after
all—Winnie or no Winnie, quads or no quads!*

17

The Observatory

Not far outside of Ambrosia, just north of the Interstate and in among the blue-green buttes that jutted up from the rising ground at the base of the Superstition Mountains, stood the rusted and rotting remains of the old McCracken silver mine. The foothills in that high and dry region were still dotted with a few splintery, tumbledown buildings—buildings put up more than a century before to serve the needs of the mining operation.

Here, late one afternoon at the end of February, the boys set up Spence's homemade telescope in an old water tank that stood towering above the wreckage of the abandoned settlement: an old assay office, a row of bunkhouses once occupied by hopeful treasure seekers, and several tottering wooden sluices that snaked down out of the stony hills on rickety wooden scaffolding, swaying and creaking in the sighing desert winds.

"It's *perfect*," said Spence, shading his eyes and looking up at the old tank as he, Mike, and Ben came to a stop within the long crisscrossed pattern of the tower's angular shadows. "And it's at a *significantly* higher elevation!"

"Tell me about it!" said Ben, collapsing on the ground and producing a can of soda that he'd brought along for moments such as this. "I didn't know hunting for Martians could be such hard work!"

Mike was bitterly regretting the loss of the quads. Without them, the three boys had been obliged to transport the components of Spence's Dobsonian all the way from Ambrosia to the McCracken mine in a wheelbarrow and a hand wagon. It wasn't a long walk, but every bit of it was uphill and over rough and rocky ground.

"Got the handsaw, Mike?" asked Spence, as he surveyed the situation.

Mike answered by pulling a canvas bag of tools from the wagon.

"Good. I'll climb the ladder and hook the rope to the old pulley. You get into the tank and cut a door in the side. I think it would be best to make another opening in the floor right next to the pulley apparatus. That way it'll be easy to take stuff up and down."

The great wooden tank was, of course, open to the sky, but its sides were much too high to see over. So Mike, at Spence's suggestion, spent some time sawing out planks at regular intervals to create windows through which the telescope could be deployed. Meanwhile, Spence got Ben to help him with the task of hauling up the tube and the rocker box by way of the pulley and rope.

Once the telescope was set up, they sat down to wait and make their plans. The sun was setting, and a chill breeze was beginning to blow up the side of the hill. Spence knelt beside his "cannon," training it on the precise spot where he expected "Planet Y" to appear in the heavens.

"If my calculations are correct," he said, sighting carefully along the length of the tube, "it should rise just about . . . *there*. North-northwest . . . azimuth 272 degrees . . ."

"What time?" asked Mike, reaching into his pocket and producing the compass. He flipped open the case and took their bearings. As far as he could tell, the telescope was pointed at the sky almost directly over the location of the hidden canyon.

"Around midnight," Spence replied. "Maybe a little before that. About an hour after Venus, and 40 minutes or so after Mars. I'm expecting a perfect night—clear with no moon."

They ate their brown-bag suppers in silence. The dusk drew down and stars began to wink above them. The fragrant desert air stirred restlessly and the night grew cold.

As he munched on cold chicken and a stale bran muffin, Mike reached into his backpack and pulled out the old copy of *King Arthur.* He switched on his flashlight and began to read:

Now when the Grail had passed again beyond his sight, young Sir Percival the Waleis, sore burdened at heart, took his leave of the Fisher King and rode forth from that marvelous castle. Then for many days and nights he pressed his search throughout the whole known world, encountering great perils, fighting heavy battles, and enduring much hunger and thirst and pain and grief. But never in all those trials was it granted him to see the Holy Vessel again.

Then upon a day it came to pass, as he rode beside a stream, that he saw a maiden approaching on a black horse with a whip in her hand. Her hair was twisted in two black braids, and her eyes shone like two stars.

"Oh, Percival!" she cried as she stopped before him, swinging her whip. "A curse on him who greets you or wishes you well! You went to the castle and beheld the bleeding lance. You sat beside the wounded Fisher King. You saw the glory of the Grail itself, so bright that it blinded your eyes. And yet you asked no Question! Was it for you such a great effort to open your mouth and speak? Had you asked, the wealthy king, so sorely afflicted, would have been cured of his wound. You do not know what will befall if he is not healed. Unfortunate was your foolish mind! Unfortunate your silence!"

"That bright reddish planet is Mars."

Mike looked up at the sound of Spence's voice. He'd fallen asleep over his book and the remains of his dinner. The night had grown very dark. Spence, a silhouette against the glow of his electric lantern, was kneeling next to the telescope, his eye pressed to the small tube that protruded from its side.

"I'll take a sighting and get her lined up for you, Ben," he was saying. "We've still got about a half hour before my new planet gets high enough above the horizon for viewing."

"This is *so* sweet!" said Ben, opening his backpack and taking out a few pieces of blank paper and a box of colored pencils. "I wonder if Percival Lowell felt this way when he looked at Mars for the first time."

Mike got up, shook himself, and stood staring up into the vast glittering dome of the heavens. He tossed a silent prayer out to the darkness: *God, help me to find out something about my dad. If there's anything at all out there, please lead me to it!*

Spence came around behind the six-foot tube and crouched there like a catcher behind home plate, rocking the telescope slightly up and down, swiveling the whole assembly this way and that on the rocker box's circular base. In a moment he stopped and peered into the eyepiece again.

"Just a bit more to the right," Mike heard him muttering. "*There!* Got it! Come and see, Ben," he said, standing up and backing away from the scope with a broad, satisfied smile on his face.

Ben knelt and pressed his eye to the little tube. For a moment he appeared to be fumbling. "I don't see anything but my eyelashes," he said.

"You're trying too hard," said Spence. "Back off a little."

Ben eased off on the eyepiece and chewed his lower lip. Suddenly Mike saw his mouth drop open and his eyebrows arch upward in an expression of wonder.

"Check it out!" Ben exclaimed. "You guys have gotta see this! It's just the way he drew it—Percival Lowell, I mean! The polar cap . . . and the . . . well, I *think* I can see the canals. . . . Quick! Where's my paper and pencils?"

Spence laughed. "I doubt that you'll see any canals. None of Lowell's successors have confirmed their existence. But it's still pretty amazing, isn't it?"

"No, wait! I do see them! I *do*!" insisted Ben. "The more I look, the more I'm sure they're there!"

Mike, too, had his turn at the eyepiece. What he saw was, perhaps, a little smaller and fuzzier than he had expected. He wasn't sure if he could see the network of crisscrossing lines or not. Still, this was clearly the very thing Percival Lowell had attempted to portray in his many Mars globe drawings. And though the image was small and distant and cold, it was undeniably real: not just a pictorial representation of something, but the thing itself—a living, pulsing disc of light out in the solar system, beckoning to them with the promise of secrets yet to be unveiled.

For the next half hour, while Ben sat at the telescope furiously sketching what he observed, Mike stood with his hands in his pockets, leaning out through one of the rough windows he'd cut in the side of the old water tank. He squinted across the darkened desert and the black hulks of the mountains at the red-orange planet that hung just above the horizon.

Words flitted through his brain:

And yet you asked no Question! Was it for you such a great effort to open your mouth and speak?

Was he asking the wrong questions? Was he looking in the wrong place? What was he supposed to do? To say?

Mike stared out into space, pondering everything Spence had said about parables and parabolic curves and the bending of parallel light rays into a sharp and tiny focal point. He remembered a lesson he'd heard taught at the Ambrosia Christian Fellowship about Jesus' reason for teaching the people in parables—*so that seeing they may not see*. What could that possibly mean?

That's when he noticed lights on the northwestern horizon: barely perceptible shimmerings, a pulsating glow, a few sudden stabbing needles of brightness . . . almost like distant summer lightning.

It's the wrong time of year for a thunderstorm, he thought. Instantly he recalled what Winnie and her grandfather had said about the Ancient Enemies . . . lights and mysterious goings-on in the hidden valley. He turned back from the window to see Spence repositioning the telescope.

"Spence," he said, "did you see . . . ?"

But Spence wasn't listening. He was at the eyepiece, focusing the image and shouting to no one in particular.

"There it is!" He released his grip on the focus rings and began gesturing excitedly. "I was right! I was right! It's there! Only it looks much brighter and closer than I expected!

"I've discovered 'Planet Y'!"

18

Discovery

Mike hurried to Spence's side. Then he knelt and fitted his eye to the tiny tube on the side of the telescope.

"Incredible!" he said when he saw it: a tiny round shape, not much smaller than the disc of Mars itself, but bright and silvery, almost metallic in the way it reflected the light. He had some trouble keeping it in view; it seemed to wobble and shift back and forth within the telescope's field of vision.

"Are you sure it's a planet?" he asked, after watching the thing for a few minutes. "I mean, it seems to move around a lot."

"I think that's just atmospheric turbulence," said Spence. He rubbed his hands together, drew his glasses off his nose, and wiped them on his sleeve. "I can't believe it! My calculations were right! There really *is* a Planet Y!"

"And it's probably in league with Mars!" volunteered Ben. He zipped his jacket up to the chin and shivered. "Oh, man! This whole thing is starting to get *hairy*!"

But Mike wasn't satisfied. He pressed his eye to the aperture again and fiddled with the focus rings.

"Wait a minute!" he said after several moments of further observation. "Spence! There's something else!"

He wasn't sure what it was, but a small point of light—a shooting star or a satellite, maybe—had zipped across the view-field just below the glittering circle of Spence's planet. "Yes—I'm positive now. *Something's* moving out there . . . down closer to the horizon. Can you aim this thing a little bit lower?"

"It's probably just meteors," said Spence. "Let me have a look."

He stooped to peer into the eyepiece as Mike backed away. Then he knelt and rotated the tube slightly downward. For a few moments he said nothing. Mike could see his jaw working and the lines in his forehead contracting as he adjusted the focus and intently studied the image in the eyepiece. Suddenly he turned and looked up.

"You're right, Mike!" he said. "It looks like some kind of aircraft! A plane or a helicopter, maybe. As far as I can tell, it was flying pretty low to the ground. And not all that far away!"

"This is it!" said Ben. "They're landing!"

"Let me see!" said Mike, pushing his way in between Spence and the scope. Seconds went by, and he saw nothing. Then, suddenly, there it was again: a pinpoint of light—or perhaps a cluster of lights—moving across his circle of vision. As he watched, a quick beam of light slanted from the moving object down toward the earth. Then the whole thing vanished.

"You're right, Spence!" he said. "It *does* look a lot like a helicopter—a helicopter with a searchlight. What would a helicopter be doing out in those canyons?"

"I'm telling you guys, it's *not* a helicopter!" said Ben, waving his hands above his head. "They're here! They're back! They'll probably re-establish their old headquarters, set up their handling machines, assemble their fighting machines, and launch an offensive against Phoenix! Or even Las Vegas!"

"Could it be some kind of military exercise?" asked Spence.

"In Navajo country?" said Mike, looking back at him. "It's possible, I guess. But I've never heard of anything like that."

"Maybe we should tell Sheriff Smitty what we've seen," Spence offered.

Mike sat back on his haunches and ran his fingers through his hair. "No," he said, looking straight at Spence and then over at Ben. "I don't think so."

Smitty was the *last* person Mike wanted to find out about this—at least for the time being. Spence's question about a *military exercise* had sparked a new idea in his mind. Maybe this whole thing *did* have something to do with the military. And if so, it *might* involve his dad somehow! His scalp tingled at the thought of it.

Maybe his dad *hadn't* disappeared in the Middle East after all. Maybe the Air Force and the government, realizing that John Fowler knew the Navajo canyon country like the back of his hand, had sent him out here on some kind of top secret mission. Maybe Ben was right—or at least partly right. Mike had read some things about UFOs and Washington cover-ups. Maybe his dad had been dispatched to check out a spacecraft sighting! Maybe one of these days he'd come walking in through the front door of the diner and explain that *this* was why he hadn't been allowed to contact them all these years. Maybe.

Then another thought hit him. The pocketknife. Perhaps *that* was why the pocketknife had been lying out there in the canyon. *Yes.* The more he thought about it, the more plausible this theory became. John Fowler *could* have dropped it there years ago, of course—back when he was a teenager. That was a definite possibility. But in that case wouldn't the knife look a lot older, rustier, and more weather-beaten? He reached into his pocket and fingered it again. It was smooth, clean, silky to the touch—almost like new. Maybe his dad had dropped it there more recently than he had imagined. He just *had* to find out. But if he told Smitty, that would be impossible. Smitty would order him to stay out of the canyon and away from the reservation. Smitty would put a stop to his investigations before they even began.

"No," he said again. "I don't think we *will* tell Smitty. Not yet, anyway."

"Then what *should* we do?" asked Ben with a blank look on his face.

"We've got to go back to that hidden canyon," answered Mike. "We've got to find out for ourselves what's going on over there! There's just one big problem."

Spence nodded. "The tunnel from the Vernon County Cliff Dwellings is blocked. And we don't know the way in from the reservation side."

"No," agreed Mike.

"Not without Winnie."

19

Wonder Woman

Rrrrriinnnngggggg!!

Mike reached the bike racks before the last tones of the bell had faded from the air. It was a warm afternoon in late winter. The sky was a bright blue, flecked with little white fair-weather clouds. The northward-slanting sunlight bounced glaringly off the pale green stucco walls of Ambrosia Middle School. Inside the small bike parking lot, the sun's rays coaxed a tarry scent from the newly resurfaced asphalt pavement. Outside the chain link fence, clumps of sage and yucca trembled slightly in the desert breeze.

"Lots of homework, Ben?" he said with a sarcastic smile as he knelt down and began fumbling with the combination on his lock. Ben was sitting on the ground beside his bike, carefully taking account of the contents of his backpack.

Just beyond the gate, a group of kids had gathered at the side of the road to await the arrival of the yellow bus. Winnie was among them—Mike could see her through the links of the fence. Her dark hair was bound up in two glossy braids and she wore blue jeans, a red hooded sweatshirt, and traditional Navajo moccasins.

She saw *him*, too. Mike could tell by the way she suddenly averted her eyes, turned her back toward the bike racks, and began gesturing and talking more animatedly with the girls around her.

I don't have time for girl games, he thought with disgust. He was in a hurry to get home. It was his day to do a two-hour shift in the diner kitchen.

"Homework?" said Ben without looking up. "Um . . . I don't think so. But you gotta see *this*!" Out of his pack, which was stuffed to overflowing with loose, crumpled, dirty sheets of lined notebook paper, he triumphantly drew a dog-eared comic book. "*Wonder Woman!* 1971! Volume 26, number 103! I got it over at Bert's for a *pittance!*"

"*Wonder Woman?*" said Mike, undoing the lock. The chain made a ringing sound as he yanked it out from between the spokes with a flourish.

"Come on, Mike! You know Wonder Woman! She's part of the Justice League of America! Companion of Batman and Superman! She's an Amazon—member of an ancient race of warrior-women!"

"Great, Ben," said Mike, wrapping the chain of the lock around the post of his bike seat and checking his own backpack before swinging into the saddle. The journal was still there. He'd been doing his best to decipher it alone over lunch and in between class periods with a short list of Diné words Pop had given him. "I'll see you later, okay?"

"Wait a minute!" said Ben. "There's something *else* I gotta show you!" Again he dipped into his backpack and pulled out a soiled, wrinkled piece of paper. In the center of the page was a drawing of a reddish globe, capped with a splotch of white and crisscrossed by a network of fine black lines.

"Your Mars globe," said Mike. "Right?"

"You got it!" said Ben. "I took it home and finished it there. This is just the way it looked through Spence's telescope. Percival Lowell was right! I could see those canals for myself—at least I *think* I could. Couldn't you? I mean, I know it was kind of fuzzy, but Spence said there was a lot of turbulence in the atmosphere. Anyway—"

"What's *this*?"

A harsh voice interrupted Ben's ramblings. A big hand reached out and snatched the paper from his fingers. Ben looked up and made a little noise like a frightened rabbit. Mike followed his gaze and saw a large Navajo boy holding Ben's drawing between the thumb and forefinger of his right hand. He was tall and heavyset, and he wore a denim jacket and had a red bandana tied around his thick black hair. Behind him stood three other young Navajo of similar size and weight—all eighth-graders, apparently.

"Looks like Bobo Ben's been *coloring*," laughed one of the other boys, a small-eyed, hard-faced youngster with a whitish scar on one cheek. "Is it a ball?" he snickered. "Did you learn how to draw a bouncy ball on *Barney and Friends*?"

"I think it's a *pumpkin*," volunteered another. "Like Bobo Ben's head!"

The whole group laughed. Mike could feel the blood rushing to his cheeks. He got to his feet and stood facing Ben's assailants. "Leave him alone," he said fiercely.

"Oh, yeah? And who's gonna *make* us leave him alone?" responded the leader. "*You*, Mikey-Wikey? I don't think so." Again the others laughed loudly.

Mike chewed the inside of his cheek, trying desperately to control the furious trembling he felt coming over him. He knew that Pop would want him to stick up for Ben. But he also remembered what Grandma had once told him about "turning the other cheek."

"Give back the picture, Johnny," he said quietly. "Give it back *now*."

Johnny didn't move. He stood holding the piece of paper just as before, with a mocking, apish grin on his face. "Give it back? Okay. I'll give it back. But *first*—"

The boy grasped the page between the fingers of both hands. Then, slowly and deliberately, he ripped it down the center with a loud, tearing sound.

"Here you go, Ben," he said with a smirk when he was finished.

"My Mars globe!" moaned Ben, taking the two half-sheets in his hands and looking down at them in horror. "I spent hours on that! You—you—"

"Shut up, Bobo Head!"

Mike could contain himself no longer. With a loud yell he lunged at the boy, striking out violently with his right fist. Johnny dodged the blow, caught Mike deftly by the wrist, and flung him aside. A burst of pain, like an electrical shock, darted up Mike's bicep and across his shoulders. Then one of the other boys jumped him from behind and twisted his right arm behind his back.

"Get his stuff!" shouted Johnny.

A third member of the group ripped Mike's pack from his back and dashed it to the ground. It burst open, spilling its contents across the blacktop. Mike saw the journal go skidding over the asphalt between the tires of a couple of parked bicycles. The blood pounded in his temples and his eyes darkened with rage. In a burst of blind fury he wrenched his arm free and made a leap for the journal. But a foot came up and caught him on the shin. He fell heavily, knocking the breath from his body and scraping the side of his face on the hot pavement.

"Stop!" rang out a voice somewhere above his head—a girl's voice.

Unable to breathe or speak, Mike opened his eyes and looked up. It was Winnie.

"Johnny Boyaze!" she said. "*Tkele'chogi! Bisodi'!* Why are you acting like a pig? And you, Sam Adsyde, and Wolly and Begai! Just *what* do you think you're doing?"

Still gasping desperately for air—his lungs felt like two deflated balloons—Mike stared up at her. Winnie's eyes flashed with fire. Her jaw was set. Her mouth was a hard, straight line beneath the proud curve of her nose. Her nostrils flared like an angry stallion's.

From her face, Mike shifted his gaze to the four young Navajo. To his surprise, all stood silent with their eyes fixed upon the ground. Not one of them answered her a word until Johnny mumbled:

"Who put you in charge of *us*, Winnie?"

"You should be in charge of yourselves!" she fired back. "You bring shame on our people! My father and my *sechai* will talk to your parents about this! Do you think I want to be pulled out of Ambrosia and sent back to the Navajo school? If the *Naat'aanii* hear about this, there could be trouble! Some of the tribal leaders aren't happy about us coming here in the first place! You *know* that."

Mike had the distinct feeling that the boy was afraid to look her in the eye. Still without looking up, he said, "Forget about it, Winnie. The bus is coming. Let's go." With that, all four bullies shuffled out of the bike yard and off toward the bus stop.

"*Klizzi! Klizzi'yazzi!*" Mike heard her muttering under her breath. She reached down, grabbed him by the arm, and slipped her other hand under his shoulders. "Get up, Mike!" she said, pulling him to his feet.

"Winnie, I—" he gasped, still struggling to breathe.

"You don't have to thank me. I have reasons of my own," she said. She picked up the journal and handed it to him. "Here. You'll be needing this."

He looked down at the little leather-covered book. "It's really not much use to me without you," he said, glancing up at her. "Winnie, I'm sorry. Do you think we could—"

She paused for a moment and cocked her head at him. There was a look in her eyes he didn't understand.

"Don't worry," she said, shaking her braids. "I'll be over. Later." Then she turned and ran to the bus, which had just come squealing to a stop at the curbside.

Mike stared after her. Then he turned and looked at Ben, who was still sitting on the ground, staring down at the torn remains of his Mars globe.

"Talk about Wonder Woman!" said Ben. "Maybe I've been wrong about her!"

"Really!" said Mike, wiping the journal on his sleeve and stowing it carefully in his pack. "I don't get it! *All* girls are hard to figure out, but she takes the prize!"

Ben got up and brushed himself off. "It's not *that* hard to figure out," he said with a strange, lopsided grin. Then, more soberly, he added, "Thanks, Mike. For sticking up for me, I mean."

"Sure, Ben." Mike pulled his bike out of the rack, shouldered his backpack, and swung his leg over the seat. "That's what friends are for."

20

Evidence

Pop was sitting at the counter talking with Gail when Mike came into the diner. They turned and looked up quickly, as if they'd been interrupted, the moment he walked through the door. It was the slow part of the afternoon, and there wasn't a single customer in the place.

Pop's face was strangely grave as he greeted Mike with a slight lift of the eyebrows. Gail was holding a Kleenex in one hand and brushing her disheveled hair away from her face with the other. She gave her son a brief, red-eyed smile before turning away and heading for the kitchen.

"I'll tell Grandma you're here, Mike," she said as she retreated. He wondered if she were having one of her headaches. It was a little early in the year for an allergy attack.

"Okay, Mom!" Mike called after her. He dropped his backpack on the counter and took a seat beside Pop on one of the red-vinyl-covered swivel stools. "Is something wrong, Pop?" he asked in a lowered voice.

Pop smiled a little. The lines at the corners of his mouth and eyes crinkled softly. "Nothing special," he said. "Nothing at all, really. Just *life*. Business as usual. You're mom's a tough cookie—a *very* special lady. But it gets hard sometimes."

Mike propped his chin in his hands and stared out toward the kitchen. "I know," he said. He sat like that for a minute or so, and then said, "Women are hard to figure out, aren't they, Pop?"

Pop chuckled. "Sometimes. Not always. How do you mean?"

"Take Mom, for instance. She misses dad just as much as I do. She even prays all the time that he'll come back someday. But when I talk about *doing* something to make those prayers come true, she pretty much tells me to forget about it."

Pop leaned back and stared down his nose. "Does she really?" he asked. "Well, for one thing, your mom worries about *you*, Mike," he said. "A lot. She's already suffered one big loss. She doesn't want to go through another."

"*Me?*" said Mike.

"That's right. You're just about the whole world to her now. She knows how to pray. I'll vouch for her on that point. And she's got more faith and courage than most people I've known in my life, and that includes the guys I flew with during the war. But she's a realist. She's wise beyond her years. Things like this do that to a person."

"But you're always talking about trusting in the Lord and *believing*. If a person really believes, don't you think they'd *act* like it?"

"Doesn't she?"

Mike resettled himself on his seat. "Pop, what if I told you that my dad is out there somewhere right now—somewhere close by. If I *really* believe that, don't you think I should go out and look for him?"

Pop folded his arms and frowned. "Before I could answer that," he said, "I'd have to ask you *why* you believe it."

"Isn't believing enough?"

"Not necessarily. People believe lots of things that simply aren't true. Real faith has to be based on something solid. Some kind of evidence."

Mike brightened and sat up straight. "Exactly! And what if I said that I've *got* evidence?"

Pop looked surprised. "I suppose I'd ask to see it," he responded.

Mike felt himself reddening. "That makes sense, I guess," he said. "But—well, maybe I'm not ready to show it to you just yet."

Pop sat forward and rubbed the back of his neck. "Mike, does this have anything to do with the journal? And the Navajo reservation?"

"Well, partly. But only partly."

"Because if it does, I hope you haven't forgotten what Smitty said. We've already been through this. That's how you lost the privilege of using the quads."

"You mean I can't *ever* go to the reservation at all? Not even to see Winnie?"

"*Winnie?*" said Pop, taken aback once more. "You want to go see Winnie? I thought she went away mad!"

"Yeah," said Mike, shaking his head. "She's the *other* female I'm having a hard time figuring out. She . . . well, you see, there was sort of this bully situation after school today, and I . . ."

Pop smiled. "And you rescued the damsel in distress. Is that it? And now the two of you are back on good terms. Well, I don't see any reason why you can't go over to Winnie's sometime if you want to. As long as you don't wander off into places where you're not supposed to go." He paused, grew sober, and rubbed the stubble on his chin. "Meanwhile, a word to the wise: 'Evidence' can be a tricky thing. Things aren't always what they seem. You've got to be careful not to jump to conclusions."

"Oh, I know that, Pop," said Mike with a wave of his hand. "I'm not dumb. Still, sometimes you just *know*. Don't you think so?"

"Sometimes. Not very often, though. At least not right at first. Take your friend Spence, for instance. Do you think many people in this town would guess at first sight that the kid's a junior Galileo? Maybe even an Einstein?"

"I guess not."

At that moment, the door opened and Ben walked in. "Hey, Mike!" he called. "Hi, Mr. Fowler! Mind if I play a few rounds of Space Invaders before heading home?"

"Be my guest!" laughed Pop as Ben made his way

back to the pinball machine. "And what about *him*?" he added, turning to Mike. "What did you think of *Ben* the first time you saw him?"

Mike grimaced. "I thought he was completely wacko," he said.

"And now?"

Mike didn't answer.

"You see, that's just my point. *Now* you've added some more evidence to your files. Now your perspective has changed. First impressions can be valuable, it's true. But they need to be tested and checked out. Carefully."

Mike was leaning forward, straining to hear Pop's voice above the ruckus of Ben's shouts and the *ping! k-chkk!* of the pinball machine. So he didn't really hear it when the door opened a second time. He was too stirred up by what Pop was saying and too intent on showing him that he wasn't just a stupid kid.

"But that's exactly what I mean to do!" he blurted out. "I found some evidence in that canyon we stumbled into. I want to go back and *check it out!*"

He hadn't meant to say it, but there it was. And having come this far, he felt he had to go on.

"That's right," he said in answer to Pop's skeptical stare. "There was something there in that hidden valley— I can't tell you what, but you gotta believe me—and Ben and Spence and Winnie and I—"

He stopped as a large hand was laid on his shoulder. He turned and looked up.

It was Smitty.

"Afternoon, Mike," said Smitty. "Afternoon, Roy. Emma wouldn't happen to have an extra piece of that prize-winning peach cobbler left over from the lunch crowd, now would she?"

"Well," said Pop, shaking the sheriff's hand and getting to his feet. "I think that's a very definite possibility, Smitty. Let me just go and see."

As Pop headed out to the kitchen, Smitty leaned down and looked Mike straight in the eye. He was so close that Mike could smell the coffee on his breath.

"Before you go looking for any hidden valleys," he said, "just remember what I told you in my office that day. I don't want anybody getting into any unnecessary trouble. Stay out of those canyons, Mike. Understand?"

Mike swallowed hard. "Yes, sir," he said.

Ben, who had stopped playing pinball when he saw the sheriff come in, followed Mike to the kitchen when he got up to begin his shift with the dishwasher.

"You see?" Ben whispered. "You see? He knows! He *knows!*"

21

Questions

Throughout most of the month of March, Mike, Ben, and Spence spent Friday nights on top of the tower at the McCracken mine.

Lying out there under the sky, Mike couldn't help dreaming of camping trips he'd taken with his dad when he was still very small—something he hadn't thought about in a long, long time. Nights on the desert in late winter and early spring were more enchanting and beautiful than he had ever imagined. The stars were like swirling snow flurries, only motionless—frozen, preserved, and mounted on the domelike ceiling of the world for all to see. Never had they looked so dazzlingly close and bright.

But though camping was fun, their astronomical observations were disappointing . . . and oddly inconsistent.

Their second outing started out like the first. As on that earlier occasion, lights appeared over the canyon country. Once again, Mike thought he could discern the comings and goings of strange aircraft. Spence's planet rose on schedule, too, about 11:15, and hung shimmering in the midnight sky, very low above the northwest horizon. But after gleaming in the darkness for an hour or so, it suddenly vanished.

Spence hadn't counted on *that*. He was as close to frantic as Mike had ever seen him. For at least half an hour he adjusted and readjusted the scope in a fruitless attempt to relocate the shining object. So they had to content themselves with studying the surface of Mars for a while before turning in to their sleeping bags.

"I don't understand it," complained Spence, as they zipped themselves in and lay there shivering. "Planets are supposed to be erratic. That's how they got their name—*wanderers*. They don't stay in one fixed position in the sky like the stars. But a planet shouldn't be *this* erratic—appearing and then disappearing like some kind of heavenly Houdini! It doesn't make sense."

When the others were asleep, Mike lay there thinking while the wind whispered and sighed through the tower's rough-cut window-holes and the crickets chirped in the surrounding brush. He thought about his dad. He thought about Martians and the Anasazi. He thought about the appearance and disappearance of 'Planet Y.' And he thought about Winnie.

Winnie. It had been nearly a month since the incident at the school bike racks, and still she hadn't come. *I guess I deserve it,* he told himself. After all, he *had* scoffed at her grandfather's tales about the Ancient Enemies. He'd questioned the traditional Diné beliefs. He'd offended Winnie. What was worse, he'd done it in the name of his Christian faith.

Now, as he lay there on his back, staring up at the stars, the *sechai's* stories came back to him with fresh force. In the darkness, with nothing but the wild rawness of the night all around him, it was easy to imagine the *Hisatsinom* dancing crazily at the edge of the cliffs, terrible in their bright ceremonial masks and turkey-feather capes. If he closed his eyes he could almost see them, calling down spears of light from heaven, conjuring up intense blasts of volcanic heat from caverns deep under the ground. He'd told Winnie that it was all just a silly fable. But now he wasn't so sure.

Now he was beginning to wonder what he might run into if he ever *did* find his way back to that hidden canyon. He'd seen the lights in the sky. *That* part of the story, at least, was real. And Ben was right: Smitty's unwillingness to tell what *he* knew was unsettling. Somebody or something was out there, and the sheriff knew it.

Mike pulled the sleeping bag up over his face, hiding from the oppressive brightness of the stars. He drifted off to sleep. . . .

<hr />

After this followed two weekends when they didn't see anything unusual at all. This didn't bother Ben, of course. He put in lots of time on the telescope, scrutinizing the Red Planet and sketching at least 15 new Mars globe drawings to replace the one destroyed by Johnny Boyaze. As for Mike and Spence, *they* spent long hours gazing out over the silent desert, throwing rocks at clumps of yucca, voicing their frustrations, and talking over theories and plans.

———✦———

By the end of the month the moon was full. It lit up the sky for most of the night, making it difficult to see any of the planets or stars clearly. On the first Friday afternoon in April, the boys met in the B-17 to discuss their options.

"Maybe it's time to pack up the telescope for a while," said Spence as he sat at the radio operator's table, entering data into his laptop computer. "It's been weeks since we've seen anything even worth mentioning. We can try again after school lets out for the summer."

Mike, who was standing beside one of the old Browning machine guns, thumbing through his dad's old copy of *King Arthur*, had a different idea. He closed the book and stuffed it into his backpack.

"Listen. The moon won't come up until about 9:00 tonight," he said. "Why don't we go out and see what we can see until then? We'll take the wagon and the wheelbarrow with us. Whatever happens, we'll quit at moonrise and haul the stuff home. What do you say?"

"Sounds good to me," said Ben, who was finishing off an after-school snack of cheese nachos and casually browsing Wells's *The First Men in the Moon*.

Spence agreed to give it one more try. And so that night, after dinner, they reconvened at the B-17, grabbed the wagon and wheelbarrow from the storage space behind Pop's garage, and headed out on foot toward the old McCracken mine.

The sunset had been rare and golden—like the light that surrounded the Grail in the castle of the wounded Fisher King, Mike thought. Now, as they traveled northward, the sky on their left hand was hot and white, fading upwards through several shades of yellow, orange, and magenta to aquamarine and turquoise near the zenith.

Spring had come in earnest. The evening was pleasant and balmy. And as Mike drank in the tonic air, he suddenly felt a deep conviction that he could do *any-thing* he put his mind to. If his dad were out there, he'd find him. He just *knew* it. He breathed deeply and trudged ahead.

That was when he saw it: a dark shape approaching from the west, out of the glow of the sunset. A horse and rider. He stopped and shaded his eyes against the after-glow.

"Ben! Spence! Wait a minute!" he called out to the others, who had been making steady forward progress while he lagged behind. "Somebody's coming."

"Mike! Wait up!"

The rider galloped up in a spray of sand and dust and came to stop alongside him.

It was Winnie. She wore overalls and a red T-shirt, and her hair was tied back in a long, dark ponytail. Mike noticed that she rode bareback, guiding Roan only with knee pressure and a light leather bridle.

"She's back," said Ben in a matter-of-fact tone. "I *knew* it!"

Winnie looked annoyed. "I came looking for you guys at the B-17," she said. "Your grandpa told me you were headed this way."

Mike felt sheepish. "We're just going to have one last look through Spence's telescope," he said. "Before the moon comes up. You want to come along?"

"Why do you think I'm here?" she asked, dismounting and taking the bridle rope in her hand.

They pushed ahead, then. Spence took the lead, while Ben pulled the wagon and Mike pushed the wheelbarrow, with Winnie leading Roan at his side.

"I'm sorry, Winnie," said Mike as dusk fell around them and the old McCracken water tower loomed up into the pale evening sky. "I'm glad you came, because I've been hoping I'd have a chance to apologize."

"Apologize?" she said, giving him a curious sidewise glance. Her dark eyes glittered in the twilight.

"For what I said about your people's stories and beliefs. I know all that stuff must be really important to you." He paused, watching her out of the corner of his eye. When she said nothing in reply, he went on. "Not that I didn't mean what I said. About being a Christian, I mean. And the truth. My dad and mom taught me to believe the Bible ever since I was little, and I *do* believe it. But—well, I guess the *way* I said all that to you wasn't quite right."

Winnie lifted her chin. She seemed to think for a moment before answering.

"Apology accepted," she said at last. "I agree. It wasn't right at all. In fact, you were a real jerk. You're lucky I didn't punch you."

Mike felt himself reddening. He was glad of the darkness. "Well," he stuttered, "like I said—sorry."

"It's funny," said Winnie after they had walked on in silence for a few minutes. "You apologized. And yet I've actually been thinking a lot about what you said. A whole lot. In fact, that's the reason I came back. Part of the reason, anyway."

She walked with her head down, staring intently at the ground in front of her moccasined feet, one hand holding Roan's lead, the other in the pocket of her blue overalls. Mike had a feeling that she was trying to avoid looking at him.

"I love my people, Mike," she said after another pause. "Diné traditions and stories and songs and beliefs—they're all *very* important to me. Part of who I am. That's why I got so mad at you. But—"

She stopped again. To Mike it seemed that she was trying to control her feelings and collect her thoughts. "This is the hard part," she continued. "I'm starting to think—maybe for the first time in my life—that some of the things I've been told may not be exactly right. That maybe they aren't the *truth*."

Mike said nothing. He peered at her through the gloom and waited.

She went on. "You remember what happened that day at school a few weeks ago?"

Mike laughed softly. "I sure do! You were great!"

The whiteness of her teeth flashed out in a quick smile. Then she grew sober again. "I told my parents what those boys did. Just like I said I would. And my parents told *their* parents. Then the *Naat'aanii*—the tribal leaders—found out. And do you know what they did?"

"No."

"They said that none of us kids from the reservation should be allowed to go to school in Ambrosia anymore! None of us! Can you believe it?"

"But that's not fair! Why should *you* be punished for what those guys did? Why don't your leaders just stop *them* from coming to school?"

"Because it's *not* a punishment! It's their way of 'protecting' us—*all* of us—from 'bad influences.' From the white man's society and the Ambrosia public schools. They say *that's* what's wrong with Johnny and those other boys."

Mike snorted through his nose. "But that's stupid."

"*I* know that!"

"So what are you gonna do?"

"My parents are fighting it," she said proudly. "My mom won't go along with them. The Navajo schools are fine, she says. But she's always wanted us to get the same education as everybody else. She won't let them stop me from coming."

"So what's the problem?"

"Don't you see?" said Winnie. "It's something much bigger than that! It's everything—my whole world! If the *Naat'aanii* can be wrong about *this*—and I think they are—then maybe they're wrong about other things, too. Maybe they're wrong about Begochiddy and the creation of the four worlds, too. And Christianity. And the Ancient Enemies. And the hidden canyon."

Mike felt as if he'd been hit in the face with a bucket of cold water. "You mean it?" he said.

She looked at him. "Yes. I—I want to know more."

"Know more?"

"About—the *truth*."

"But what about the hidden canyon?" Mike fumbled in his pocket. His fingers slipped past the Bible as he felt for the knife. When he spoke again, his voice trembled slightly with excitement. "Would you really be willing to show us the way back to the hidden canyon? In spite of what your grandfather and the tribal leaders say?"

She took her time answering. "Yes," she said at last, very slowly. He couldn't see her face in the dark, but he thought her voice sounded oddly subdued. "I guess so. But I—"

"That's great!" said Mike. "And you'll help me translate the words in the journal?"

"I already *told* you I'd do that," she said—a little distantly, he thought.

"Good! *Now* we're starting to get somewhere!"

Winnie said nothing as they came up under the

water tower. She tied her horse to the timbers at the base of the structure and followed Spence up the ladder. Mike wondered why she had suddenly become so silent and subdued.

———⊛———

Sir Percival rode forward, full downcast in spirit, until he passed beneath the eaves of a dense wood. Deep within that forest he came at last upon a spring that bubbled up beside a rocky cell where dwelt a holy hermit.

"Well met, sir knight," said the hermit. Then he led Percival into his grotto, where stood an altar stone all bare of its cloth, in keeping with the Good Friday observance.

"Sir," said Percival when the holy man had shared with him of his meager fare, "four-and-a-half years have I sought the Holy Grail in vain. Only now do I realize how long I have been wandering with no sense of direction. And I will tell you more: I am deeply resentful of God, since He stands godfather to all my troubles."

"Say not so!" answered the hermit. "For I know that you beheld the glory of the Holy Vessel itself, sitting in the presence of the maimed king. And yet all that you achieved there was shame: for though you saw the marks of his suffering, yet you failed to ask your host, 'Sire, what ails you?' Through youthful inexperience you asked no Question, and so let slip a golden opportunity."

"It's there!" shouted Spence, leaning away from the telescope and swinging around to face the others. "It's back! Back in the very same spot—just where I expected it to be! But . . ."

"What's back, Spence?" asked Mike, looking up from the pages of *King Arthur*. He'd been sitting and reading by flashlight while Winnie crouched beside him, examining the journal.

"The lights!" Spence answered. "And Planet Y—if that's what it is! But it's risen about two and a half hours earlier than it should have—at least by my calculations."

"Lemme see!" said Ben, elbowing past Spence and taking control of the telescope. "I'm telling you guys," he said in a moment, gesturing with one hand while keeping his eye glued to the eyepiece, "it's *not* a planet. It's an invasion! It's an all-out attack! And somebody needs to *do* something about it. Hey!—there's one of those shuttle pods or fighters we saw before!"

"Can I take a look?" asked Mike, gently pushing Ben aside. He rotated the tube just slightly downwards toward the horizon and put his eye to the hole. He saw light—waves of undulating light, pierced at random by shafts of sudden brightness. And then, so abruptly that he might easily have missed it, a black object, small but very clear, flitted across his field of vision.

"A Huey!" he exclaimed, turning to Spence. "I'm almost certain I just saw a Huey!"

"What's a *Huey*?" said Ben, scrunching up his nose.

"A helicopter. A Bell UH1H Iroquois. The kind they

flew in Vietnam. I've got pictures of them back in the B-17—in my *Jane's Pocket Book of Helicopters*. What do you think of that, Spence?"

"Maybe it *is* some kind of military exercise," said Spence. "Or—"

"But there aren't any military exercises going on in Navajo country," said Winnie flatly. She put her finger in the journal and stood up, leaning out through one of the tower's window holes. "If there were, I'd know about it. Anyway, that just wouldn't happen.

"But those lights!" she exclaimed, squinting out across the desert. "They're the same ones I told you about—that night we met down in the canyon. I've seen them before. The lights of the *Hisatsinom*!"

"Martians," corrected Ben.

"There *aren't* any Martians, Ben Jones," said Winnie.

"Oh, yeah?" he responded. "And where do you think all those Navajo stories about 'Ancient Enemies' came from in the first place? Huh? Some people just don't know anything! I saw an episode of *True Mysteries* that was about something just like this. Did you realize that the Egyptian pyramids were originally air traffic control towers for UFOs?"

"Give it up, Ben," said Winnie. "This is serious."

"I think Winnie's right," said Mike, growing very solemn. "I don't know exactly what it is, but I've got a feeling we've stumbled on to something *very* serious. Maybe even dangerous."

"Now he tells us!" laughed Ben. "*Dangerous?* Hello!

How about 'the end of the world as we know it'?"

"It's not like that, Ben," said Mike. "But it is—well, funny or fishy, if you ask me. It's also something important enough for Smitty to want to keep it hushed up."

"So what are you thinking, Mike?" Spence asked, stepping up to take another look into the telescope.

"I'm thinking that it *might* be military after all—at least partly. A *top secret* military operation. It might even have something to do with invasion or national security."

"*What?*" Winnie turned to him with a look of disbelief in her eyes. "You've been listening to Ben too long! What are you trying to say?"

"Two things," said Mike. "Two things that *could* be linked together somehow.

"Number one: I think there's *evidence* that we're up against something really *big*.

"Number two: I *believe* it might be connected with my dad."

22

Revelations

"Your dad!"

Ben's voice was shrill with exasperation. "Why is it always about your dad?" he wanted to know. "*Your dad* this and *your dad* that! It was *your dad* at the observatory and *your dad* at the Cliff Dwellings. Then it was *your dad* in the hidden canyon and at the hogan. Why can't we search for Martians or look for new planets without talking about *your dad* all the time? Your dad and his journal! It's like you're obsessed, Mike!"

Spence squatted beside the telescope. He took off his glasses, wiped them on his sleeve, and gave Ben a keen, serious look.

"Look, Ben," he said. "Mike's been trying to find his dad ever since the day we met him. We all know that. Maybe you and I would have an easier time understanding that if *we'd* lost *our* dads too. We're not so different from him—we've just got different quests, I suppose. But I can tell you this: Mike's search for his dad has brought the four of us together. And I think that's a good thing."

Winnie stepped away from the window and sat down again. She opened the journal and laid it in her lap. "I agree," she said.

Mike, too, seated himself on the tower's rough wooden floor. He looked gratefully at Spence.

"You're right, Spence," he said. "We've each got our own quest. I understand that. I realize that maybe I've been—well, pushing *my* agenda a little too hard. But don't you see what I'm trying to say? I've got this feeling that it all fits together somehow! Ben's Martian thing, 'Planet Y,' the 'Ancient Enemies,' the canyon, the lights, the Huey, whatever it is that Smitty's working on! I think it's all linked together like a chain. And I really do believe that it might have something to do with my dad!"

Ben looked sheepish. "Sorry, Mike," he said. "I didn't mean what I said. I'm glad we're friends, too. I'll help you with your quest. Really I will! *After* this Martian thing blows over!"

Winnie rolled her eyes.

"So it's settled," said Spence. "We're with you, Mike. We're on your side. And we'll help you if we can. But"— he leaned forward—"well, maybe you wouldn't mind explaining yourself. I mean, I hate to be a wet blanket and all, but—how on earth can Martians and lights in the canyon and 'Planet Y' have anything to do with your dad?"

Mike got up on his knees. "The Air Force told us that my dad disappeared somewhere in the Middle East," he said. "I've always *known* that wasn't true. But I could never explain why. Until now."

"Keep talking," said Spence.

"Before Pop opened up the B-17 and I found the journal and the *National Geographic* article, I had no idea that my dad was so familiar with the Cliff Dwellings and the Navajo canyon country."

"So?" said Ben. He reached into his backpack and pulled out a bag of onion-garlic potato chips.

"So it's obvious that something funny—something big—is going on in that canyon. It's not every day—or night—that you see a Huey flying around. They're military helicopters! And if something big *is* going on, and if the military is involved, it just makes sense that the government would pick *him*—my dad—to go on a special secret mission to check it out. I mean, he's a top Air Force pilot, and he knows the land around here like the back of his hand!"

"I get it!" mumbled Ben, crunching thoughtfully. "So your dad came out here and *then* the Martians captured him! And *that's* why he's been missing so long! That makes sense."

"What *I'm* thinking," said Mike, "is that this whole thing is such a top, top secret operation that *nobody*—not even my mom or my grandpa or me—is allowed to know *anything* about it. So they tell us that he's missing in action. See? Then, as soon as it all breaks loose—as soon as it's all over—he'll come home. But right now everything depends on secrecy. That's why Smitty won't talk."

"That's brilliant, Mike!" said Ben through a mouthful of chips. "Why didn't *I* see that?"

"I'm not so sure," said Spence, hugging his knees. "It's a nice theory. But it sounds like a lot of wishful thinking. Like something in a movie. What evidence do you have that *any* of this is true?"

Mike pursed his lips. Then he reached into his jacket pocket and drew out the pocketknife.

"This," he said, holding it out to them. "I found it the day we stumbled into the hidden canyon. Right after the rock slide. Look at it—see the initials on the case?"

"A pocketknife?" said Winnie, training her flashlight upon the object.

"Yes. But not just any pocketknife. Look at it!"

Ben bent close to the pocketknife and examined it closely. A potato chip dropped half-eaten from his fingers to the floor. "*J. F.,*" he said.

"That's right. *J. F.*"

"Cool! What does it mean?"

"*John Fowler,*" said Mike conclusively. "Don't you get it? It's my dad's! It *has* to be! At first I thought he must have dropped it there years ago. But just look at it! It's so clean and shiny! Almost new! It can't have been lying there very long. That's what makes me think that he's out there somewhere in those canyons *right now*!"

Spence scratched his head. "I still don't know," he said slowly. "How many other *J. F.'s* do you think there are in the world?"

"Not many who've ever been in that hidden canyon! Didn't Winnie's grandfather say that nobody ever goes there? Nobody is ever *allowed* to go there! Right, Winnie?"

They all turned to look at the Navajo girl. At the sound of her name, Winnie lifted her face from the journal, which she'd been studying intently by flashlight. She tucked a stray lock of dark hair behind her ear. Then, with a look of conviction in her dark eyes, she said:

"Mike—I'm starting to think that this might make sense after all. At least some of it."

Mike scrambled over and knelt beside her. "Really? How do you mean? What does it say?"

"If I'm right," she answered, "it's a pretty ingenious system. Like this section right here—the one we were looking at in my kitchen that night." She pointed to the page. "If I take these Diné words—*thanzi cha dzeh jadholoni tsah t'kin ma'e ahnah*—and translate them into English—*turkey, hat, elk, kettle, needle, ice, fox, eye*—and *then* take all the first letters of those English words . . . t-h-e, k-n-i- . . . see? It starts to spell something."

Mike's heart was pounding. "What?" he said. "What does it say, Winnie?"

She looked up at him, her eyes gleaming in the light of the full moon.

"It says,
At dawn the sun goes down
To where the treasure lies.
The knife points the way."

23

Thunderstorm

They set out for the hidden canyon very early the next morning. Winnie met them just beyond Interstate 40, on the very edge of the reservation, looking like a Sioux or Cheyenne warrior astride Roan in the half-light of dawn.

Above the pulsing line of pale blue on the horizon a few persistent stars still trembled at the top of the chill morning sky. Mike zipped his jacket up to the chin and walked alongside Winnie's horse as she turned and led them down into a dry arroyo, then up onto a red table-land that rose and climbed in gradual steps as they crossed it to the north.

Soon a tiny spark flashed out in the east. Flames of bright red leapt up at their feet and flowed out across the desert. Blossoming mallow and Indian paintbrush caught the brilliant level shafts of the rising sun and reflected them back in a thousand scarlet pinpoints of light. Here and there the budding canopy of a solitary cottonwood, a bright cloud of gentle April-green mist, hovered in the air just above the rocky ground. Saguaro cactuses stood like motionless green sentinels, watching the travelers pass. Towering rock mesas and monuments, white and gold and copper in the morning, presided over the silence like Gothic cathedrals.

When they were about a mile southwest of Winnie's settlement, they stopped at a large, flat rock to eat their breakfast. It was broad daylight by that time, but the sun had gone behind a spreading cloud. The desert around them, so brilliant with color only moments before, lay under a dimly luminous pall.

Mike unzipped his backpack and produced the breakfast food of his choice: cold toaster tarts. Raspberry. Tearing open the silver foil, he licked his lips and took a bite. Then he pulled out the old worn copy of *King Arthur*, leaned back against the rock, and began to read:

Sore abashed at the holy hermit's words, young Percival rode out again upon his perilous quest. And when he had ridden through many lands and passed through divers trials and combats, it befell that he came upon a narrow stone bridge that spanned a swiftly running beck. And he was ware where a strange knight in black armor came riding against him from the far end of the bridge, with shield raised and lance lowered. Then Percival too set lance in rest and bare down upon his opponent, so that they met in the midst of the bridge with a great din of clashing steel and a shattering and splintering of spear shafts. And Percival fell before the black knight's lance.

Anon he jumped up lightly and drew his sword.
And when the other in like manner had dismounted
and drawn his blade flashing from its scabbard, then
did those two heroes fly at one another with such a
great hewing of helms and shields that fire sparked
from their swords and their bodies failed of breath.

At length Percival smote the other a great buffet
upon the helm, so that the knight was driven to his
knees; but the sword of Percival burst asunder with the
force of the blow. Then was the black knight magnani-
mous; for he said, "Little do I doubt me, brave and
warlike man, that you would go on fighting without
your sword if need be. But let there be a truce betwixt
us till we have rested our limbs."

So they sat down together upon the green grass. And
when they had unlaced and removed their helms, Sir
Percival saw straightway that his worthy opponent was
none other than his own half-brother, Feirefiz. For Feire-
fiz was a piebald man: half black and half white, like a
magpie. And thereby did Sir Percival know him. . . .

"Are we getting close yet, Winnie?"

Mike looked up at the sound of Ben's voice. "Good
question," he said. "How much farther?"

Winnie held up a hand as she swallowed a mouthful
of fry bread.

"Not far at all now," she said. "Just over that rise."
She pointed off east toward a rocky swell of ground covered with spiny gray-green clumps of yucca and topped

by a small copse of juniper and piñon. "Once we're on the other side, you'll see the edge of the canyon. But you probably won't *know* that you're seeing it. They don't call it *hidden* for nothing."

As it turned out, she was right. When they topped the ridge and came out through the thin growth of spindly evergreens, Mike looked out and shaded his eyes. Away below them stretched a land so rough-cut, so multilayered, cross-divided, and riddled with lights and shadows, that a herd of dinosaurs could have hidden there without being seen. There were undulating hills and jagged orange outcrops, like the walls of ancient cities. There were abrupt red and ochre monoliths and spear-points of rock jutting up out of the earth like the bones of giants. There were dips and holes and lines of brown and dark green where shrubbery marched along the edges of arroyos and dry riverbeds. If there *were* a canyon nearby, Mike certainly couldn't see it. On the other hand, the whole place could have been nothing *but* a massive honeycomb of deep-cut canyons. He remembered what Winnie had told him about the Diné's six points of direction: north, south, east, west . . . and up and down.

———※———

At last Winnie slid down off her horse, removed her pack from his back, and gave him a sharp slap on the rump. "Go home!" she shouted. "It'll be easier if I go the rest of the way on foot," she said in answer to Mike's inquiring look. "From here on, there's a lot more up and down than east and west. Look!"

She turned and pointed down the face of a sheer, steep cliff to a broad band of flowing reds, oranges, and yellows far below—the hidden canyon itself.

Mike caught his breath. He felt as if he were standing on the edge of the world. Just below their feet a narrow path slithered through the stones and dry grass, switchbacked its way down a stair of serrated sediments, and then plunged straight over the cliffside. The boys shouldered their backpacks and followed Winnie down the trail.

At the bottom of the canyon they stopped for another short rest.

It was just past noon. The four of them took their midday meal in a little alcove of rock set into the canyon wall not far from the foot of the cliff.

"So where was it that you found this knife?" asked Winnie, stepping out from under the rock and turning her face up toward the sky. Though the thin veil of the early morning overcast had burned away, it was quickly being replaced by a troop of big, puffy, blue-shadowed cumulus clouds. They came swiftly up out of the west like a fleet of tall ships under full, billowing sails.

"Back that way," said Mike, pointing up the canyon. "A long walk. That's why we should get started *now*."

"Funny," said Spence, glancing up. "If this were July, I'd say we were in for a downpour. But it's a little early for thunderheads."

Winnie nodded and glanced anxiously from one side of the canyon to the other. "The Diné say that the Ancient Enemies have power to control the wind and rain," she said.

Farther down the canyon they came upon the footprints they had discovered on their first trip through the canyon. They were still there—lots of them. And it looked as if the surrounding sage and scrub oak had been trampled by the passage of feet.

Mike knelt down to examine the tracks. Then he glanced at Winnie's moccasined feet.

"If there are any *Hisatsinom*—or Martians—down here," he smiled, "it looks like they buy their shoes at your grandma's store, Winnie."

Winnie scowled down at him. "It's no joke, Mike," she said. "I told you: The Diné don't come down here!"

"Whatever," said Mike, straightening up and brushing the dirt from the knees of his jeans. "All I know is what I see."

"Hey, guys!" Ben's voice came echoing to them from over against the canyon wall. He was standing in a space between two quaking aspens and a stunted juniper tree and pointing to a spot on the ground at the base of the cliff. "Look! Someone made a fire over here!"

Mike, Spence, and Winnie ran over to join him. Again Mike knelt and fingered the charred remains of what looked like a small cook fire.

"It's cold," he said, "but it can't have been here very long. Someone must have been camping." With a glow of rising hope in his chest, he reached into his pocket and felt for the pocketknife. Then he got to his feet. "Come on!" he said.

They trudged ahead, then; and as they went, the sun, which had been shining out bravely through gaps between the clouds, was suddenly blotted out. A darkness, strangely deep for that hour of the day, dropped over the canyon like a curtain. At the same instant, a gust of sharp, cool air, laden with the scent of rain, struck them in the face and stirred the dust at the base of the cliffs. The swallows that had been swimming in the river of air above their heads disappeared into clefts and niches in the rock. Cedars, junipers, and piñons trembled in the wind.

"It may be only April," Spence said, "but it sure feels like a thunderstorm is coming on." He unzipped his backpack and withdrew a small plastic envelope, from which he produced a clear plastic rain poncho.

"Don't worry about it," said Mike. "Just keep going!"

Soon the canyon took a sudden turn to the left. Mike looked up to where the tops of the cliffs glowed red-orange against the thick gray of the sky.

"Look! Spence! Ben!" he called, pointing upwards. Above their heads, jutting skyward from the cliff's highest point, rose the tall, sharp pinnacle of rock Mike had seen on the morning of their first excursion—the formation that marked the place where the landslide had buried the mouth of the tunnel. "This is it! We're almost there!"

Even as he spoke there came a bright flash, followed by a few scattered drops; and then, as if from a great distance, a grumbling roar of thunder.

"Looks like I was right," said Spence.

Together they pressed forward into the rising wind. Soon large drops of rain were slapping them in the face, plopping heavily into the dust, and spattering on the rocks. Spence donned his poncho while the others pulled their jackets up over their heads. Sensing that the darkness had suddenly intensified, Mike picked up the pace and began running, leaping over rocks and roots, slowing only to clamber over large boulders or fallen trees that lay in their path.

"It's ahead of us on the right!" he shouted back to the others, pointing up at the sharp pinnacle of rock. "Just below that—"

But at that moment a forked and fingered bolt of lightning knifed down out of the gray-green clouds and struck the tip of the pointed tower of stone. For a fraction of a second the entire formation stood out sharp and bright against the black backdrop of the sky. A shower of pink sparks burst from the face of the rock and fell gracefully through the air, like the petals of a flower or the glowing remnants of fireworks on the Fourth of July. Mike felt a hand clutch his arm. He turned to see the light just fading from Winnie's face. Her eyes were wide, her forehead arched and furrowed, and her lips parted in an expression he couldn't understand—either of wonder and disbelief or of sudden realization.

"M-Mike," she stuttered. "That rock! I think I . . ."

But her words were drowned out by the following crash of thunder. So overwhelmingly and shatteringly close was it that it stopped all of them in their tracks and caused Ben to set up a howl. As soon as the last cracklings and rumblings of its angry voice had faded away, the rain began to pour down in unrelenting sheets.

"Run!" yelled Mike, pointing in the general direction of the tall, sharp rock. "That way!"

They did. But it was only a matter of moments before each and every little rill and rut in the canyon floor had become a rushing stream. Rivulets of foaming reddish-brown water sprung up on every side of them. And as the streams joined together to become a violent torrent, Mike happened to look up and see a break in the opposite wall of the canyon—an opening, about 10 or 15 feet wide.

It was the entrance to the gorge he had noticed on their first visit to the canyon, the archway that led into the rough and narrow arm of the canyon that branched off of the main valley toward the northeast. It lay up a short rise, out of the water's reach, just below the pointing pinnacle of rock. *We've made it, then!* he thought. *This must be the very spot where I found the knife!*

"There!" he shouted, grabbing Winnie by the sleeve and pointing to the gap in the cliff. "We'll have to look for shelter up there! Come on!"

Up the slope they dashed, slipping through the mud and flowing gravel, falling to their knees, getting up again, and stumbling over stones and debris, until they had climbed under the arch onto a shelf of higher and drier ground beneath an overhanging section of the cliff. Here they huddled for shelter while the thunder rolled and the sky poured down over the edge of the cliff like a waterfall. So thick and heavy was the veil of rain that they could see nothing of their surroundings, but sat stranded as if in the middle of a blinding fog.

The first fury of the storm passed quickly, and yet the rain continued to fall for a couple of hours. Mike sat with his back to the wall of the canyon and his chin on his knees. He felt unbearably cold, stiff, and cramped. He couldn't help envying Spence, who seemed to have succeeded in staying relatively dry under the expansive tent of his poncho. Ben sat with his head under the skirt of the poncho, wet, bedraggled, and with a look of disgust on his round, red face. Winnie stared out into the rain from under the hood of her sweatshirt, her dark eyes still as deep pools, her face a smooth, expressionless veil over her inner feelings.

At last the storm slowed to a complete stop. The sun broke through a space between the spent and scattering clouds, setting the whole dripping world ablaze with the glitter of a million rubies, amethysts, and diamonds. A double rainbow arched across the sky beyond the red bluffs of the cliff. And as the light grew and the air cleared, Mike lifted his head and looked out across the canyon.

"Spence," he said in a quiet but urgent voice, "let me see your binoculars!"

Spence complied. "What is it?" he asked.

Mike seized the binoculars eagerly, stood up, and aimed them at a spot on the opposite canyon wall, about 50 feet up the side of the cliff: a dark place, still under the shadow of a passing cloud, like a huge hole or the mouth of a gigantic cave among the rocks.

"I'm not sure," Mike answered. His voice trembled with excitement and exhaustion.

All at once the cloud passed. The sun shone full on the face of the cliff. Mike let out a gasp. Sure enough, back in the dim recesses of a high-arched alcove in the face of the orange rock was what appeared to be an ancient and perfectly untouched Anasazi pueblo, twice, maybe three times the size of Dinétah House.

Mike bit his lower lip. The black rectangular windows of the square houses stared out at him from across the airy canyon like the empty eye sockets of a hundred speechless skulls. Was it possible? Could this really be the ruin his dad and Harrison Lasiloo had been expecting to find? It *had* to be. *The knife points the way. . . .*

"It's a ruin!" he shouted to the others. "We've found the ruin my dad was looking for! Can you guys see it?"

"You're right!" said Spence, taking the binoculars and pointing them up at the cliff. "From here it looks like a particularly fine example of late thirteenth-century Type III masonry. Seems to be almost perfectly preserved, too. I think I can even see a way to get up there—handholds and footholds in the face of the rock!"

"The journal was right!" said Mike, giving Spence an

enthusiastic clap on the shoulder. "I told you guys! It was right!"

Winnie stood gazing up at the cliff dwelling, shading her eyes against the glare of the sun. "Mike . . ." she said, reaching over and taking hold of his sleeve.

"Not now, Winnie," he responded, shaking her off and reaching down to pick up his backpack. "We've got to go check this out. Right now! Come on!"

With that, he jumped down from the shelf of rock and dashed into the gorge.

24

Celestial Object

The sun was slipping below the western rim of the canyon. A blue shadow rose upon the opposite wall. Soon it would engulf the alcove and the silent cliff dwelling.

Mike saw all of this as he led the others across the gorge. Just below the ruin it widened out into a broad, level sandy space crossed by a deep arroyo that was running high and strong with thick brown rainwater. Their shoes were like mud pies by the time they reached this gurgling stream.

"One thing's for sure," said Spence, as he vaulted across. "We won't be finding any more moccasin prints now."

Mike glanced around at the sodden, rainwashed canyon floor and nodded. "You're right," he said. "It's a good thing the cliff dwelling itself is protected. We ought to be able to find some more evidence up there."

Once across the arroyo, he led them toward the spot where Spence had seen the steps cut into the rock. It was farther away and harder to get to than they had expected.

Near the foot of the cliff the ground broke up into a series of stony rivulets, sandbanks, and clusters of red boulders, all of it awash in swiftly rushing rain runoff. There were fallen trees, too—piñons, cedars, and junipers. Beyond this grew a barrier of brush, weeds, and sharp, spiky yucca.

Carefully they picked their way through this obstacle course. The ground rose steadily as it approached the foot of the cliff. Up and up they climbed, breathing in the cool and fragrant air, which was heavy with the smells of rain, wet earth, and crushed sage and cedar. By the time they reached the actual cliff face and saw the first handhold—a narrow horizontal slit in the rock—the sun had gone down and darkness was gathering quickly.

"All right," said Mike, reaching up and laying hold of the rock. "I'll go first. You follow me, Ben. Then Winnie and Spence. Got that, Ben? Ben?"

It was clear that Ben hadn't been listening. He was standing at the foot of the cliff with his face turned up to the sky and his wide brown eyes focused on something above Mike's head—something far up in the pale blue strip of air beyond the canyon's rim.

"Look!" squealed Ben. "It's a . . . It's a . . ." He was beginning to tremble. "It's a . . . I don't know what it is! But it's probably from Mars!"

"*Ayi!*" muttered Winnie under her breath, squinting up into the gathering dusk.

"*I* know what it is!" said Spence with a wry smile. He drew the binoculars from his pack and pointed them skyward. "That's my celestial object! *That's* 'Planet Y'!"

Mike looked. There above the cliff edge, almost directly above his head, a small, round, silvery object rose into the dim air, catching and reflecting the remnants of the sun's red afterglow like a miniature moon. It was as bright as any star. Certainly, Mike thought, anyone viewing it from a distance would have thought that it *was* a star. But it wasn't. Because of his experience with Pop on the airstrip and his keen interest in all things aeronautical, Mike knew exactly what it was.

"That's no planet," he said. "It's a *weather balloon*! Somebody has just sent up a weather balloon! With a light attached to it!"

Spence frowned. "You're right. And from the look of it, I'd say that, whoever they are, they're somewhere close by. Up there in that ruin. Right now."

"It's a signal of some kind," said Mike. "It must be."

"A signal for what?" asked Winnie.

"Who knows for sure? But my guess is that it has something to do with the Huey—the helicopter we saw through Spence's telescope. Something military, maybe."

"Yes," agreed Spence. "That level space at the bottom of the canyon would be the perfect place to land a bird of that size. Especially if you're trying to do it secretly. The balloon is probably there to guide night-flying pilots."

"Exactly," said Mike. He straightened himself and shrugged. "Well, whatever it is that's going on out here, I think we're about to put our foot in it."

"If we haven't already," said Winnie.

Ben's face was pale. His lower lip was quivering.

"So . . . does this mean we're going home now?"

"Going home?" said Mike. "No way! We've got to check it out!"

"What's to check out?" said Ben. "You don't know what you're saying! The Martians have landed! They're calling in their reserve troops! Another cylinder or two will probably come crashing down here any minute. They'll be checking *us* out before you know it. I'm not hanging around for that! *I* know what they do to the people they catch!"

"Maybe Ben's right," said Winnie. "Maybe we *should* go back."

"I'm sure that's what Sheriff Smitty would say," offered Spence in response to Mike's look.

Mike glared at them. He felt his cheeks begin to burn.

"Okay," he said at last. "If that's the way you all feel about it, fine. But *I'm* not chickening out now! I've got the journal, I've got the knife, and I'm going on to find my dad! Or whatever there is to find! I'll see you all back in *Ambrosia*!"

He turned back to the cliff face, laid hold of the first slot in the rock, and hoisted himself up. *Friends!* he thought. *Who needs them anyway?*

Gritting his teeth, he began to climb. Hand over hand, up the steeply slanted rock, past delicate and fragrant sprays of spreading cliff rose, sharp outcrops of ochre stone, and little running trickles of rainwater. At last his fingers touched a course of level, square-cut stones, like a low wall. Grunting, he gripped the edge with both hands and hauled himself up, sending a small shower of gravel and pebbles down behind him.

"Hey!" came the voice of Ben, plaintive and petulant, from somewhere down below. "Cut that out!"

Mike got to his feet. He turned and looked back down the cliff. There, just below him, Spence was stretching up to grasp the top of the stone ledge with his right hand. Behind him came Winnie and Ben. Mike brushed his hands off on his jeans, wiped the sweat from his forehead, and smiled in spite of himself.

"You changed your minds?" he said, as Spence clambered up.

"I don't know about anybody else," answered Spence, "but *I* want to find out who's behind this weather balloon thing! I mean, how's an astronomer supposed to know what's what with people sending up unauthorized weather balloons all over the place?"

"We gotta stick together," huffed Ben as Mike and Spence gave him a hand up. "We all promised. Anyway, it's getting dark! *I'm* not going back now! Not without *you*, Mike. Those Martians could be anywhere!"

"And you *know* you'd be lost without *us*," added Winnie with a kind of smirk as her head emerged above the cliff edge.

"Maybe," said Mike as he and Spence pulled her up. "Maybe not."

Once all four of them were on their feet, they turned around and looked up at the ruin. What they saw took their breath away.

They were standing on a low wall or shelf of yellow-brown masonry at the edge of an expansive structure of interlocking walls of sandstone block, built into a high, deep, arching alcove in the face of the upward-sweeping cliff. The ceiling of this massive cave soared some 90 or a hundred feet above their heads. Its floor was completely filled in with stonework of the most precise and meticulous design.

"Fascinating!" said Spence. "It's like a cross between a castle and a maze!"

The whole complex was laid out in the shape of a huge **D**. Mike, Ben, Spence, and Winnie stood at the very edge of the letter's outermost curve. The left half of the **D** was divided up into a series of circular wells and square stone chambers or cells—ancient kivas and houses, now stripped of their roofs and exposed to the open sky. On the right side was a smooth, level courtyard of broad, flat flagstones, skillfully shaped and set close together between seams of gray mortar. In a few places square holes or trapdoors pierced the pavement and led down to black hollow places somewhere below.

Beyond this level space rose the houses of the ancient cliff dwellers: row upon row and rank upon rank of square-built apartments and storage chambers, all with rectangular or T-shaped windows and doors and cedar roof-poles, eaves, and lintels. These boxlike rooms or houses filled the cave to its rear wall; they rose three, four, or in some places even five stories high, until they touched the ribbed and fluted ceiling of the alcove itself.

Mike stood and stared. Here and there a shelf of rock projected from a wall below one of the mysterious darkened windows. Through the gloom, he thought he could make out a pear-shaped jar or pot sitting on one of these shelves—apparently where the owner had left it some five or six centuries before. In another place, a frayed rope of yucca fiber dangled from a ridgepole and fluttered in the breeze. The place breathed an atmosphere of timeless detachment and solitude.

"Mike!"

There was a hand on his arm—Winnie's.

"Look!" she said in a tense whisper. "Lights! In one of the rooms!"

"She's right!" said Spence, peering through the darkness. "Somebody *is* here!"

Mike looked. Directly across the courtyard a chamber doorway flickered with red firelight.

"What did I tell you?" said Ben, his voice trembling. "They're here!"

"This is it, then," said Mike, reaching into the inner pocket of his jacket and feeling for the knife. "This is what we came for. Whatever it is we're going to find in there—Martians, or *Hisatsinom*, or a secret military outpost, or . . . or whatever—*this* is the time to do it. What do you guys say?"

All three answered with a silent nod.

"Okay," he said grimly. "Let's go!"

25

Caught!

Slowly, carefully, they began to make their way across the open courtyard. Behind them the velvet curtain of the heavens, a mosaic of turquoise and ultramarine, was beginning to sparkle with the jewels of the gathering night. In front of them the orange light in the T-shaped doorway of the stone chamber pulsed, flickered, and glowed, casting eerie snakelike shadows out across the courtyard.

"Get down!" Mike whispered to the others. "Stay low! We don't know who or what is in there! Let's try to stay out of sight until we have a better idea what we're dealing with."

"Maybe we should split up," suggested Winnie.

"Good idea," agreed Spence. "Two by two."

"I'm with *you*, Mike!" said Ben.

"Okay!" said Mike. "Spence, Winnie, you swing around that way and come up to the door from the left side. Ben and I will circle the big square hole with the ladder sticking up out of it and approach from the right.

If you see any sign of trouble, run for it. We'll catch up with you back at the steps."

"Got it!" said Spence.

Mike and Ben turned their backs on the others and made a wide detour around the square opening in the pavement—probably the entrance to a subterranean kiva, Mike thought. Out of it protruded a ladder of long spruce poles.

With slow steps and anxious care the boys avoided this obstacle and stole forward through the darkness. Flashlights were out of the question. The blood was pounding in Mike's ears. Sweat was trickling down the back of his neck. He bent low beneath the weight of his backpack, doubled up almost as if he were crawling, and crept along silently on the rubber soles of his tennis shoes.

"Down!" he hissed to Ben as they drew near to the light. "Stay down! We don't want them to—"

He stopped. He stared. A face—he'd seen a face in the doorway of the chamber! For a split second it hung there in the mystic firelight, swiftly imprinting an image upon his fevered, racing brain. The strong jaw and firm mouth. The high forehead and prominent cheekbones. The regulation haircut, cropped on the top and shaven on the sides and back. It hovered there for a moment, like a fluttering shred of a fleeting dream. Then it was gone.

"Dad?" he whispered to himself. Then, as if empowered by a will of its own, his voice rose up and burst from his throat. "Dad!" he shouted. "Dad!"

Standing up straight, Mike dashed forward toward the light. Two steps. Three. His toe caught the edge of a loose paving stone. He stumbled and fell heavily, crying out in pain and surprise.

"Mike!" yelled Ben. "What happened? What's the matter?"

Immediately there arose a commotion inside the lighted chamber. In the next instant several dark figures—grotesque, faceless silhouettes against the flickering red glow of the firelight within—rushed out and stood hesitating on the flagstones just in front of the threshold. Quickly, without thinking, Mike rolled into a shadowed corner and hid himself.

Then a strange voice—a man's voice—rang out from somewhere behind him:

"Quien es?" it called.

Out of the corner of his eye Mike saw another dark figure—a guard or sentinel, he thought—come dashing out of a dark space somewhere off to the right. He saw Ben begin to run as the figure bore down upon him.

"Aahhh! Mike!" yelled Ben as the man seized him. "They've got me! Mike!"

"Ben!" hissed Mike through tightly clenched teeth. His fists and the muscles in his arms were like knots of steel. Cold fear and desperation coursed through his body and paralyzed him. For what felt like an eternity he lay there staring at the nightmarish scene, trying fruitlessly to jump-start his brain into some kind of action.

Like a pack of wolves, the dark silhouettes in the doorway sprang forward, converged upon Ben, and dragged him into the lighted chamber. When they were gone, Mike jumped to his feet and ran.

"What happened?" asked Spence, as he and Winnie ran up and met Mike at the top of the stone stairway.

"No time now!" Mike blurted. Glancing back over his shoulder, he gave Spence a shove toward the edge of the alcove. Shouts and footsteps reached his ears from the direction of the lighted chamber. "Go!" he said fiercely. "Over the edge! You too, Winnie! I'll tell you when we get to the bottom! Hurry!"

Without another word, they did as he told them. Mike followed them over the edge, swinging himself over and stretching out with his right toe. As soon as he found the foothold he began to climb, down, down, as fast as he could, hand over hand and foot over foot, his heart in his throat and a thrumming in his ears.

As soon as they reached the canyon floor, they made a desperate dash for cover. Through the thick brush they ran, past the hulking black shapes of the boulders and the crowding clumps of yucca, over the flooded arroyo, and back across the broad, open sandy space in the middle of the gorge. They didn't stop until they reached the shelf of rock on the other side where they had taken shelter from the rain.

Mike threw down his backpack and leaned against the wall of rock. His fingers were scraped and bleeding from his hasty climb down the cliff face. He fought to catch his breath. Lightheadedness overtook him and pictures swam before his mind's eye: dark shapes—men, Martians, demons, whatever they might be—converging on Ben and dragging him away. Sweat poured down his forehead and stung his eyes.

Spence stumbled over and fell to his knees beside him.

"So what was it?" he said. "What happened?"

For a moment Mike couldn't speak. He struggled to breathe. "It was—my fault," he gasped at last. "I—I saw a face! I thought it was . . ."

He trailed off. Winnie came over and peered into his face. She looked scared, he thought; worried; confused. There was a crease across her forehead like the one his mom got whenever she was anxious about him.

"You thought it was *what*?" she asked. "What did you think it was?"

Mike couldn't answer. His lip began to tremble. He had to bite the inside of his cheek to keep back the tears.

"Well, whoever those guys were," Spence said in a moment, "they weren't friendly. It's a good thing we were able to get away when we did. They don't seem to be following us." He sighed. "Nothing ventured, nothing lost, I guess."

"Wait a minute," said Winnie. There was a tone of urgency in her voice. She put a hand to her forehead and glanced around. "Where's Ben?"

"That's just it," said Mike mournfully. "Something *was* lost! *Him!*"

Winnie gripped him by the sleeve of his aviator's jacket. "What are you saying, Mike?"

"They got him! Those guys caught Ben!"

"What?" said Spence.

Mike leaned his back against the stone wall and slid to a sitting position. He put his head in his hands. "They caught him! I never meant for this to happen! I thought it was my dad! If I'd have known that . . ."

"How?" said Winnie impatiently. *"How* did they end up grabbing Ben and not you?"

"I saw a face," Mike answered. "A face in the firelight. I—thought it was him! I called out. I ran toward it. Then I tripped and fell, and someone grabbed Ben, and then they all dragged him inside. They didn't see me. I—I didn't know *what* to do. It was like I couldn't move!"

"And you just . . . ran away?" The look in Winnie's eyes made him feel like he was shrinking inside.

"I told you! I didn't know what to do!" he protested. "And we had agreed to meet back at the stairs if we ran into trouble. What would *you* have done?"

The lines in Winnie's face softened. "I don't know," she answered softly.

"The real question," said Spence, "is what to do *now*."

Mike stood up and brushed himself off. He straightened his shoulders and pushed his sweat-soaked hair back from his forehead. "I've already got the answer to *that* one," he said. He picked up his backpack and handed it to Spence. "Here—take this for me. I can't afford to carry any extra weight."

"You're not going back up there? *Alone*?" said Winnie.

"I've got to. And you two have to go back to town—quick as you can—and bring Sheriff Smitty."

"Right," said Spence. "What do you want us to tell him?"

"Tell him I was an idiot! Tell him he was right! I don't care! The only thing that matters now is rescuing Ben. So whatever you tell him, just make sure he gets back here fast! I know it's a long way, but . . ."

"Don't worry," said Spence. "We've got our flashlights. We'll be okay."

"And I know the way," said Winnie, laying a hand on Mike's shoulder. "Remember? North, south, east, and west . . . up and down."

"Go on, then," said Mike grimly. "Go up and get help!"

The two of them turned and trotted off toward the arch.

26

Through the Roof

For a moment Mike stood watching Winnie and Spence as they disappeared down the canyon. Then he turned, recrossed the open space at the bottom of the gorge, and jumped back over the rushing stream.

Sticking close to the canyon wall, he picked his way over rocks and roots, darting from bush to boulder, always keeping his eyes fixed upon the flickering light halfway up the cliff face. He didn't dare use his flashlight, and it was slow going without it.

He hadn't gone 50 paces when the air around him began to stir, raising the hairs on the back of his neck. In the next instant a flight of bats burst out of the cliffside just above his head and swept skyward in a storm of squeals and dusky wings. For a moment he stood staring after them into the night sky, his heart pounding wildly. Then, just as unexpectedly, an explosion of thoughts flitted crazily through his brain.

Maybe he *should* have gone back with the others. Smitty's face rose before his mind's eye. He thought about his mom and cringed. Even now he could see that little furrow deepening across her forehead. He knew what *she'd* say. But what was he supposed to do? Just *leave* Ben there? That wouldn't have been King Arthur's way. Nor John Fowler's.

Then another idea struck him: the Ancient Enemies! What if the *sechai's* stories were true? Was it the *Hisatsinom* who had got hold of Ben? Or the Martians? *Stupid!* he thought. And yet somehow, down in that blackened canyon, nothing seemed too far-fetched to be real. He felt hungry, weary, and faint.

Mike stopped and stared up at the arched alcove in the rock, its walls shimmering with the pale orange dancing light. Shaking himself, he reached into his inner pocket. The compass, the Bible, the knife—he fingered them for a moment, taking some small comfort and courage from the knowledge that they were still there next to his chest. Then, biting his lip, he set out again, feeling his way along the ribbed and crumbling surface of the canyon wall.

Stony spurs jutted across his path at irregular intervals. Always he kept the glow of the firelight directly in his line of sight. On and on he trudged, wiping the sweat from his eyes, stubbing his toes on piñon roots, and pricking his legs against the tips of the yucca leaves. At last he came to a place where the light seemed to be just above his head. He stopped and ran his hand along the cliff wall.

With a sudden thrill he realized that he'd found

them, even in the dark—the handholds! Yes! There could be no doubt about it—his fingers touched a deep depression in the rock. Jamming the toe of his left tennis shoe into this hollow, Mike reached up, laid hold of another with his fingertips, and began to climb.

A shower of gravel and pebbles skittered down the rocks behind him, but he pressed on, shoving his right foot firmly into the next foothold and pushing himself up. He could feel the pocket Bible inside his jacket, slapping against his chest as, deftly and nimbly, fingerhold by fingerhold and step by step, he slowly made his way to the top. The heavy, labored rhythm of his breathing drove all conscious thought from his brain.

The light—a wavering, watery glow framed within the chamber's T-shaped door—came into view again as Mike's eyes cleared the top edge of the cliff. Hoisting his left knee onto the ledge, he heaved himself up and lay flat on the pavement of the broad courtyard. Slowly he crept forward.

He could see them clearly now . . . black shapes edged in red gold . . . the silhouettes of men hunched around the fire just inside the narrow opening. And he could hear their voices—low, intense, subdued—though he couldn't make out any words. He had to get closer somehow, but couldn't risk showing himself at the door. How to get nearer without being seen?

Quickly he scanned the cliff dwelling for another avenue of approach. Through the darkness he saw again the two square holes, like wide trapdoors, yawning between the flagstones on either side of the courtyard. From each of them a long ladder of cedar poles slanted up into the night air. Between these two openings lay a third one, smaller and narrower—a black mouth leading down to unguessed depths below, this one without a ladder or any means of descent. *Not there,* he thought. *I'm looking for a way up.*

To his right, beyond these entrances to the subterranean kivas, rose the square stone towers of rooms and houses, one above the other, sheer to the arched ceiling of the alcove itself. But to the left, where the fire flickered, the ruin climbed in a random series of low, scalable steps to a wide ledge of rock. From Mike's perspective, the ledge appeared to be lined with a row of small storage chambers. And the second of these chambers seemed to stand directly above the room inhabited by Ben's captors. He decided to try and reach it.

It wasn't a difficult climb. His biggest problem was avoiding the loose unmortared stones that threatened to come clattering down behind him at any moment, warning the occupants of his presence. But he proceeded with great care, until at length he had reached the ledge. Slowly he edged his way to the opening of the little room and ducked inside.

He saw at once that his guess had been correct. Through a thin opening in the floor of the chamber shone a narrow strip of reddish light. There was smoke, too—a thin, trailing wisp of smoke—smoke from the fire that burned in the room below.

Mike took the knife from his pocket and began scrabbling in the dust around the slit. It only took a few moments to break through the layer of dirt, rubble, and rushes that covered the floor. Below that lay a subfloor of spruce poles, very old and dry, clearly bearing the marks of ancient stone axes. The rotted material came away easily; Mike tossed it aside by the handful. Then he knelt and put his eye to the hole.

Just below him stood a group of 12 men. Their jet-black hair reflected the reddish glow of the dancing firelight. Mike could see Ben sitting cross-legged in their midst, his back to the flames. He looked very hot, very uncomfortable, and very scared.

To all appearances, the men were Navajo. They were dressed in the traditional Diné fashion—like Winnie's *sechai* and his friends. What could it mean? Winnie had been so adamant about insisting that the Navajo *never* came to this place.

He got down on all fours and pressed his face to the hole. There could be no mistake: big, blousy shirts of velvet and calico, cinched at the waist with belts of sheepskin; here and there a glint of silver and turquoise; loose-fitting trousers of white homespun; moccasins of soft leather. *Moccasins!* thought Mike with a little wry smile.

Then one of the men began to speak. At the sound of the voice, Mike twisted his head and pushed his ear to the opening, straining to catch the words. At first he could make nothing of the confused jumble of sounds that reached him through the hole. Then, gradually, recognizable syllables began to emerge. It was all strangely familiar somehow. Definitely not Navajo. *Ojala . . . trabajo . . . del Norte . . . de la policiaca.* An odd, incongruous picture took shape in his mind's eye—the face of Mrs. Gutierrez, his Spanish teacher. That was it! These men were speaking Spanish!

His curiosity roused, Mike peeled back a few more inches of the flooring. Again he peered through the opening and caught sight of two new figures. A couple of men in blue jeans and denim jackets had just stepped into view—Americans . . . Caucasians. One was tall, longhaired, unkempt, and beer-bellied. The other . . . but Mike couldn't see the other very clearly. He strained to get a better view.

Suddenly the men in Navajo garb began to raise a ruckus. The tall, longhaired American shouted them down. *"Ay! Silencio! Yo tengo hombre tambien!"* he yelled with an irritable wave of the hand. *"Silencio!"*

The other voices subsided. Mike pressed his eye to the hole and squinted. That's when he saw it.

That face again! The face he had seen in the doorway! It belonged to the other American—the trim, fit, athletic-looking one. He could see it quite distinctly now, and he realized instantly that it wasn't his dad's face at all. In a flash of almost joyous recognition, he understood that it was, instead, the face of that *other* man who looked so much *like* his dad. The man in the diner. The man who had tipped him so generously at the gas station. Eagerly, Mike leaned forward against the opening with all his weight.

And then—*Crack!* Before he knew what was happening, a piece of the floor gave way on the left side of the hole. Mike's hand plunged through into empty space. *Crunch!* In a shower of dust, grime, and rotted wood, his whole head and shoulder burst through the opening. For a brief moment he could see 15 bewildered faces staring up at him.

And then with a *crash* he was falling!

27

Coyote

Mike opened his eyes. He was lying on his back, looking up through a haze of smoke and dust at a shifting ring of animated brown faces. Shafts of red firelight pierced the clouds of swirling motes, striking the rough stone walls at unsettling angles, weirdly framing and highlighting the dark shapes that surrounded him. He rolled over onto one side and winced—there was a sharp pain in his left shoulder.

Vaguely, slowly, he became aware that the room was filled with a confusion of shouts and laughter. Above the din, Ben's frightened wail was unmistakable.

A pair of rough hands grabbed him by the sleeves of his leather aviator's jacket and yanked him to his feet. The pain darted down his left arm and across his back. *"Oooh!"* He sucked the air in sharply between his teeth.

"Looks like our little friend here invited a guest," said the longhaired American, pushing Mike into the center of the room. *"Ayudame!"* he shouted to the men who were dressed as Navajos. "Bring me the other one! *Pronto!*"

A couple of them dragged Ben from his place by the fire and deposited him heavily at the man's feet. Ben looked up and gave Mike a weak smile.

"Hey, Mike," he said. "Nice of you to . . ."

"Shut up!" drawled the tall, beer-bellied man, punctuating his command with a savage kick to Ben's right leg. A smoldering cigarette dangled from one side of his large, loose-lipped mouth. "No talking until Coyote says so!"

Ben clutched his leg and whined. Mike looked down at him with a sick feeling in the pit of his stomach.

As he stared, he saw a pair of well-worn hiking boots step up and come to a stop directly in front of Ben. Slowly, Mike lifted his eyes—past the faded jeans above the boots, past the denim jacket and white cotton T-shirt. At last his gaze rested upon the face . . . the face with the calm blue eyes, the strong, square jaw, the high, clear forehead.

A feeling of desperate hope and relief leapt up inside him. So it *was* him!

Then another thought flashed across his mind: maybe this person knew something about John Fowler. He was obviously a military man himself—that seemed clear from his haircut and the neat, trim lines of his body. Maybe *he* was part of the secret military operation too! Maybe he could tell him where to find his dad. . . .

Mike lifted a hand and timidly stretched it out toward the man. "I know you!" he said. "Remember me? I saw you at the—"

Slap! Sting! Stars and darkness . . .

The next thing Mike knew, he was looking up at the

object of his hopes and expectations from the floor. He reached up and rubbed his jaw—it smarted terribly from the backhanded blow he'd received. How could it be? Dazed, he glanced around at the mocking, laughing faces that surrounded him. He felt sick and faint.

"Now get up," said the trim young American, reaching down and grabbing Mike by the collar of his jacket, "and tell me just exactly what you kids are doing here."

A fit of dizziness set the room spinning around Mike's head. He put a hand to his forehead. Everything was reeling, but he forced himself to focus on the face. He heard his own voice speaking:

"You—you let my friend go!"

From somewhere in the room came raucous laughter.

"Don't talk back to Coyote!" spat the gangly, beer-bellied man. He drew the cigarette from his mouth and tapped it over the boys' heads, showering them with hot ashes.

Coyote frowned. "Let your friend go?" he said, wrinkling his forehead and thrusting his nose down into Mike's face. His breath was heavy with alcohol. "Go where? To do what?"

Again Mike reached up and rubbed his sore jaw. Gradually, his head was clearing and his sense of bewilderment beginning to fade. He eyed Coyote carefully as the room around him ceased to spin and settled back into its place. Suddenly a realization hit him. All at once he knew: A man might *look* like John Fowler *without* being good and trustworthy and kind.

"Why do you want to know?" said Mike. "Do you have something to hide?"

"I'll ask the questions!" Arching one eyebrow, Coyote pushed Mike away and took a step backward. For a moment he studied both boys narrowly. "Now," he said, "I want to know what you kids are doing down in this canyon. What is it? Hmm?"

Ben wiped his nose on his sleeve and squinted up at him. "Looking for Martians?" he said in a small voice.

"Martians!" spluttered Coyote's gangly assistant. The cigarette dropped from his mouth as he let out a guffaw and rubbed the stubble on his bony chin. "Tell me another one!"

"Quiet, Bly!" spat Coyote. He jammed his hands deep into the pockets of his jeans and adopted a detached, skeptical air. Mike watched as the man's gaze move slowly around the circle of Latinos dressed as Navajo—for such, he now realized, they must surely be: illegal immigrants on the run, under the guidance and protection of these two American smugglers.

Coyote's eyes came to rest on the dark space outside the open doorway. He seemed to be looking for something in the star-spattered sky beyond the mouth of the alcove. "Search them!" he said at last. "Time's short, and we can't leave without finding out what they've been into. Too risky."

Bly moved with surprising quickness. "You heard the man!" he said, reaching down and pulling Ben to his feet. "Put 'em up!"

"But I haven't been into *anything!*" whined Ben. "*Really!*"

Mike stood stock-still, bracing himself to resist.

"I *told* you!" Bly hunched up his shoulders, thrust his right hand into the pocket of his faded denim jacket, and produced a small silver pistol. "Hands *up!*" he repeated, dropping his voice to a low growl. "I don't wanna have to get nasty!"

Immediately Ben's hands shot straight up over his head. Mike lifted his more slowly. Then, pistol cocked and ready, Bly approached and began frisking the boys with his free hand. Mike shuddered when the man's fingers touched his jacket pocket. Bly open his mouth to speak. Mike bit his lip. *I won't give them up*, he thought. *Not without a fight.*

"Wait!" shouted Coyote, pointing to a small object that glittered in the dust at Mike's feet. "Just a minute! What's *that?*"

Mike glanced down. His mouth went dry and his throat tightened. There on the floor—just where it had fallen when he came crashing down through the ceiling—lay the pocketknife. Instantly he dropped to his knees and made a dive for the precious thing. But Coyote was too fast for him. Mike saw the man's strong, sinewy hand close around the knife's pearled handle just as Bly seized him by the collar and yanked him gasping to his feet.

"Well, well!" A slow smile spread across Coyote's face as he studied the treasure in his hand. "Looks like our young friend has found something that belongs to *me!*"

"You?" Mike blurted.

"That's right!" The steel-blue eyes fixed Mike in their gaze. "I'd been wondering where I lost it. Sure wouldn't want the *wrong people* to find *this* lying around. Thanks, son!"

Son. Something inside Mike stretched out painfully and desperately in response to that word.

Again Coyote smiled broadly and eyed the object that lay gleaming in his open palm. Then, for the first time, he laughed—laughed like a man who seemed curiously relieved.

Like a bolt of desert lightning, another thought flashed through Mike's head: *Whoever he is, this guy does know something about Dad! Somehow or other, he got hold of his knife! He must know where he is!*

Mike stuttered, groping for words. *Better not say too much!* he thought. *Better not let on!* At last he found his voice. "I don't believe you!" he said.

He felt a sharp nudge in his ribs and turned to see Ben giving him a miserable, plaintive look. Mike shook his head violently and forged ahead.

"It *isn't* yours!" he challenged, looking Coyote in the face. "*I* found it while exploring the canyon . . . days ago! It's *mine*! Give it back!"

"No," said Coyote. "I don't think I'll do that."

A rush of air swept through the door, stirring the dark hair and bright Navajo clothing of the men who stood crowded together in the small chamber. The flames of the small fire on the hearth guttered, wavered, and leapt upward. This was followed almost immediately by a rhythmic mechanical rumble, distant at first—*chuka chuka chuka*—but churning closer and growing louder by the second—*thud thud thud thud*. Bly, accompanied by several of the phony Navajo, hurried to the door and peered out. Suddenly the canyon outside the door was filled with light—a swirling, churning hurricane of flashing light.

"*Mira! El avion!*" Mike heard someone say. "*El Norte y la libertad!*"

Bly turned and looked back at his boss. "The bird," he announced.

Then came a steady, relentless beam of light and a veritable storm of wind. Through the narrow T-shaped opening Mike saw the helicopter, a vintage Huey camouflaged in various shades of green, brown, and gray, slowly descending just beyond the mouth of the cave.

Mike shot a glance at Ben. Ben's eyes were wide and staring.

"Whoa!" said Ben in a barely audible whisper.

Coyote closed his fingers around the pocketknife. Keeping his eyes fixed on Ben and Mike, he took two sidelong steps toward the wall of the chamber, reached into a shadowy nook, and brought out a semiautomatic rifle.

"Get the passengers on board," he instructed Bly. "I'll be along in a minute—as soon as I've taken care of these two."

28

The Kiva

Bly hurried the 13 Mexicans through the narrow door and out across the open courtyard. Mike watched them go with a pounding heart. Glancing over at Ben, he saw that his friend's face had gone very pale and that his lower lip was trembling. Ben, in fact, looked for all the world as if he were about to faint. Mike reached over, squeezed his arm, and gave him what he hoped was an encouraging nod. Then he turned and locked eyes with Coyote.

"What are you gonna do to us?" he said.

Coyote scowled. The corners of his mouth turned upward in an expression of pure disdain. "Out!" he ordered, indicating the doorway with the barrel of the gun. "No arguments."

As they emerged into the chill desert night, Mike could see the last of the men disappearing over the cliff edge. They were descending, he knew, the same stairway of handholds and footholds that he had climbed only an hour or two earlier. The dull chopping sound of the helicopter's engines reverberated down in the canyon. Clouds of dust, eerily illuminated by the aircraft's flashing lights, swirled madly in the space beyond the high-vaulted alcove. Across the canyon, clumps of yucca and sage waved and twisted weirdly in the clefts of red rock, tossed this way and that in the wind-torrent stirred by the whirling blades.

Between the boys and this nightmarish vision stretched the pueblo's flagged courtyard, a pavement as neat and level as Pop Fowler's back patio. Even at a moment like this, Mike couldn't help but marvel at the skill of the ancient builders. The moon had risen, and the flat stones shone clear and smooth in its pale light, the regularity of their pattern interrupted only by the three square openings that led down to the kivas. Over this pavement Coyote drove them at gunpoint, jabbing the rifle barrel into Mike's ribs every so often, until they had reached the center hole—the one without a ladder.

"Hold it!" he said sharply. His lips were pressed firmly together; his mouth was a grim straight line. "Now turn around—nice and slow. That's right. Backs to the hole."

Ben began to whimper. "I don't think this is such a good idea," he offered. "Couldn't we just—"

"Quiet!" hissed Coyote. "Just do as I say!"

"You never answered my question," Mike piped up boldly. "What are you doing to us?"

"Just stowing you away," the man answered. "Nice, neat, and comfortable. Where you won't be able to tell anyone . . . about *this*"—he waved the pocketknife—"at least not for a while. Not until we're long gone!"

Again the thought crossed Mike's mind: *He must know something about Dad! Why else would he be so concerned about that knife?*

"W-we won't *ever* tell!" he heard Ben pleading. "Honest!"

But Coyote didn't respond. Instead, he took a step forward, lowered the gun, and pointed it at Ben's chest. Ben gave a yell and stumbled backward toward the open hole. Mike clenched his fists. His muscles tensed.

Then, as if a new idea had just occurred to him, the man's face suddenly relaxed. He stopped, raised an eyebrow, and frowned; then, looking like an investor carefully weighing his options, he judiciously placed the knife between his teeth.

"On second thought," he said, speaking out of the corners of his mouth, "it might be better to take one of you along. Just in case. C'mere, Big Boy!" He seized Ben by the elbow. "We're going for a ride."

"Wait a minute!" Ben protested loudly. But Coyote paid no attention. In one swift, rough motion, he yanked Ben from Mike's side, twisted his arm behind him, and held him firmly.

That's enough! thought Mike. *I can't just stand here and let this happen!* He poised himself to spring.

But Coyote saw it coming. Gripping Ben tightly with his left hand, the man reversed his rifle and jammed the butt of the stock straight into Mike's stomach—just below the spot where the ribs divide. Mike gasped as the air in his lungs was forced out of his mouth in a voiceless scream. Then, feeling like a deflated balloon, he staggered backwards and flopped straight down into the square black hole in the pavement.

Into the darkness he plummeted, down a rectangular shaft of hand-hewn stone so narrow it was a wonder he didn't crack his skull against its sides. Fifteen feet or more he fell, grasping his aching shoulder, until he landed in a cloud of dust on something large and soft and very dirty. Mike coughed violently as airborne particles of grime and rotting fiber invaded his mouth and nostrils. For several minutes he lay there in a daze, staring up at the square hole above him. Then, surprised to find himself unhurt, he raised his head and peered into the surrounding blackness.

It only took a few moments for his eyes to adjust. When they did, he saw that he was lying on a pile of filthy debris: dirt, rags, broken bits of wood, strips of some kind of cloth, sharp pieces of rock or broken pottery, maybe even some bits of bone—he couldn't be sure. His hand touched something hard and smooth with sharp, broken edges—a piece of a shattered pot. He picked it up and ran his finger over its finely crafted surface. Then, pocketing the shard, he squinted again into the darkness. Slowly he began to discern gradations of shadow; then a picture emerged, etched in shades of gray.

Mike sat up and drew a deep breath. He was sitting

in a small stone cubicle, looking out through a narrow rectangular arch or doorway into a large open space. Everything was very dark, and yet gradually he began to gain an almost intuitive sense of his surroundings. Oddly enough, it felt as if he, like Santa Claus, had fallen down a chimney, right into someone's fireplace!

Just outside the "fireplace," just where the spark screen might have been, stood a rectangular stone, about two feet wide and four feet high. Carefully, hesitantly, Mike poked his head out of the opening; then, gingerly, he dragged himself out.

He pushed beyond the rectangular stone and staggered to his feet. Steady currents of air swished past his face. Though still unable to see clearly, he could tell that he was standing in a big circular room. A dim, diffuse light fell from above. Mike lifted his eyes in search of the source of the light.

His heart leapt. An opening! And a ladder!—a tall ladder of spruce poles that ascended to a pale square of moonlit sky. So that was it! Mike was inside a kiva! He had fallen down the ventilation shaft and was now standing between the deflector stone and the hearth. And there was a way out! Coyote must not have realized! Maybe there was still time to catch him!

Despite the pain in his shoulder and his shortness of breath, Mike scaled the ladder like a chimpanzee. He emerged at the level of the courtyard just in time to see Ben, about 10 feet away, struggling desperately against Coyote, who was shouting in frustration and straining to drag the boy toward the edge of the cliff. *Good old Ben!* thought Mike. He could be as stubborn as a mule when he needed to be! And this time, his stubbornness had given Mike just the chance he was looking for.

With one last burst of effort, Mike vaulted out of the hole and catapulted himself toward the grappling pair. Catching Coyote just below the knees, he propelled himself forward with all the strength he had left. The man released his hold on Ben, tottered, swayed, and crashed to the pavement on his back, shouting a curse as he fell. His rifle bounced and skidded over the stones toward the cliff edge. The pocketknife skittered away in the opposite direction—back toward the entrance to the kiva.

"Ben!" shouted Mike, tightening his grip on his opponent. "The gun!"

"The gun?" spluttered Ben, looking completely bewildered and as white as a sheet.

"Yes! Get rid of it!"

A light dawned in Ben's eyes. With surprising speed and agility, he dashed toward the weapon, reaching it just as Coyote broke free of Mike's grasp. Mike saw Ben give the rifle a swift kick and send it spinning over the cliff edge, down into the smoking, echoing canyon below. Then Mike himself made a desperate lunge for the pocketknife. His hand closed around it.

"Look out, Mike!" screeched Ben.

In the next instant Coyote was upon him. Mike tightened his fingers around the smooth pearl case and held it fast as the man wrestled him to the ground, jamming a fistful of knuckles into his face. For a moment, everything went dark. Then, in a sudden and unexpected explosion of furious energy, Mike gave his right knee a swift upward jerk. Coyote reared up with a sharp cry, holding his stomach, the look of a wounded animal on his face. Immediately Mike rolled to one side, grasped the top rung of the ladder, and pitched himself down into the kiva.

This time he landed on his feet, directly in the center of the ancient hearth or fire hole. Staggering from the force of the fall, he tumbled backwards in another cloud of dust and fine ash, coming to rest with his elbows on the edge of the pit. His mind raced. He remembered that kivas were often connected by narrow underground passages. Getting up and stumbling to the wall, he began feeling his way along the low stone shelf that ran around the perimeter of the room. If only he could find an opening!

Crash!

His search was interrupted as Coyote, in a storm of shattering wood and stone, came hurtling to the floor of the dim underground chamber. The ladder had collapsed under him! His heart pounding, Mike turned back to the wall and renewed his desperate groping for a way of escape. He could hear his pursuer cursing and fuming as he struggled to his feet. At last he found it— an opening in the wall!—just as the shadowy form of Coyote came hurtling toward him with arms outstretched. Without hesitating, Mike plunged into the hole and scrabbled deep into the darkness on his hands and knees.

Blackness. Nothing but solid blackness. He fled straight into it, the sweat stinging his eyes. Blood pulsed and throbbed in his temples. Ghostly, clinging shreds of some dry, filthy, fibrous stuff brushed his cheeks and caught in his hair. The stone floor scraped his knees and knuckles until they bled. And still he crawled blindly forward, the knife clutched tightly in his right fist.

Without warning, Mike's head burst through a tangle of dirty cobwebs and into a rush of free-flowing air. So he'd been right—it *was* a connecting tunnel! And he'd made it through! Before him lay another circular chamber, almost exactly like the one he'd left behind, complete with fire pit, ladder, and square opening in the ceiling. Grasping the two sides of the opening, Mike braced to pitch himself forward. But to his shock, he couldn't move. He was stuck fast.

Again he pulled. So that was it! His jacket had snagged on something—something sharp that protruded from the passage wall. Yes, he could feel it now. Just another sharp tug, and—

"Ahhh!" he cried hoarsely. There was a hand around his ankle! His heart pounded in his chest like a drum. Again he tugged at the jacket—it came free! Then, with a sharp kick, he shook off his attacker's hand and leapt forward, tumbling head over heels into the airy kiva. His hands shot forward instinctively to shield his face, slapping the cold stone floor as he fell. The pocketknife flew through the darkness and struck the opposite wall of the chamber with a loud "chink!"

"Ha!" came a mocking laugh from the narrow crawl space behind him. Mike looked up to see Coyote stepping over him and leaping to the other side of the kiva. He struggled to his feet and caught sight of his adversary kneeling in the dusty murk at the foot of the wall, desperately pawing the rubble-strewn floor in search of the disputed object.

Mike jumped. Too late.

"Got it!" shouted Coyote triumphantly. Then, dodging to one side and waving the pocketknife in his upraised left hand, he leapt to the ladder and clambered to the top.

Hands and knees bleeding, eyes bleared with sweat and dirt and cobwebs, his heart in his throat, Mike watched the man disappear through the dim opening. Then he sank back into the angle between the wall and the floor, crumpled into a ball, and groaned. Despair overwhelmed him. He'd fought—and lost. Lost the only clue he'd ever found as to his dad's whereabouts. Worse than that, he'd let the criminals get away with Ben!

But no! He just *couldn't* let that happen! He couldn't sit back while the first and best friend he'd ever had since coming to Ambrosia became a kidnapping victim! With another surge of unlooked-for energy, he thrust himself to his feet, hopped onto the ladder's lowest rung, and fought his way to the top.

What he found there nearly made him laugh out

loud with surprise. Not three feet from the opening lay Coyote, facedown and spread eagle on the pavement. Standing above him with a long spruce pole in his hand, obviously rummaged from some other part of the ruin, was Ben. Good old Ben! He must have monitored the subterranean chase from beginning to end and positioned himself to trip Coyote as soon as he emerged from the hole. About a yard from Coyote's hand, gleaming with a pearly sheen, lay the knife.

"Way to go, Ben!" shouted Mike. With a single bound, he cleared the prostrate form of his opponent, seized the prize, and backed away, putting a safe distance between himself and his enemy. For the space of a single breath he stood smiling grimly to himself and gazing down at the two initials that burned like silver fire along the casing—J. F. The quest was not lost after all! The knife had been regained. And once Coyote and his gang were behind bars, they'd find out everything he knew about Mike's dad.

In that moment three things happened at once— three things that changed Mike's whole situation in the blink of an eye.

First, a wild and disconcerting cacophony of thuds, crashes, shouts, and roaring engines suddenly broke out in the canyon beyond the cliff's edge. The wildly swirling lights began to flash again. A sudden rush of wind ruffled his hair and Mike turned his head to see the helicopter rising to the level of the courtyard. Bly was at the controls. The side door was thronged with the shapes of yelling and gesticulating men. *"Policiaca!"* Mike heard some of them yell. *"Venga pronto!"*

Second, in that brief moment of confusion, Coyote jumped to his feet, deftly disarmed Ben, twisted the hapless boy's arm behind his back, and drew a revolver—a revolver Mike hadn't realized he possessed.

Third, a shot rang out at the entrance to the alcove. Mike froze as the report echoed hollowly throughout the ruin and the bullet ricocheted off the wall somewhere among the highest rooms at the back of the cliff dwelling. Apparently someone was ascending the cliff face—someone with a firearm.

Bly was shouting and gesturing wildly from the cockpit of the helicopter. A couple of the other men tossed out a rope ladder; it landed with a slap on the courtyard pavement.

Mike stood transfixed as Coyote, jamming the revolver up under Ben's chin, began backing slowly toward the edge of the courtyard. Beyond it hovered the helicopter, a bright, roaring, monstrous portent in the moonlit sky. Dirt, sand, and stray bits of dry sage and yucca leaves whirled around their heads in the tornado created by the flashing blades. When Coyote and his captive were standing about five feet from the ledge, they stopped. The man squared his jaw, pursed his lips, and nodded.

"Now," he called to Mike in a cold, sharp-edged voice, "just toss me that knife and I'll be off."

"No!" said Mike, clutching his treasure defiantly.

"It's not yours! You know something about . . . the *real* owner. And I'm gonna find out *what*!"

Ben shuddered and cried out as the man shoved the barrel of the revolver into the soft flesh under his jaw. "The knife!" demanded Coyote, his jaw tensing, his voice rising in pitch and intensity. *"Toss it over and I'll let your friend go!"*

Mike started. Then he looked down at the knife that lay in the palm of his hand. His dad's pocketknife—for *Ben*? What should he do? That knife was the only piece of evidence he'd found in all his long months of searching. Along with the journal, it represented the best hope he had of finding his dad.

Dad! With his other hand, Mike reached into his pocket and touched the compass and the Bible he always carried there. Sudden images, like patterns of light in a distant mist, flashed through his mind: his dad standing behind him, knee-deep in icy rushing water, showing him how to cast a line into the stream; his dad sitting by his bedside, telling a story or reading to him from the Bible; his dad's face, pressed up against his own, laughing as he wrestled Mike to the floor and shoved his nose into the fuzzy warmth of the living room carpet. Give up this link with all these precious memories?

"I don't have time to wait!" Coyote was shouting. "Neither does your pal here! Just toss it over here and he goes free!"

Mike's eyes met Ben's. He saw the fear, the absolute terror, that made them stand out so vividly in the boy's pale, round, pasty face. What was he supposed to do? He wanted his dad back. But he couldn't throw Ben to these wolves!

Then another thought struck him. What if the man were lying? What if he took the knife and kept Ben too? What then? *I don't know*, he thought, fighting back the tears. *But it's a chance I'll have to take.*

Gritting his teeth, squeezing his eyes tight, and giving his head an angry shake, Mike released his grip on the knife. Hesitantly, reluctantly, he let his arm swing forward. The satiny pearl casing slid smoothly over his fingertips. A second later, the pocketknife clattered on the stones about three feet in front of Coyote.

The man shoved Ben roughly to the ground and took a step forward. Immediately another shot rang out from the edge of the cliff. For a split second, Coyote stood still, a look of fear and confusion contorting the features of his handsome young face. Then, leaving the pocketknife where it lay, he turned quickly, sprinted to the rope ladder, and clambered aboard the helicopter.

Away flew the great thunderous bird just as a third shot sounded at the alcove entrance. A figure emerged over the top of the cliff.

It was Smitty.

29

Sunrise

"Mike! Ben! Are you all right?"

The sheriff's heavy boots pounded the flagstones as he crossed the courtyard at a run, his pistol at the ready, an expression of impatient anxiety on his weathered brown face. "What in the blue blazes have you kids been up to?"

Behind Smitty came six armed deputies. One after another they flung their booted feet up over the edge of the cliff, scrambled to a standing position, and unslung their rifles. Behind the deputies came two smaller figures.

"Spence!" called Ben. "Winnie! Boy, I never thought I'd be so glad to see *you*!"

Winnie, still the proud, full-blooded Diné in spite of her bedraggled appearance, curled her lip at him. "You better be!" she said.

"We did it!" called Spence, running up and extending a hand to Mike. He had shed his jacket and poncho somewhere, and his khaki pants and blue golf shirt were saturated with muddy water. "Looks like we got here just in time, too! I've never run so fast, gotten so muddy, or fallen down so much in my whole life! It was great! Almost as exciting as building a telescope or discovering a new planet!"

"We called Smitty from my house," Winnie explained. "Good thing my mom insists on having a phone—*in spite* of what some of the *Naat'aanii* say!"

Mike laughed and embraced his mud-encrusted friends. Then he bent, picked up the knife, and deposited it in his pocket. He turned his face up toward heaven with tears of relief and thanksgiving flowing down his dirty cheeks. And as he did so, he noticed for the first time that the ceiling of the stone alcove was beginning to glow, as if with a rosy luminosity of its own.

Outside, in the open space beyond the cave's great arch, the sky was growing light. Above the topmost crags of the cliffs on the other side of the canyon a thin line of bright yellow trembled at the edge of the world, like a river of molten gold. Above it waved rippling bands of mist—red, blue, and purple, like the stripes of a fluttering flag. Then, like the firing of a bright but silent shot, the sun itself flashed out, sending a blinding ray straight down to the square, black hole that led to the great kiva where Mike had struggled with Coyote during the long, dark night. The last ragged shreds of cloud melted away as the golden disc began to push its way into the blue air.

"I oughta horsewhip you kids!" said Smitty, who had dispatched his deputies to conduct a thorough search of the cliff dwelling. He pushed his hat back and wiped his forehead. "Didn't I tell you to stay out of this area? Now you know why! What in the world were you trying to prove, Mike?"

Mike looked up at him and brushed a tear from his eyes. "Funny you should put it that way, Sheriff Smitty. I guess I really *was* trying to prove something—though not in the way you think." He glanced around at Ben, Spence, and Winnie. "We *all* were, I suppose. I guess we just went about it all wrong."

One of Smitty's deputies came up carrying an armload of weapons and dragging a large canvas duffle bag. "Looks like they left in a real hurry, Sheriff," he said, laying the guns on the pavement. "They took off and left all this stuff behind. And more. Hard narcotics. Cash, too."

"They probably thought it was safe here," said Smitty, rubbing the stubble on his chin and casting his eyes around the ancient pueblo. "After all, who was likely to find it? An undiscovered ruin in a hidden canyon, protected by Navajo taboos. They've probably been using this as a base of operations and rendezvous point for a long time. They bring the people and the loot up here from the border, traveling by way of the Indian reservations as much as possible—Papago, Gila River, Fort Apache. Then they take them by helicopter—an old military surplus Huey—wherever they want to go. A foolproof scheme. But they didn't figure on Mike Fowler and his gang!"

Mike hesitated. "So—are these the guys you've been looking for, Smitty? The 'coyote' the state police have been chasing?"

"Appears that way," Smitty replied, holstering his pistol and opening the mouth of the canvas sack. "Look at this—bundles of money. All big bills, too. And Colombian cocaine."

"They looked like Indians," volunteered Ben. "Not the leaders, but the other guys. The ones I thought were aliens." He grinned sheepishly.

"*Illegal* aliens," said Smitty without looking up. "Headed north to find work. All part of the same operation. I imagine some of this stuff was the price they paid for the coyote's services."

"Well, they weren't Diné. That's for sure!" said Winnie.

"No," said Mike. "They were speaking Spanish."

"Mexicans, Guatemalans, Salvadorians, probably," said the sheriff. "*Posing* as Navajo."

Another deputy—a thin man with a narrow, nut-brown face, sparse, graying hair, and wire-rim glasses—approached with a metal cash box. "More of the same, Smitty," he said, setting the box down in front of the sheriff and wiping his hands on his pants. "But if you ask me, the *real* treasure hasn't even been touched yet." He smiled and glanced up at the towering ranks of square stone houses and storage chambers behind them.

"Dr. Philip Seher," said Smitty, by way of introduction. "Dr. Seher's an archaeologist from the University of Arizona. He's been living in Ambrosia for the past six months. A volunteer sheriff's deputy, too. I brought him along because of his knowledge of Anasazi ruins. Dr. Seher, meet Mike, Ben, Spence, and Winnie."

"Pleased, I'm sure," said the doctor, extending a hand to each of them in turn.

Throughout Smitty's description of the Coyote's operation, Mike's heart had been pounding and burning within him. What did it all mean with respect to his dad? Where did the knife fit into the picture? Had Coyote and Bly kidnapped his father? Or was John Fowler hiding out somewhere in the adjoining canyons, spying on the criminals' activities for the government? The time had come to find out.

"Smitty," he said, as the sheriff and the doctor examined the contents of the cash box, "there's something I need to show you. Something I found out there in the canyon."

He reached into the inside pocket of his jacket and felt for the pocketknife. The compass was there. The Bible, too. His fingers touched the knife and the piece of broken pottery he'd picked up down in the kiva. Then, all at once, it hit him.

The journal. The journal was *gone!*

Mike blanched. What could have become of it? Where could he have dropped it? Where was the last place he remembered having it?

With a sick feeling in his stomach, he realized that it could be almost *anywhere.* Down in the kiva. Lying in the subterranean darkness of one of the connecting tunnels through which he had crawled. Buried under ashes and rubble in the room where he had fallen through the ceiling into the middle of the Navajo imposters. Hidden at the base of the cliff, among the sage and the yucca and the scrub oak. Washed away in the rushing waters at the bottom of the arroyo.

He felt the color drain away from his face. Lights danced before his eyes. Hunger and weariness joined forces with the pain in his shoulder and assaulted him with a horrible faintness. He leaned his head forward and held it in his left hand.

"What is it, son?" said Dr. Seher, laying a hand on his shoulder. "What have you found?"

"Oh—well, there was *this*," said Mike, fighting to recover his composure. He pulled the shard of pottery from his pocket and handed it to the doctor. "And—and this knife. Smitty, do you think"—he said, extending the precious treasure toward the sheriff—"do you think this knife might belong to—"

"*J. F.!*" exclaimed Smitty, dropping the metal box to the ground with a clatter and seizing the proffered pocketknife. He held it up between the thumb and forefinger of his right hand and examined it closely. "*Jackson Fox*! So *he's* the one behind all this! Well! I should've known! That makes perfect sense! That provides the puzzle's proverbial missing piece!"

"*Jackson Fox?*" said Mike, lightheadedness descending upon him once again.

"Fox has a record as long as an orangutan's arm. Drug dealing, smuggling, car theft, extortion, racketeering—wanted in five states, but especially here in Arizona and New Mexico. Only thing is, he's never been involved in running illegal aliens before. So he wasn't really a prime suspect. Until now."

"The coyote's real name is . . . *Jackson Fox?*" Mike still couldn't take it in. He felt as if he were standing in the middle of a bizarre dream . . . or a nightmare. The light of the rising sun was shining straight into his eyes and blinding him with its brilliance. He stumbled forward and caught hold of Smitty's arm.

"That's right," said Smitty. "At least there's good reason to *believe* so. At this point, I'd say all the evidence points that way. And your knife here is the missing link that brings the whole case together. I guess I owe you a debt of gratitude—even if you *weren't* supposed to be here in the first place. But, hey!—Mike! Are you okay?"

The sheriff's face was growing fuzzy. The doctor came over and put an arm around Mike's shoulder. "The boy looks faint, Smitty," he said. "Here—let's get him to lie down for a moment."

Mike lay on the flagstones with his face turned toward the hole that led down to the kiva. And as he lay there, he heard the doctor say:

"I don't want to cause you any more excitement than is absolutely necessary, my boy. But this potsherd—it really is a most remarkable find."

"Really?" said Spence. "Can I see?"

"Certainly." Dr. Seher handed the shard to Spence before continuing. "If I'm right—and I believe I am—it points to one of the oldest Anasazi caches ever to be found. Possibly the very site your father was on the point of unearthing before he . . . well, went away and got involved in other things."

"Fascinating!" said Spence. "Do you really think so?"

"I'm almost positive of it. This is early eleventh, possibly even late tenth century if my eye does not deceive me. Most remarkable indeed."

"It—wasn't made by Martians, then?" asked Ben.

The doctor turned and looked at Ben with a strange, uncomprehending smile.

As for Mike, his heart was pounding once again. "You mean *you* know something about my dad?" he asked.

"Well, of course! Everyone in the southwestern archaeological community knows about John Fowler and Harrison Lasiloo and their famous discovery of site number 429! *National Geographic* write-up and all! And *everyone* knows that they believed they were on the verge—the very cusp, mind you—of uncovering even *bigger* treasures. Some think they had already stumbled upon them and were only waiting for the right moment to go public with their findings. Very exciting stuff, all that. And it looks like you've inherited a portion of it!"

Again Mike began to feel woozy and queasy. So bright was the rising sun in his eyes that he had to hide his face in the crook of his elbow.

Suddenly he sensed Winnie's presence. She knelt beside him and took his hand.

"Mike!" she whispered urgently. "It all makes sense now! They *had* found it! Your dad and Lasiloo! Don't you see how the sun shines straight down into that kiva?"

Mike uncovered his eyes. "Yeah," he said feebly. "So what?"

"Don't you remember what the journal said?

At dawn the sun goes down
To where the treasure lies."

Mike groaned. "The *journal*! The journal also said *the knife points the way*!"

"Yes!" said Winnie. "Exactly! That's just it!"

"What's just it?"

"I tried to tell you! But then the storm came, and after that I never had a chance. You know that big rock formation at the top of the cliff? The tall, sharp one right above the arch that leads into this canyon?"

"Yeah?"

"I remembered something when we were looking up at it during the thunderstorm yesterday afternoon. Just at the moment when the lightning struck it. The Diné know that rock formation! They have stories about it! They call it 'The Knife'!"

Again Mike groaned. Then he covered his face once more and rolled over on his side.

"Smitty," he said, "can we go home now?"

30

The Last Chance Detectives

*Then arose Sir Percival and took his brother by the
hand. And he embraced him, and wept upon his
neck, and the two of them made many a profession
of manful brotherly love one for the other, for that
each had been full fain to find the other all the days
of their lives.*

*"Now," said Percival, "here is a great marvel:
that in failing of the Grail Quest, I should yet have
found you after all these years, my brother! And so
it comes to pass that in great sorrow my joy has
been made full!"*

*Then was he ware where a dark-haired maiden
came riding toward them on a palfrey. And she lifted
up her voice and cried out, "Happy are you, son of
Gahmuret! Now God is about to manifest His grace
in you! For in embracing your brother in such hum-
ble and charitable wise, you have indeed fulfilled the
true Quest, though all unwittingly. Though you raised
a brood of cares in tender years, the happiness which*

*is on its way to you has dashed their expectations.
For still it lies within your power to return to the
noble, gentle Fisher King and present him with the
Question that will heal his wound and banish all his
agony."*

Then rode Percival and Feirefiz by many roads
and by-paths, over field, meadow, and mountain,
until at last they came again to that fair and shining
lake, and above it on a hill the Castle of the Grail
and the wounded Fisher King. And they entered in
and were greeted right graciously by the knights and
maidens of the Grail, and made to sit upon round
carpets with scarlet cushions of down. Then were
they feasted upon venison and quail and made to
drink from goblets of pure gold.

At last they were led before the sorrowful king,
who lay in the sling-bed beside the fire, making
great moan because of his incurable wound. Then
Percival wept. And when he had done weeping, he
rose to his full height and said, *"Dear Sir, what is it
that ails you?"*

Then through the asking of that Question, by
the grace and mercy of God, the Fisher King was
raised up and made well and whole again. And the
strength of his limbs returned, and the luster of his
complexion, and he stood upon his feet and blessed
them. And so it happened that Sir Percival was
given the king's daughter to wed, and it was granted
to him that he might become King of the Grail Castle

after him. And as for Feirefiz, he was led to the font
and received the grace of baptism that very hour; for
he had been an Infidel until that day.

Mike closed the book and shoved it down into his backpack. Then he picked up his fork and poked at the last few fragments of meat loaf and mashed potatoes on his plate. They were cold. He pushed the plate to the other side of the counter and squinted into the golden sunlight that was pouring in through the diner's windows.

Gail came out from behind the counter, sat down beside him, and laid a hand on his arm.

"You *do* understand why I had to ground you—don't you, honey?" she said.

"Yes, Mom."

"Even though I *am* very proud of you for the way you handled yourself. And what you did to help your friend."

Mike nodded. He looked up at his mom's face and saw the little worry-crease on her forehead. A faint, kind smile hovered at the corners of her lips. But the expression in her brown eyes was deeper than he could fathom: a look of almost desperate joy mixed with a lingering sadness. He knew what it was. He knew what he'd put her through while he was out there in that canyon chasing his fleeting dream. She thought she'd lost *him*, too. Only now was it beginning to dawn on him what that might really mean to her.

"But does it *really* have to be for a whole month?" he

asked plaintively, laying down his fork and resting his chin on his hands. "What do you think, Pop?"

Pop, who had just come out of the kitchen, sat down on the other side of Gail.

"That's up to your mother, Mike," he said. "Though, to be honest, I'm afraid I'd have to back her on this one. Sneaking out without telling anyone. Disobeying the sheriff's orders. Endangering yourself *and* your friends. That's pretty serious stuff."

In spite of everything, Mike couldn't help smiling. *Your friends.* He liked the sound of that.

"I know, Pop," he said. "But do I really have to wait a whole month to see Ben and Spence and Winnie again?"

Gail shook her head. "You'll see Ben and Winnie at school," she said. "And they can all come and visit you *here* whenever they want. I just don't want you traipsing off across the desert and stumbling into some criminal's hideout again. At least not anytime soon!"

"As a matter of fact," said Pop dryly, "Ben, Spence, and Winnie are grounded, too." He laughed at Mike's wide-eyed reaction. "No joke! I know, because I've checked around. Sounds like there were some *real* fireworks over at the Teepee Motor Lodge when they found out what Ben had been up to. But that's not the end of the story. I used my influence to work out a deal with all the parents. The whole crew has been granted leave to stop by and see you tonight." He looked at his watch. "I imagine they'll be arriving any minute."

Mike grinned. "Thanks, Pop."

At that moment the front door opened and Smitty walked in.

"Evening, Gail—Roy," said Smitty, taking off his hat and hanging it on the rack beside the door. He strode over to the counter and perched himself on the stool next to Gail. "So what'll it be, Mike? Cherry pie? Apple fritter? Donuts? Chocolate cream cake?"

Mike turned and gave him a dumb look.

"Didn't I tell you?" said Smitty, scratching the back of his neck. "Dessert's on me tonight!"

"Really?" laughed Gail. "What's the occasion?"

"Roy knows," he answered with a grin and a wink. He stroked his mustache and raised an eyebrow. "A *red-letter* day for the Ambrosia sheriff's office, for one thing. Seeing as how *we* provided the clue that led to the Coyote's capture. They'll sit up and take notice of that down in Phoenix!"

"You mean they *caught* him?" came a familiar voice from behind them. *"Woo hoo! All right!"*

Mike turned to see Ben, flanked by Winnie and Spence, standing in the open doorway.

"You better believe it, Ben!" laughed Smitty. "Thanks to you crazy kids—and yours truly, of course—Jackson Fox is officially behind bars. Once we knew exactly *who* we were looking for, everything began to fall into place. Only took a few days to track him down and corner him. Those state troopers were *pretty* impressed, I can tell you. And I've never seen Arlene so excited! She even forgot to eat her lunch!"

Ben stared in disbelief.

"Well? What are you kids waiting for?" said Smitty, waving them over to the counter. "C'mon! Sit down! As I was just telling these folks, dessert's on me."

Ben stood gaping. "You mean I can get *anything* I want?"

"Anything."

Ben crossed the black-and-white checkered floor in three big steps and vaulted onto a red-vinyl-covered stool. "Can I see a menu, please, Mrs. Fowler?"

Grandma Fowler had just come out of the kitchen. She wiped her hands on a towel, hung up her gingham apron, and approached Ben with a doubtful expression on her face.

"Why, Ben Jones!" she said, her eyes wide, her forehead wrinkled upward, and her mouth drawn into a tight little circle. "Do you mean to tell me that you don't already *know* what you want? I thought you'd committed that menu to memory!"

"That doesn't mean it isn't fun to look!" he shot back.

Spence sat down beside Ben. "Just a fruit cup for me, Mrs. Fowler," he said. "Thanks very much."

"Come on, Spence!" Mike reached over and gave the young scholar a good-natured punch in the arm. "Loosen up! How often do you get a free dessert?"

Spence stuck out his lower lip and frowned thoughtfully. "Well," he said slowly. "How about frozen strawberry yogurt? With granola?"

Gail jumped up to grab a handful of menus from behind the counter. Winnie immediately took possession of the seat she had vacated—the one between Mike and Pop.

Smitty laughed and slapped the counter with the palm of his hand. "Everybody order *whatever* you want! I mean it, now! I figure you kids'll be treating *me* before too long." He gave Mike a sly sidewise glance. "What with all that *reward* money, I mean. Not to mention your share of the cash the museum is forking over for the Anasazi stuff they found down in that kiva. Sounds like quite a stash."

Mike stared at him. "You mean they've already excavated it?"

"They've made a good start."

A bright ray of hope shot through his heart. "Did they—find my dad's journal?"

Smitty shook his head. "Sorry, Mike. No. But they *have* discovered some extremely old—and very valuable—artifacts. Things your dad would have been real happy to find. He'd be proud."

Pop was smiling like a Cheshire cat.

"And they're giving *us* a share of the money?" Mike stammered.

"That's right. Dr. Seher insisted."

"*And* a reward?"

"Well, now, that's a whole different matter. There's been a price on Fox's head for the last four years. That just comes with the territory."

"Who'd have thought it, eh, Mike?" said Pop. "Grounded and rewarded all at the same time!"

"Sounds like the story of my life," said Mike, running his fingers through his sandy brown hair.

"Kind of takes the punch out of my punishment, doesn't it?" said Gail, putting on an exaggerated pout. "Oh, well. You can't blame a mom for trying."

"That's pretty much what *my* mom said," observed Winnie.

Gail and Grandma took the dessert orders. Despite Smitty's urgings, everyone exercised admirable restraint and good sense. All except Ben. *He* put in a request for two banana splits and a piece of peanut butter cheesecake. Then he talked Spence into joining him in a round of Space Invaders while they waited for the food to show up.

"Funny, isn't it, Pop?" said Mike, as the *Pings!* and *chk-chk-k-k's* mingled with Ben's ecstatic shouts. "I mean, what a way to crack a case! The whole thing was just one big mistake from beginning to end! We were all looking for the wrong thing. And we all went about it in the wrong way!"

Pop just nodded. But there was a twinkle in his eye.

"I mean, there was Ben and the Martians. And Spence with his theory about 'Planet Y.' And you, Winnie—" He stopped, hesitated, and felt his cheeks grow hot. "Um . . . what was it *you* were after?"

Winnie scowled. He thought he could see a flush of red on her neck. "How can you say that, Mike

Fowler?" she asked. "Especially when it was *you* who got me started! You and those things you said about the 'Truth.' "

"Oh, right," Mike said, feeling a bit flustered. "Well, anyway, then there's me. I guess I'm a lot like Sir Percival. *His* mom didn't want him to go off on his quest, either, but he went anyway. And he got into all kinds of trouble and made all sorts of stupid mistakes. He really botched everything up. He didn't just read the evidence wrong. He didn't even know enough to ask the right Question! He bungled everything that could possibly *be* bungled—just like me! And yet . . ."

Pop smiled. "And yet, somehow, it all came out right in the end."

"Yeah." Mike stared out the window at the B-17. The setting sun was rippling along its sleek silver sides in bright streams of flowing gold. "Pretty amazing, isn't it?"

"Amazing. Yes," said Pop, leaning back and striking a reflective pose. "It *is* amazing. But not as unusual as you might think. You said it yourself: It's the story of our lives. At least when the Lord's involved."

Smitty glanced up from the cup of steaming black coffee and the wedge of apple pie that Grandma had just set down in front of him. "I don't know about that," he said, taking a judicious sip. "But I'll tell you one thing: We couldn't have solved this case without you kids. Maybe it *was* all a big blunder on your part, Mike. I didn't want you out in those canyons in the first place. You know that! But—well, in the end, it was as fine a piece of *accidental* detective work as I've ever seen. And I mean that!"

"Detective work?" said Ben, who had come running as soon as his dual banana split appeared. "Did you say *detective*, Sheriff Smitty? You oughta see my collection of *Detective Comics*! I've got every issue from August 1968 to February 1973! And Bert's working with me on getting the rest. Did you know that *Detective* is one of Batman's nicknames? Like *Dark Knight* and *Caped Crusader*?"

"No," said Smitty with an indulgent chuckle. He stopped to admire the piece of pie on the end of his fork before popping it into his mouth. "I sure didn't."

Ben sat down in front of his dessert and picked up a spoon. Then, with the suddenness of one who has just seen a vision, he dropped the spoon, clapped his hand to the side of his head, and jumped up again.

"What is it, Ben?" said Winnie, a tone of alarm in her voice. "Are you okay? Leave it to Ben to choke on a banana!"

Ben's face was aglow with the light of inspiration. "What an *incredible* flash!" he said. "*Detectives*! Mike! We're *detectives*! Real, true-to-life, honest-to-goodness detectives! Don't you see? Sheriff Smitty said so himself!"

"Take it easy, Ben," laughed Mike. "What's your point?"

"Why not make it official? Why not incorporate? Why not draw up a list of bylaws and organize ourselves into a real Detective Agency?"

Mike looked at Winnie and Spence. "Not a bad idea, Ben," he smiled. "Not bad at all."

"Not bad! It's *great*!" enthused Ben. "Just look at the talent we've got in this group. There's Spence—he's the genius. And Winnie—even I have to admit that she's got guts, and she knows the desert better than any of us. And *I* can do just about anything I put my mind to!"

Mike grinned.

"And then there's you, Mike. You're a born leader! You're a true adventurer! And that's not all. You're a *friend*—the best friend a kid like me ever had!"

Mike felt his lower lip begin to tremble. He laughed out loud to hide it from the others.

"I agree," said Spence, pouring a cup of granola over the top of his strawberry yogurt. "One hundred percent. Detective work *could* be extremely challenging. I might even get to use my telescope once in a while."

Winnie nodded. "I guess searching for truth is what detectives do best," she said. "You can count me in. As soon as I'm off being grounded."

Mike glanced around at the others with a warm, comforting glow welling up from deep inside him. "Well, then," he said, "I guess it's settled."

Out of his pocket he drew the blue lanyard with the shining silver key at its end. "This," he said, holding it up in the light, "is for all of you. I'll keep it in a drawer here in the diner—just behind the counter. The B-17 will be our headquarters. You can all come and use it anytime you want. We'll put Spence to work on the old radio. We'll collect maps and books and newspapers. We'll put together a file of information on every strange and suspicious thing that happens in Ambrosia—good old Ambrosia! But most of all," he concluded, with a bold glance at his mom, "we'll continue the search for my dad. We'll search until we *find* him."

Ben was beaming. "So what are we gonna *call* ourselves?"

Mike thought for a moment. At last he said, "That seems obvious, Ben. Last Chance Diner. Last Chance Gas. What else can we call this outfit except 'The Last Chance Detectives'? All in favor, say 'aye'!"

The vote was unanimous.

Explore faith and other mysteries/adventures

With the "Last Chance Detectives"®

All-New Audio Adventures!

The Day Ambrosia Stood Still

What in the world is going on in Ambrosia? Car horns beep on their own, radios blare on and off and Jason Whittaker's car careens wildly out of control. Things are just as haywire at the Last Chance Diner, where the silverware suddenly moves across the table! From the producers of "Adventures in Odyssey" comes the first installment of the "Last Chance Detectives," an all-new audio adventure. Produced by Focus on the Family, *The Day Ambrosia Stood Still* teaches about standing up for what you believe. Each exciting audio adventure in this new series encourages kids ages 10 to 14 to think through faith for themselves.

Mystery of the Lost Voices

The Last Chance Detectives are hot on the trail of a 40-year-old mystery: what happened to a hugely popular rock band whose plane vanished without a trace! Buddy Lewis and the Cats got on a plane and were never heard from again. The fearless foursome discover the plane's wreckage in the desert. But the case takes a strange twist when Mike, Spence, Ben and Winnie encounter a desert hermit with mysterious ties to the band's disappearance. Part of an exciting new audio adventure series, *Mystery of the Lost Voices* teaches a valuable truth about contentment.

Last Flight of the Dragon Lady

Something goes terribly wrong after the Last Chance Detectives join Pop to help deliver a DC-3 to a friend. They have no idea that hidden on the plane is some hot cargo, and sinister forces will stop at nothing to terminate their flight! The real terror begins when Pop slumps over at the controls and Mike has to fly the plane—with no radio and a fuel gauge on empty! The hair-raising episode of the "Last Chance Detectives," a new audio adventure series, delivers a powerful punch about trusting God even when things look their worst.